DEDICATION

Each year millions of individuals, women, children, and
men are taken and sold as sex slaves or work
slaves around the world. They are taken by business people.
People that are part of a multi-billion-dollar slave trade.
These victims are stolen from their loved ones, and the lives they
were meant to lead. They are sold, abused, tortured, and murdered.
I dedicate this book to all those who have been
taken, abused, and tortured around the world.
We will never stop looking for you. We pray for everyone,
and we pray God will always be with you.

ACKNOWLEDGEMENTS

I would like to acknowledge and thank those that have been so generous with their encouragement, their time, and their talent without which this series would never have been possible.

To my husband and children who stepped up and took over the responsibilities of the housework, meals, appointments, not to mention the endless readings, I thank you.

To Author Marie Crist, your support and ambition carried me through. Your energy and determination kept me on point. Your help was without end and still is. I couldn't have done this without you.

Justifiable: Oregon

Copyright:

Justifiable: Oregon
TERRIBLE Tilly
By Pamela Crist-Wright

JUSTIFIABLE OREGON
TERRIBLE TILLY

By Pamela Crist-Wright

PROLOGUE:

TILLAMOOK ROCK LIGHTHOUSE
SEASIDE, OREGON

He worked swiftly, the order of dispensing with the body down pat. There was a certain amount of pride in a job well done. There was relief in knowing that he had total dominion over the crematorium and that no one would or could disturb his work without his permission—or at least without his knowledge. The trip to the rock alone took thirty minutes, longer on rough water.

Closed circuit monitors and video kept him assured of his privacy as he gathered the intel he needed to pass on to those who needed it to continue their missions. His mission was always the same. It never varied. Many would find his work unsettling, unnerving, but not him. He knew his work was all that kept so many others safe and out of harm's way.

Terrible Tilly, as the lighthouse was known, rose from the sea on craggy slabs of jagged rock. Native American folklore believed the rock looked like a sea monster to protect the evil spirits that dwelt beneath the depths of the ocean. More than one soul lost his life while Terrible Tilly was being constructed more than a hundred and forty years ago.

Supposedly, many of the lighthouse keepers lost their mind and self-control as they kept the lights shining out to sea. The history of the lighthouse was fraught with stories that only Hollywood usually thought up. Even now, the old girl was steeped in intrigue. And on a clear night with the stars shining, smoke could be seen wafting out to sea as the crematorium housed inside Tilly consumed one more soul's lifeless body.

Loved ones and friends weren't likely to venture out to Tilly, to see the tiny little cubicle that held the ash remains of their dead. The only visitor who had ever ventured out to the rock in a speed boat had become violently ill from the choppy surf. Once inside the lighthouse, insidious little sea worms that infested the porous surface of the lighthouse had fallen onto the poor guy. He couldn't get back to shore fast enough.

A pest control company was called but before the infestation was under control, three trips to the lighthouse had to be made by the company.

No, no one else ever wished to pay their respects in person to Terrible Tilly. This fact played well with the new caretaker of the crematorium. On foggy nights and most are dark dank foggy nights, the smoke from the furnace was lost at sea.

The room was set up like any other autopsy room complete with instruments, drains, tubes, etc... Cadavers aren't intimidated. However, to the regular guy, the one who's still breathing, it can be scary as hell. Especially the way the caretaker liked to introduce them to the room and the equipment. Most of these guys are the ones who have been on the other side of terror. These guys are the ones that have taken great pleasure in inflicting pain and fear on their innocent victims.

The caretaker took no pleasure in the pain. He did take a great deal of pleasure in watching them turn from cocky, arrogant, tough sons of bitches into blubbering cowards that would tell him things they didn't even know in the hopes of securing their freedom.

Their freedom was not an option for many reasons. First and foremost, their freedom would destroy the ultimate mission. Second, their freedom would ensure the pain and suffering of countless victims and their families. And that was unacceptable to the team. The team's mission was to save lives, to save innocents, and to rid the world of the scum that preyed upon others.

These animals always knew of other traffickers, they were like packs. They delighted in hearing of each others conquests. They taught each other the tricks of their trade. They helped each other to trap, torture, and often kill their victims. No, the caretaker felt no remorse in his work.

The interrogations were always performed during daylight hours. The windows in the tower let bright light into the work area. Additional lighting would not be detected from shore or home telescopes. Nor could the interrogations be witnessed because the windows were few and high above the room. The constant crashing of the waves hitting the rock on which Tilly was perched blocked all other sounds. All and all the lighthouse offered the perfect place for these procedures.

The furnace was large, loud, and incredibly efficient as it worked under cover of night. So, the unauthorized cremations were virtually unnoticed. The lighthouse had its own mega generators and did not require local utilities. No record of power use was ever recorded. In the end, the ash left behind was dispersed among the foamy sea-caps leaving one less monster to prey upon the weak.

The team delivered the three subjects to him as usual. At night and sedated. By the time the first subject was regaining consciousness the caretaker had him strapped to the autopsy table. With all the tools of the trade spread openly on high tables within sight of the subject. Mirrors were carefully placed for the maximum view of the entire room and its intended purpose.

This part of the interrogation was critical. And the time it took varied greatly from subject to subject depending on many factors. He needed the subject fully conscious and completely aware of his surroundings.

"Water, I need water."

The subject was clearly coming out of sedation. The caretaker stood silent and in full view of the subject. He didn't move a muscle. He waited patiently, quietly.

"Hey, water. I need water."

The subject's voice was a little stronger, slightly annoyed.

"Where am I? I'm thirsty. What the hell!"

The subject struggled against the restraints. The caretaker could see the confusion and concern flicker across the subject's face.

"Where am I? Where am I?"

The caretaker remained still and silent letting the subject's predicament settle in.

"Dammit, I asked you a question! Answer me! Where am I? Answer me, damn you!"

The table held steadfast but shook as the man struggled violently against his restraints.

A few more minutes and the subject would take notice of his surroundings. The table, the instruments, the tubes already attached to his I-V, the mirrors, and of course his interrogator. Every interrogation was very much the same in the beginning. Confusion, annoyance, demands, and eventually extreme fear.

"Was I in an accident?"

The question was more to himself than to the interrogator.

"Wait, wait a minute. This isn't a hospital."

The subject was taking note of his surroundings now. The stone walls and the damp cold musty scent of the room added to his confusion. The mirrors he stared into reflected all the tools of the trade. Normally never seen by its clients. The drain that flowed along the edges of the table he found himself strapped to drew a barely audible gasp from the subject.

The subject slowly turned his head to stare straight into his captor's eyes and he knew. He knew just as his victims had known, there was no way out. Not a sound was made. Not by either of the men, not even as the interrogator stepped closer to the table all the while returning his stare.

The interrogator calmly and quietly took a clipboard from the instrument table and began to scan the document. He had read it numerous times prior to the delivery of his newest subject. He knew every victim, every evil inhumane act perpetrated against each young girl. This part was important. It was important for him to be in the right mindset, to be reminded of the absolute necessity of this work. The photos of the innocent girls set his jaw in a clench, and the subject took note of his captor's clenched jaw as their eyes met again.

The interrogation began.

CHAPTER 1

THE OREGON COAST

The yacht had returned from Baja the night before. Dropping anchor in a cove down the coast south of Tillamook Head. There was no way ever to have seclusion along the coastline. The best one could hope for was an inlet with no beach access road leading to the shore. The 101 highway was sprinkled with wide spots in the road where people could pull over for a scenic view of the Pacific.

The yacht could be spotted by any number of sightseers above, but even the very best binoculars couldn't give away the secrets below deck. Above deck, sunbathers and Grey Goose gave the appearance of lucky people living a luxury costal life.

The captain strode periodically about the ship. Crisp white jacket and navy-blue slacks lending prestige to the scene above deck. Sunbathers draped dreamily on the expensive chaise lounges, shot glasses at their fingertips.

Captain Snell stopped and adjusted a sun-sail over the top

of a sleeping bank executive. The banker snorted and twisted slightly on the chaise.

Very soon now the banker would come to and expect delivery of what he'd paid for.

"Luxury at its finest."

That's what the banker had called it, the catalog that is. The banker had spent a great deal of time perusing the inventory, eyeing something of interest only to be carried away by a new find.

To the banker they were dolls really, life sized dolls presented for his playing pleasure. The little beauty with the long dark lashes had his attention right away but the tiny little blond with a dimple just above the corner of her mouth captured his imagination and his imagination was going wild with possibilities.

Eventually a decision was reached, and the fee had been wired to an account in the Cayman's. This time though he would be more careful, he would take his time. Last time it had ended all too quickly, he had miscalculated his strength; she had been so small after all.

The banker had set aside a few days of vacation time to fully enjoy his new acquisition. The staff at the bank had been told of his much-anticipated diving trip to the Grand Cayman Islands, a ruse insisted upon by the sellers of his luxury purchase.

Grey Goose never had this effect on him before. Groggy and listless, he lay a little longer on deck. It was mid-morning, and he knew his new toy was on-board by now. Excitement and anticipation stirred his emotions, helping him clear away the fog of the drink from the night before.

Ted had boarded the ship after dark along with two other buyers in Baja. The limo driver had begun by serving them champagne on the drive to the docks. The three buyers met for the first time in the limo and were a little uncomfortable with each other at first.

The champagne followed by the extravagance of the yacht and flowing liquor loosened everyone up and soon the three began sharing stories of wild escapades that lasted well into the night. By morning, each one passed out on deck and unaware that the ship had dropped anchor along the calm Oregon coastline.

Ted struggled to stand; his legs wobbled beneath him. The captain informed his employer of his guest waking.

"Good morning, Mr. Anderson."

Ted jumped at the unexpected and unheard arrival of his host behind him

"Ohh…good morning, Mr. Jackman. Has my purchase arrived?"

"Yes, it has. If you will follow me to the main salon."

"The salon… I though… I would rather..."

"Would you prefer your cabin, Mr. Anderson?"

"Well, yes actually. I would prefer my privacy."

"Very good then, follow me to the main salon for a coffee while I instruct the crew to have your purchase placed in your cabin. Did you sleep well?"

"Not really, I'm still a little groggy from the liquor I guess."

"Sea air, expensive liquor, and good conversation will exact its toll, Mr. Anderson."

Dark Colombian coffee filled the main salon with its scent. And, Ted Anderson, was ready for a cup or two.

"Black no sugar, please," Ted instructed.

"As you wish."

Jackman extended the cup and saucer, and Ted gratefully took the cup and breathed in the rich aroma before taking a sip. The coffee was strong and seemed extraordinarily delicious to his taste.

"It must be the sea air," he mused.

He poured a second cup and again drank deeply. He felt revived and the anticipation of seeing his new toy was foremost on his mind.

Jackman hung the phone up.

"I believe all is ready, if you will follow me."

"I can hardly wait. But first, tell me how we are to dispose of … of the…merchandize when I'm done?"

"That's of no concern for you, Mr. Anderson. Your package deal is all inclusive and those worries are ours to incur."

"I want to know for peace of mind, you do understand."

"Very well, Mr. Anderson, we have an understanding with the Mexican government. There is a lucrative market for secondhand merchandise in Mexico. We sell to Mexico and the merchandise is shipped all over the world, without a trace. Are you ready?"

"Absolutely," Ted said smiling.

He whistled a lively little tune and strutted eagerly behind Jackman. The ship was large, and the walk seemed somewhat endless. Just as Ted was about to ask Jackman exactly how much longer it would take, Jackman came to a halt in front of a row of cabin doors.

"About time," Ted muttered under his breath.

Jackman opened the door to the cabin and entered ahead of Ted. Ted entered and anxiously looked around. Irritation and confusion scowled his face as he watched, Jackman close the door and turned to face him.

"Well?" Ted waited for Jackman to respond.

Jackman said nothing. Ted's eyes narrowed to slits.

"If you think you can swindle me out of a shit load of money, you're... you're..."

Ted swayed unsteadily on his feet though the ship was calm and still.

"I want what I paid for!"

Ted felt groggy and light-headed just as he had when he woke earlier.

"The coffee, the coffee had... You...you'll...."

"Never get away with it. I know Mr. Anderson. Everyone says that—funny really—coming from men like you."

"They'll know I was never in the Cayman's!"

"Mr. Anderson, you're upset, it's understandable given your circumstances. You do remember buying a coach airline ticket, don't you? You went to the airport. You checked your baggage, and you even spoke to the agent when you showed your documents at customs, as per our instructions."

"Yes," Ted's voice rasped.

"You were instructed to go to the men's room and change clothes, yes?"

Mr. Jackman kindly nodded his head to his own question and, Ted, slowly mimicked his movement.

"You were asked to drop your ticket into the trash receptacle along with your clothes. I assume you did so?" Mr. Jackman's methodical voice encouraged a response.

"Yes," Ted whispered.

"Well then, there it is, don't you see?"

"I never got…"

"On the plane… I know Mr. Anderson. Our Mr. Anderson got on that plane. Our, Mr. Anderson, who bore a striking resemblance to you. He wore your discarded clothes, retrieved your ticket from the trash bin, boarded your flight and promptly took a nap, conversing with no one. Upon landing, our Mr. Anderson went to the men' room. Changed clothes, put on a ball cap, and boarded a return flight using documents we prepared for him."

Both men were quiet for a moment. Mr. Jackman waited

for the expected question, the same question they all asked.

Ted's voice shook. "Why? I paid you; I paid you a great deal of money!"

"Indeed, Mr. Anderson, a great deal of money. Money that will serve a great many causes and we are very appreciative."

"The other two, they'll know. They paid you too."

"Yes, yes they did. And when they wake, in good time, they will be as you are now."

"And exactly how is that?"

"Facing your demons, Mr. Anderson. Making restitution, as it were."

"Who are you to judge me? Who the hell are you to exact restitution from me?"

Ted struggled to stay on his feet, his face contorted with rage and fear. Mr. Jackman watched the drug take over and Ted slid into a crouch. His legs numb and crumpled beneath him.

"There never were any kids for sale in that catalog were there?"

"No, Mr. Anderson, there most certainly were not."

Ted's eyes closed as he slumped over on the floor of his cabin.

Jackman studied the pig at his feet and wondered how this damaged piece of refuse could stand to be in his own skin. He wondered how a man could become so evil, as to order human beings from a catalog just as one orders a meal from a menu.

Jackman studied, Ted Anderson, crumpled on the floor of the cabin and another thought came to mind. The damage his own soul was caused through the work he chose to do. The work he was compelled to do. The work he knew he would always do regardless of the law or the condition of his soul.

Three interrogations would take place tomorrow morning inside the dank walls of Terrible Tilly. However, tonight after dark, the ship's small outboard would take out the trash. The beautiful yacht would glide away in the dead of night and soon a new set of buyers would be wined and dined aboard Duplicity.

CHAPTER 2

SARAH

BOSTON-Nearly a year ago

Sarah Knight stood at the massive windows of the penthouse overlooking the park. People spoke in hushed tones among themselves, occasionally glancing her way and sadly shaking their heads. Sarah did not hear any of their quiet conversations; she was lost in her memories.

Last week she and Greg spent days secluded at their cottage on the Vineyard. They left the cottage to walk to the Black Dog restaurant for dinner a couple of times and to pick up some wine for their cozy nights by the fire.

Today she kissed Greg for the last time. *How is that possible*, Sarah thought, *how can any of this be happening?* Sarah's arms were wrapped around the waist of her simple black dress, and she felt cold, empty, and completely alone in this room full of people. People she and Greg knew and spent time with as a couple. Now, she just wanted them all to go away so she could lie down, to sleep, and to forget that Greg was gone. And nothing would ever be the same again.

***

"Sarah, it's been three weeks since the funeral. We need to talk. The estate needs to be settled."

Ben balanced the phone against his left ear while thumbing through Greg's will. Ben had been, Greg's lawyer, his friend, and very much a father figure to him since, Greg's own parents had died many years ago.

"I know, Ben. It just felt too overwhelming, too final, I guess. I've been avoiding this and I'm sorry. This is hard for you too. We both loved him. I know you have other responsibilities, and you want to wrap this up."

"No, that's not true, Sarah, I'm happy to give you all the time you need. Really, it's just that you've been avoiding your friends as well, and people are starting to worry."

"Well, they needn't. I've just needed time to adjust to being alone. But it's so hard, Ben. I woke up this morning and I thought…I need to tell Greg. And then it hit me, Greg is gone. I can't tell him anything ever again. I feel like I'm going crazy."

"Sarah, what you've described is very normal. You're going through the grieving process and it's going to take a long time. Maybe you should talk to someone, a professional in grief counseling or something. I could ask around if you want me to."

"No, Ben, thanks though. Set up a time and I'll come in and take care of Greg's estate."

Sarah knew she and Greg had been more than comfortable financially. Sarah knew Greg was part-owner in a lucrative software design company. A company that designed very popular games.

What she didn't know was, Greg's share of the company was worth millions of dollars, and his partners wanted to buy her out. She had no interest in trying to stay on in a company she had no ability in, so she sold her interest and, Ben, helped her set up her own investments over the next few months.

***

"It's been six months, Sarah, do you have any plans for your future?"

"Well, Ben, I believe you've helped me plan for my future very well."

"I mean do you have any plans to travel or get involved in something. You know plans to move on. It's OK to do that, Sarah."

"Yes, I know its OK and yes I have been thinking about something but it's pretty drastic and they say you shouldn't make any drastic changes for at least a year after you lose someone."

"Who are they?"

"What?"

"Who are, they, that's always offering unsolicited advice?"

"Oh, the experts I guess, why?"

"Because, Sarah, you are the only one who can decide

when you are ready to move on." Ben smiled as he put the phone to his other ear.

Tears welled in her eyes, and she nodded to herself. Yes, she was ready. Ready to begin again. But first she would have to go back, back to the beginning, to Seaside. The first place she had ever felt safe and happy. Until her world fell apart.

CHAPTER 3

SEASIDE: THE OREGON COAST

20 years ago

Sarah slammed her locker. She was late again, and her psychology teacher was a vicious angry spinster who enjoyed making public examples of anyone who shows up late for her class.

Like most sixteen-year-old girls, Sarah had an aversion to being singled out in front of a classroom full of peers. Especially when she was the new girl in school and not quite sure of where she fitted in with the various groups or clicks.

The jocks had spotted her from day one and some were making bets on who would hook up with her first. Sarah didn't know that, but the cheerleaders did. And they were making their own bets as to who's boyfriend would stray first. When you look like Sarah, and you are the new girl in a small school, your stock is raised by the jocks looking for a new conquest.

Robbie was little for a jock, but quick and he had an

unbeatable jump shot.

"Are you going to the pit on Friday?"

Sarah jumped when he spoke to her; she hadn't heard Robbie come up behind her. She'd seen him around and knew enough about his standing to know he was popular with just about everyone.

"I don't know, what's the pit?"

"It's where we hang out. You know, with a keg and loud music."

"Oh. Who's going to be there?"

"Everyone that matters; you want me to pick you up?"

"I'll let you know, thanks…I've got to go."

Sarah gathered her books from the locker and headed to her next class.

Sarah wanted to fit in more than anything. She had lived in more states than anyone she had ever known. Not that she had known anyone for very long. Her father always had a new plan, a new adventure to set out on, and that meant the family was always on the move.

Sarah had listened to her parents talk about Seaside many times. Her dad was a good carpenter, and he was sure he could make a lot of money building condos on the coast. Building condos would take a long time, Sarah was sure they would finally stay somewhere long enough to enjoy friends and maybe even long enough to have a boyfriend.

Robbie was cute but Sarah just wasn't very attracted to

him. She could go to the party with him but what if he thought that meant they were together. If Sarah turned him down, she was afraid that she would miss her chance to fit in. Friday was two days away. She didn't know what to do.

At lunch, Sarah sat alone for about five minutes before, Chuck Reynolds sat down across from her.

"Hey, Sarah, right?" Chuck knew her name. "I'm, Chuck. Where'd you move from?"

Sarah knew Chuck was major and if he was interested in someone, then she was in.

"Alaska."

"You're kidding, right?"

"No, it is in North America you know."

"Yea, but isn't there about one person per square mile of land?"

"Yea, so?"

"I just never met anyone from Alaska before; did you like it there?"

"I don't know, I wasn't there long enough to find out."

"Well, listen, I'm going to the pit on Friday, and I just thought you might want to go."

"Yea, I want to go."

"Great, a bunch of us are going in my ride. I'll pick you up around 7:00."

"Great, thanks. I live…"

"I know where you live. It's a small town, remember."

Now all she had to do was clear it with her parents, not that she could mention the pit or the keg. She'd think of something before Friday.

Friday night was the beginning of Sarah's first real home, her first real school, and her first real friends. She had never been happier in any place they had ever lived, before moving to Seaside.

Even her dad seemed to settle in as he developed big plans to build his first condo. Before long, he had a business partner and financing to begin his new project. The months flew by, and Sarah's family finally had a place to call home.

Chuck was the first boyfriend Sarah had. And while he was fun to be with, Sarah just wasn't ready to get too close or at least not as close as Chuck wanted to get. During summer break, Sarah worked as a bus girl at Harrah's. A very up-scale restaurant along the turn-a-round, close to the beach. Chuck surfed and got close with one or two college girls enjoying their break at the beach.

Come September, Sarah looked forward to her junior year and soon joined a couple of clubs. She wasn't even too torn up about, Chuck, straying. Other guys were already lining up to make their move. Sarah was going to take her time and enjoy the attention.

Homecoming turned out to be the best week of her life. She couldn't wait to get to school each day to be with her friends and Sarah had just started going out with Dan, a tall, very good-looking senior.

Dan was a defensive guard on the football team and not pushy like Chuck had been. Sarah found herself really falling for Dan, and she hoped he felt the same way about her. Weeks passed and Dan became a familiar guest at her house.

Weekends were rarely spent with their friends from school. They didn't party at the pit and even having a beer was seldom. They were happy to spend their time talking about future goals and dreams. The possibilities were endless for them.

Talking usually turned to kissing and soon kissing was not going to be enough. It was only a matter of time before she would decide that sex was right because, Dan, was right. Right for her. Sarah didn't tell him any of this because she knew her resolve to wait a little longer would dissolve the moment she shared her thoughts with him. The moment Dan's mouth found hers, the rush of her blood coursing through her knocked any common sense right out of her head.

On Friday, Sarah got home and saw a dark sedan in the drive. Her father was also home, which was very unusual for 3:30 in the afternoon on a weekday. When she entered the house, Sarah could tell something was very wrong. Her mother had been crying and her father looked worried…no…scared. He looked very scared. Who were these guys and what was going on? Before she could form a single question, Sarah's mother quickly came to her and took her arm.

"Sarah go to your room, please!"

"But…"

"Now, Sarah!"

Her mother ushered her to her room and closed the door. When she heard her mother's footsteps quickly retreat down the hall, she put her ear to the door but could only hear bits and pieces. Occasionally a voice would rise, and she would hear her father's denials, but denials of what?

When her mother finally came to get her, she knew. They were moving again, and nothing could have devastated her more than losing the only home she felt she had ever had.

CHAPTER 4

SEASIDE: NOW

Portland International was not as big as, Sarah, had imagined it would have been. Luggage was across from car rental, and she had everything wrapped up in minutes. With GPS uploaded, Sarah maneuvered the little rental through traffic and finally hit Sunset Highway to the 101.

The scenery was more beautiful than she had remembered. Breathtaking glimpses of glittering expanses of azure water spread before her.

The road hugged cliffs so high she felt herself tremble as she took the curves. At Otter Bay she had to pull over and get out of the car. Otter Bay was nothing more than a wide space in the road for a scenic view and photo op.

The view made Sarah want to cry. She almost did until a mini-van full of hyperactive kids and their cranky parents pulled into the parking space beside her car.

The side door flew open and kids poured out as parents scrambled to keep the kids out of the highway. Sarah watched in amazement as the parents quickly lined the kids up at the guardrail and the dad began snapping photos.

"Do you mind," the father asked, Sarah.

He held the digital camera out to her.

"No, no, I'd be glad to."

Sarah stepped forward taking the camera.

"Just look through here and press there and you're done," the father instructed.

Sarah took the shot and handed the camera back.

"Are you on vacation?" she asked.

She smiled at the kids as they squirmed to get loose from the grip their parents had on them.

"No, thank God," the mother explained. "We're going down the coast to Garibaldi. My parents live there and we're taking the kids fishing."

"Fishing, fishing," the kids squealed in unison.

"Well, have fun."

Sarah stepped back giving the parents an out for a quick exit, and they took her up on it. They were no more anxious to get back on the road than Sarah was for them to leave. She smiled and waved as the minivan pulled back onto Sunset highway.

Sarah wanted another minute or two to breathe in the misty cool air coming off the ocean. Across the road from the scenic viewpoint was a water fountain offering fresh spring water from the mountain behind it. She remembered drinking from one of these fountains when she was a kid. Her parents had stopped for picture taking along the coast when they moved to Seaside with her.

Sarah hurried across the road and pressed the fountain lever. The water was ice cold and nearly froze the back of her throat, but it was so great. She smiled at the good memory it brought back.

The rest of the trip could have taken forever if, Sarah, hadn't forced herself to refrain from stopping every ten minutes to take in the incredible beauty of the ocean and cliffs spread before her. Did she just appreciate beauty more as an adult, because she couldn't remember being this infatuated with the sea when she was a kid?

"I can't believe the cannon's still there," she said.

As she passed the turn that leads to Cannon Beach. Cannon Beach is a fantastic little beach town full of artists and writers, and one or two actors that have beach cottages by the sea. The locals say that the cannon washed up on the beach over a hundred and fifty years ago and that is how the village got its name.

Haystack Rock came to mind. Sarah had loved climbing around the base of Haystack when the tide was out in Cannon Beach. Starfish, crabs, and other creatures were caught in small pools of water in the crevices around the massive rock jutting out of the sea.

The tourists loved coming to Cannon Beach and to Seaside. But the locals were as much a part of the sea as the creatures caught in the tide pools. Once you're captured by the magnificent vastness of the ocean and the scent of the sea, it becomes part of who you are and who you want to be. No other experience can match or fulfill what the sea has to offer your senses. Coming back to Seaside, coming back to the sea, was coming home to, Sarah.

Seaside had grown so much she hardly recognized it. Many of the old stores were gone and new ones had taken their place. No one would have remembered, Sarah, but the faces of those she had been forced to leave behind were still clear in her mind. Maybe because she had held on so tightly to the faces of the place she had felt so connected to. Maybe because her parents had refused to allow her to stay in touch with any of her friends, once they had left Seaside. So quickly and under such stressful circumstances.

Sarah overheard her parents talking once about Seaside. The bits and pieces she overheard scared and hurt her. Before then she had never had a reason to feel shame toward her parents and certainly not shame for her own name.

That day long ago, the day she came home from school to find a dark sedan in the drive with government tags on the license plate was the beginning of years of moves and dingy little apartments.

Finally, the stress and unhappiness of the family grew so

thick that her mother packed their things and moved them both to live with her grandparents in Boston. Sarah's mother resumed her maiden name and changed Sarah's as well. Both she and her mother went by the name of Crawford, after that. Her father visited occasionally but eventually stopped. After a few years, Sarah learned he had drunk himself to death.

After graduation, she worked during the day in a little antique store called, *Three Honest Ladies*. At night, she took classes at the local college. Photojournalism was her passion, as was history. Her studies helped occupy her time.

Sarah wasn't sure what she wanted to do with her future, and that turned out to be moot because she met Greg when he came into the store one day. Greg was looking for antique doorknobs for a massive mahogany door he had purchased through an estate auction the week before.

Greg was thirty-one years old, about six feet tall with blond hair and blue eyes that crinkled at the corners when he smiled. He smiled a lot, and his teeth sparkled as if he belonged in some toothpaste commercial.

Greg took her sailing, fishing, and antiquing along the cape. One day, they sailed to Martha's Vineyard and explored the little villages. And rode scooters around the island. After a lunch of lobster and fresh clams, Greg took her hand and walked her back to their rented scooters.

"I want to show you something," Greg said, flashing that smile of his.

"What is it?" Sarah asked as she strapped it in her helmet.

"It's a surprise, just follow me and I'll show you."

Twenty minutes later, they were in Edgartown. They slowly inched around tourists and of all things, an ox pulling a small cart over the cobbled street in front of the whaling museum. Greg turned down a side street and soon stopped in front of a lovely two-story cottage. It was white with a narrow front stoop, inches from the cobbled street.

"What's this," Sarah questioned?

"You'll see."

Greg took Sarah's hand and led her up the steps before he took a key out of his pocket and unlocked the door. Greg opened the door and pulled her into the bright cheerful living room. It was filled with overstuffed furniture and antiques prevalent in the whaling days of the 1700 and 1800's of the island. Sarah didn't know what to say so she looked at Greg and waited for him to explain.

"Well," Greg exclaimed!

"Well, what," Sarah questioned?

Greg looked exasperated. "What do you think of the place?"

"I think it's beautiful, how could I not? Is it yours?"

"No, Sarah, it's ours, if you'll have me… and it. We're a packaged deal."

No words came forth as Sarah stared at, Greg, shocked. Stunned silence filled the foyer. Greg's heart sank into the pit of his stomach.

"It's OK, Sarah, really. I shouldn't have sprung it on you like this. I... um... lets go, ok?"

Sarah was instantly in his arms laughing, crying, and talking onto his shoulder in unintelligible words. Greg lifted her face and covered her mouth with his.

"Is that a yes," he asked when he finally pulled away from her?

Her answer was to wrap her arms around his neck pulling his head down to her mouth.

"Yes," she whispered as she kissed him again and again.

The next few weeks were a blur as Sarah and Greg planned a quiet low-key wedding. There was no one for her to invite anyway except her mother, grandparents, and the three honest ladies.

Her mother had remarried and moved to Connecticut after her senior year of school. She had wanted Sarah to move with her and her new husband. Sarah had refused, and her grandparents had intervened on her behalf. Her mother resigned herself to the fact that, Sarah, had enough moving and she let the issue go.

The wedding was small and elegant. Performed by a bishop in a small white church and attended by family and a few friends. Sarah's mother and grandparents liked Greg very much and could see that Sarah was happy and in love with her new husband. There was no doubt in anyone's mind that Greg adored his bride.

Greg had wanted to take, Sarah, on a Caribbean honeymoon but, Sarah, asked to honeymoon on the Vineyard. She wanted to capture the feel of home, her home by the sea. Life was joyous and demanding.

Greg's work was primarily in Boston but afforded them luxury time on the Vineyard. Sarah often thought of Seaside and planned to take Greg there for a getaway. He had been on the west coast but only in California. She wanted him to see the magic of the Cascade Mountains and the Northern Coastal Mountain cliffs overlooking the white-capped swells along the Oregon coast.

Never could Sarah have imagined that the years and their life would fly by so fast or that their time together would end so quickly. She had taken for granted the happy times and assumed they would simply go on forever.

Most people never imagine the unthinkable until it happens. Sarah wouldn't leave the hospital. The nursing staff would bring her food trays that she left uneaten. Sarah showered in Greg's hospital bathroom and took only small breaks to walk outside while he remained in a coma after the horrific car crash.

The doctors tried to tell her there was no hope, but she wouldn't listen. The day Greg died was the day Sarah shut down and closed herself off from the rest of the world. Now, months later and back in Seaside, she felt ready to live again.

CHAPTER 5

THE GLASS HOUSE

Sarah pulled into a parking spot in front of what used to be an arcade along the turn-a-round. Now, it was a group of upscale boutiques filled with swim-ware and beach clothes. Seaside was gearing up for the summer tourist trade. The beach was chilly in April, so Sarah grabbed a sweater out of her overnight bag and put it on.

Cold sand squished under her feet, and she began to shiver. She didn't let the water ebb under her feet because she knew it was freezing cold. Few people were combing the beach, and most were wearing coats. She wished she had her jacket on.

Sarah took in the expansive view of the sea and smiled as her eyes settled on the lighthouse. She remembered the lighthouse from years ago. There was a write- up in the newspaper, The Seaside Signal. Apparently, some infestation of sea worms had embedded itself throughout the lighthouse and the caretaker refused to return until they were exterminated.

They say it took the pest control company several trips to the lighthouse before the worm infestation could be controlled and eliminated. However, the caretaker was long gone, and the lighthouse was sold to a Portland investor who turned it into a crematorium. Sarah shuddered a little at the thought of a motorboat gliding a casket out to the lighthouse. The thought of it took on a Gothic and cryptic note.

To the south of the lighthouse were the gorgeous cliffs of Tillamook Head, with a small smattering of very expensive homes. The house that caught Sarah's eye had a wall of gleaming glass and massive multilevel decks complete with a swimming pool. And it sported an enclosed tram on a motorized lift that brings the tram down to the beach and back. That was the house she wanted to buy. That was the house she would call home.

The water was calm and the day clear. Gulls cried overhead as she made her way back to the promenade entrance on Broadway. Excitement filled her as her heart raced. *What if the owner wouldn't sell, what if…?* Sarah stopped thinking about the negatives and took a deep breath. She would call Ben.

Ben would check it out and she could remain in the background, anonymous. This was, after all, a small town and word spread fast if someone was looking to purchase an expensive property on Tillamook Head. Ben listened as, Sarah talked and drove up the winding road to Tillamook Head. She hoped to be able to pinpoint the house she'd seen from the beach.

"Sarah, do you think you may be rushing into this too fast?" Ben's voice was concerned.

"Ben, this is like coming home and for the first time since Greg's death, I actually feel excited and hopeful about life."

"Well, it's like I've always said, only you can know when you're ready for the next step. If you can get me an address, I'll call one of the local Realtors and see what I can do."

"Thanks Ben, I knew I could count on you."

In the meantime, Sarah set herself up in an ocean-side hotel room and enjoyed her beach combing in the mornings and midday lunch on the terrace.

Afternoons were spent getting re-familiarized with the shops and surrounding areas. Including Cannon Beach and Haystack Rock. Sarah wondered if she could remember the spot where she had been thrown from a horse named Comanche, that she had rented from the riding stables. A wayward gull had spooked, Comanche, as she galloped toward Haystack Rock.

For ten days she laid flat on her back in a hospital bed with a cracked pelvis bone. Which had nearly drove her crazy, especially when her mom declared no more horseback riding! Of course, her mom relented, and Sarah could enjoy endless gallops through the sand and surf with Comanche.

Sarah searched the phone book and saw that many of the kids she had gone to school with were still living in Seaside. Some even owned a few of the newer shops in town.

Chuck Reynolds was not listed in the phone book, but

Robbie Worthington was, and he owned a little coffee shop on Broadway. Josh Baker and his wife owned a great shop that sold everything from kites to skateboards, bikes, and sand-sail beach crafts. One of the cheerleaders owned a beach boutique where Sarah had recently bought a sundress.

Sarah couldn't bring herself to look up, Dan. It felt a little disrespectful to Greg, and she wasn't sure she wanted to know who he might have married.

She had been right; no one had recognized her when she'd come face to face with them. She remembered them and certainly had an advantage over them. Sarah wasn't about to disclose her past with them. Her father may have harmed them or their families in some way. And she wasn't about to destroy her home with any bitter feelings they may harbor toward her or her family.

The town was buzzing with gossip. Who from Boston has just purchased the most expensive property in Clatsop County? Ben had outdone himself, as usual. The house Sarah just bought was a source of contention between a divorcing couple. And neither one could wait to unload it and part company as quickly as possible. Though sparsely furnished, the furniture that was there had been part of the sale and had allowed Sarah to move in right after the closing on the house.

By now, Sarah had been tagged as the buyer of the glass house and shops she frequented couldn't help her quickly enough to spend her money. She slowly established casual friendships over the next few weeks. She even had a couple of lunch dates with Cindy, an ex-cheerleader and with Josh and his wife. Sarah was even thinking of having a small cocktail party at her home.

Security at the house was state of the art and Sarah enjoyed using the tram to get to and from the beach. When the tram was up, Sarah could flip the power switch off which ensured the tram couldn't be accessed. The property was enclosed with a security fence, and closed-circuit cameras were placed throughout the house and around the property. Sarah felt safe and secure in her glass house overlooking the sea.

The night before her cocktail party, Sarah took a dip in the swimming pool and was grateful for the solar heater. Wrapped in a thick terry robe, Sarah walked over to the telescope on the deck and scanned the water.

There were no distant lights from passing ships on the dark waters. She drew a line at spying on neighbors, but she did check out the lighthouse and there was a flicker of light at the base of the rocks. A moment later the light went out and when Sarah scanned the area around the rocky edges it was dark. *It must have been a reflection from the town lights* she thought and went back into the house.

CHAPTER 6

THE CARETAKER

He couldn't use the flashlight anymore. Someone might see it from town, and his associates would most certainly not appreciate it if he brought undue attention to the lighthouse.

The wet body was unbelievably heavy and cumbersome to move over jagged rock. Thirty more minutes and the oven would be hot enough and as luck would have it, a scheduled cremation was to take place tonight, as well.

CHAPTER 7

SETTLING IN

Friday night's cocktail party was in the works and Sarah wondered what in the hell she was thinking of when she invited so many people to her glass house.

She hadn't even hired a caterer to help her out. Yes, she knew her way around the kitchen. But she was a nervous wreck, and the party was in five hours.

Somehow, Sarah pulled off baked brie in puff pastry, baskets of French baguettes and seafood dip, chicken satay with peanut sauce, and lobster rolls, along with a few bought items at the local specialty shops.

Her bar was fully stocked, and Josh had agreed to act as bartender to get the party started. With two hours left before guests were due to arrive, Sarah decided to relax in a hot bath with a glass of chardonnay.

Guests arrived right on time and Sarah looked radiant in

her pink Armani slip dress. Those who hadn't met Sarah yet were anxious to greet their hostess. Most were curious about her sudden appearance in Seaside and why she had left Boston. Soon everyone was enjoying themselves and the conversation turned to local issues.

"Joe and James Bartlett never did have any sense," Josh stated. "Even in high school they were always over the top. Getting high, getting drunk, it didn't matter what it was it was excessive."

"What happened," Sarah inquired?

Josh's wife, Melinda, exclaimed, "They got drunk and tried to row out to the lighthouse last night. The boat tipped over and Joe drowned!"

"That's horrible!" Sarah's hand automatically flew to her mouth.

"I'm surprised it didn't happen sooner. The way they drink and drive, drink and sail, drink and everything."

"Mike!" Cindy glared at her husband hoping to shut him up.

"What," Mike frowned? "You know it's true."

Cindy let out a deep breath. "Anyway, James is in the hospital, and their parents are beside themselves with grief."

"I'm sure they are," Melinda said quietly.

Sarah remembered the flicker of light she had seen at the base of the lighthouse the night before. *What time did she see the light;* she tried to recall the time? When she came back into the house, she had turned on the TV and local news was just coming on. So that meant it was 11:00 p.m. She had seen the light at maybe around 10:50.

"What time did they take the boat out?" Sarah spoke to Mike.

"What?"

"When Joe and James took the boat out on the water, what time was it?"

"I don't know, why?" Mike asked.

"Well, it's just that I was using the telescope last night and I thought I saw a light flicker at the base of the lighthouse." That got the attention of her guests.

"Maybe, James, was searching for, Joe," Melinda offered, "Or it could have been the Coast Guard."

"No," Sarah said, "The light lasted for just a second and it was small, very small, like a flashlight. The Coast Guard would have huge lights and lots of them, right?"

"Right," they said in unison.

"What time did you see the light, Sarah?" Mike asked.

"It was around 10:50. Just before the news came on. That's why I wanted to know when they put the boat in the water."

"I don't know what time they put the boat in the water. But the Coast Guard will have a record of when they got the call about the guys," Cindy offered. "I'm sure, James, spent some time looking for, Joe, before heading to shore to get help. Maybe he was searching the base of the lighthouse just hoping, Joe, made it there. I can't imagine what he was going through. Freezing water, his brother missing…"

"Yea, and very, very drunk," Josh said dryly.

"Do you think, James, will be held responsible for, Joe's death?" Melinda questioned.

"Surely not," Josh frowned. "They're grown men who made wrong choices and, Joe, paid the ultimate price for his choice. Most of us are just surprised it took so long to catch up with them."

"Josh, that's a little harsh isn't it?" Mike chided.

"It's not as harsh as it would have been if they had killed anyone else during their escapades. They each have had several DUI arrests over the years, and we all drive the same roads as they do… or did."

"Do you think they'll ever find his body?" Cindy whispered.

A quiet hush fell across the room and suddenly the party was over.

CHAPTER 8

DAN

The next morning, Sarah drank coffee, black, and read the Seaside Signal at the kitchen counter. Joe's body was lost and never recovered by the Coast Guard. James was not to be charged in the case, and no reference was made regarding alcohol or past transgressions.

A memorial service was set and most of the townspeople wanted to show their love and respect to the family by attending. Followed of course by Joe's buddies filing into the local pubs to raise a glass or two, in his honor… of course.

The toasts raised to Joe, eventually gave way to other talk. And as the patrons got buzzed their jovial spirits turned to remember when's, and soon everyone was laughing and drinking to less serious times.

"Hey," someone shouted, "Remember the time we had a funeral service for, Fred!"

The bar crowd went wild with laughter!

"Fred's funeral was the best. Man, that was a good time wasn't it?"

Of course, everyone offered their version of what really happened to Fred, which led to the best funeral service Seaside had ever held or was likely to ever hold according to the bar flies. For the few in the pub that weren't present for, Fred's funeral, those who had been reveled in the opportunity to tell and retell the story.

Fred was an old one legged drunk. He never had any money to buy his own drinks but was never without a friend who'd spring for a beer or two in any of the pubs along the turnaround. Even the bartenders bought him a round nearly every day.

Fred must have had a liver the size of a marble because one day as he sat on the bar enjoying his beer, he simply keeled over dead as a doorknob. Fred most likely died of cirrhosis of the liver though no one will ever truly know for sure. No autopsy was performed and Fred was buried in a simple coffin carried through the streets by his friends and patrons of the pubs he hung out in.

Fred's final resting place wasn't so final because the pallbearers dumped his body into the river that fed into the Pacific and, Fred, floated out to sea as his friends cheered and waved goodbye.

"Yea," one of Fred's bar buddies sighed, "That was the best funeral we ever gave for anyone. I sure do miss buying beer for that little one-legged drunken seagull!"

The bar went wild again, and laughter spilled out onto the promenade and passersby smiled at each other as they strolled along the beachfront.

Since Fred's days in the pubs, the ATF became more stringent in enforcing the no fowls allowed rule and the protected seagulls were once again safe from contributing to the delinquency violations.

The week after the cocktail party flew by and Sarah was feeling welcomed and comfortable around town. Many of the locals already knew her by sight and took an active interest in her comings and goings. Plus, they wanted to be included in her next party.

The weather was warming, and early morning beach combing was coming alive again. Sarah had taken to scanning the beach early each morning with her telescope. When someone would stop to inspect a find, Sarah would try to focus the scope to determine what the find was.

When she tired of her snooping, she would take the tram down to the beach, remove the key and pocket it before taking off up the beach. Most mornings Sarah would end up on the promenade waiting her turn outside the always busy bakery.

If I don't watch out, she thought. I'll gain a ton of weight. Mmm… black coffee and caramel apple twists on a cool morning at the beach. What could be better?

Sarah took her time strolling back to the tram. Her sandals

laced through her fingers, her toes leaving prints in the wet sand. The walk back to the tram was slow and easy leaving plenty of time to think about, Greg, and how she wished she had shared Seaside with him before he was gone. He would have loved it here just as she did.

The gulls cried and dipped toward the beachcombers, hoping they would throw their bakery goods to them.

"Tough," she said.

As she popped the last morsel of buttery goodness into her mouth followed by the last of the coffee. *How many* laps *in the pool burn 450 calories of pastry* she wondered as she pulled the key to the tram from her pocket and stepped into the Plexiglas enclosure.

Sarah had swum laps until she could swim no more.

"Damn that caramel apple twist," Sarah said aloud.

As she stood under the needle like spray of the shower in the master bathroom. The phone began ringing just as she took a large dollop of moisturizer out of the jar.

"Hello."

Sarah held the phone in her left hand with the cream in her right hand.

"Hi Cindy, what's up?" Sarah paused to listen. "Dinner, I'd love to, what time?" A night out is exactly what she needed. "I'll be there, thanks for inviting me. I'll see you soon, bye."

Sarah took her time getting ready for dinner with Cindy, Mike, Josh, and Melinda. Dinner at the Partee room was always nice. There was no ocean view of course because it was on the golf course high above the first green, six blocks inland.

The chef was French and gifted even though he had to tone down the sauces. Chocolates and creams, etc.—to accommodate a more healthy and fit lifestyle among the locals as well as the tourists.

The cocktails were perfect, and the staff did not intrude with constant comings and goings. Once their orders had been given to the waiter the conversation turned to more interesting topics.

An hour or so later coffee was served with an assortment of tiny French pastries. Sarah faked not being interested in the pastries while she sipped her coffee.

Mike had said something about a fundraiser and the conversation paused waiting for her response. But Sarah was lost in time. Twenty years ago, to be exact, she watched Dan enter the Partee room.

He was tall and slender with strong wide shoulders and a mat of thick dark hair. Sarah remembered everything about, Dan, from all those years ago. The first time she saw him, the first time he'd called her, the first time he had kissed her.

"Sarah, Sarah."

"What, oh I'm sorry. What were you saying?"

"Never mind that," Cindy said. "How do you know, Dan?"

"I, I don't," Sarah quietly stammered.

"ok then… do you want to know him?" Cindy grinned

mischievously.

A deep shade of crimson started at the base of her throat and spread across, Sarah's face, leaving her cheeks flushed. Mike smiled at the deeply embarrassed, Sarah, and looked across the room to see who Dan was with. He was alone and that was unusual. Not that, Dan, saw anyone steady. He was kind of a free spirit since his divorce, and he seemed to like it that way.

Dan had noticed Sarah, the moment he entered the dining room. This was not the first time he had been aware of her presence in Seaside. Seaside was a tourist town, yes, with lots of new people all the time. However, little escaped the locals. Especially a newcomer capable of purchasing a property like the glass house.

Sarah thought she was unknown. She thought no one would remember her from high school. Sarah's time here in school may have been short but for, Dan, it was very memorable. He didn't know why she was not forthcoming about her time here before but for the time being he would respect her privacy.

Just then, Dan looked over at their table and Cindy waved him over. Sarah was at a loss of what to do, so she simply smiled as he walked over. His gaze never leaving her eyes and she knew. She knew he remembered her.

"Dan, would you like to join us?" Cindy was quick to offer. "We've already eaten but please join us for coffee and dessert."

Dan nodded, pulled up a chair and sat down.

"Sarah this is, Dan Morrison, Dan, Sarah Knight," Mike introduced them.

The others had known him their whole lives.

"Sarah," Dan said as he reached for her hand and gave it a little squeeze.

The others glanced at each other but said nothing. The next hour or so was spent discussing the upcoming fundraiser and speculation regarding summer trade in a tourist town.

Occasionally, Dan's eyes would meet Sarah's, and her heart would skip a beat. The feelings she had for him in school were not lost in time. Whatever he had that had attracted her to him before was very much here now. Charisma, charm, or pure sex appeal drew her to him and him to her. Sarah was in trouble and she had the distinct feeling that she was ready for it.

Dan sat at his desk the next morning, coffee at hand and the financial report in front of him. He'd read the report numerous times and hadn't a clue to what the final figures had been.

His mind was not on the financial s, it was on Sarah Knight. Why the secrecy and why the facade of being new to town? Whatever her problem, Dan wanted to know, he wanted to help, but most of all he wanted to reconnect with her.

To hell with it, Dan thought as he grabbed his car keys.

The drive along Sunset Blvd. was bright and sunny with glimpses of incredible ocean views that always made the drive a pleasure. Most locals often took their home and city for granted, never fully enjoying what they had. The tourists on the other hand often dreamed of leaving their hectic lives for a lower key and relaxed way of life.

Human nature is, never to fully appreciate what you have right in front of you. We always seem to be looking for the next big thing or the next exciting venture to come our way. Dan wanted the new romance that just moved to town.

The gate was closed at the end of Sarah's driveway. Dan drove close to the intercom and pushed the call button. Sarah was startled by the unfamiliar sound of the call button on her security system. Though she had heard it before, when she was customizing herself with its features, she had never actually had anyone call her on it before. The gate had been left open for guests and service people because she was expecting them. Sarah froze as she stared at Dan's face on the monitor. Once again, Dan pressed the call button.

OK do something, she thought.

Pressing the response button, Sarah said, "Hi Dan, come on up."

Sarah buzzed the gate open and Dan drove through. The glass house was just as impressive from this angle as it was ocean-side.

The couple that had it built had hopes of resurrecting their failing marriage. The house did not fix what was wrong in their relationship. The husband had never had to work a day in his life. Trust fund babies often bank on the money at their disposal to solve all the ills in their life.

The wife was bored and lonely and used the money to fund whims and short-lived hobbies. They even bought a plane so she could take flying lessons. The only lessons learned were never to trust your bored and lonely spouse to a bored with his wife, flight instructor.

The back of the house posed impressively making it difficult to judge which side was truly the front side of the house.

Ornate landscaping created a lush private retreat. To the right of the drive a driving range and putting green stood at attention, the flag on the green cheerfully waved as Dan passed.

A circular drive of finely placed brick brought Dan's car steps away from the wide tri-level porch and Sarah, as she had stepped out to meet him.

"Sarah," Dan greeted as he came up the steps to her.

"It's good to see you, Dan," she smiled.

They looked at each other for a moment longer. "Please, come in."

They stepped into a foyer and Sarah crossed the room with Dan behind her.

"Would you like a coffee or something?"

"No, thanks though," Dan's voice was warm and familiar.

"Please, have a seat."

Sarah motioned for Dan to sit on a deep sofa facing the glistening sea. Nothing was said for a moment as they each stared out the floor to ceiling glass to the amazing vastness of the ocean before them.

"I have wondered about you, Sarah. I've thought about you often."

"Me too, I've always thought of you here in Seaside. I couldn't really picture you anywhere else."

"Why is that?"

"I don't know. Maybe because you and Seaside were the only happy memories I carried with me wherever I went."

"Why didn't you come back when you were an adult and when you could make your own decisions?"

"Dan, I created a life for myself in Boston. A happy life and it's one I'll always be grateful for."

"I heard that you're a widow."

"Yes, my husband Greg died in a car accident nearly a year ago."

"I'm sorry, Sarah."

"Thank you. Greg was a wonderful man, and I miss him very much."

"Why all the secrecy and why haven't you mentioned to anyone that you used to live here or that you went to school with the people you now spend time with?"

"Dan why do you think my family moved away in the dead of night without notice to anyone?"

"I don't know. Why did they?"

"I don't know either!"

The next few hours were spent with Sarah, explaining all she did know and the suspicions she had to, Dan. In the end, all the questions that surrounded her childhood remained. And neither Dan nor Sarah knew just what acts, illegal or otherwise her father had been involved in. Sarah explained that if her father had been involved with something illegal that had hurt any of her friend's families, she wasn't prepared to deal with it just yet.

By coming to Seaside fresh and unbiased, she hoped to build a new life for herself. A fresh start in a familiar memory. One that held such promise for her before, and she hoped would again. Before Dan left he asked Sarah to have dinner with him.

"Can we make it tomorrow night instead?" Sarah smiled up at him.

"Of course, tomorrow night it is."

Dan took one last look at the sea.

"I was here for the housewarming the Carter's had when this house was built. It was the talk of the town for months while it was being built."

"I do love this view," Sarah mused.

.

CHAPTER 9

TERRIBLE TILLY

The caretaker took meticulous notes. Facts had to be checked, investigated, and verified. There was no room for error. Mistakes would make the team vulnerable. Mistakes would make the team guilty, guilty of harming innocents. And that would make the team unfit to fulfill their mission. Lucky for him these facts were verified and re-verified before a subject ever arrived on Tilly.

His main goal was to gather intelligence from each subject, on yet to be discovered perpetrators. Pedophiles always know other pedophiles. They're like cockroaches gathering in dark grimy places, contaminating all they touch. His job was to uncover their hiding places and then the team would work together to exterminate the nests of vermin.

The three subjects arriving together were routine, and the setup in the lighthouse was effective. The caretaker simply kept each one sedated in a separate room until their turn for interrogation.

Ted Anderson was wracking his brain. There had to be something, something to bargain with. What did this guy want? Events of the night before were coming back in bits and pieces. Ted watched, fear gripping him to his bowels. He watched as his captor picked up a clipboard and studied the contents. Ted's stomach lurched as he took note of his captor's clenched jaw as their eyes met again.

"Shall we begin?" the interrogator quietly asked Ted.

"I, I want to cooperate! Just tell me what you want!"

The interrogator stood silent and very still. He was staring always staring, unblinking. His countenance was commanding, and terror erupted deep within his subject.

"Please, I have money."

Cold calculated silence met his offer.

"I'm a Banker, I have connections."

Silence filled the room.

"I know something, something big, something worth billions of dollars and I'll let you in on it."

The interrogator remained silent…but an almost imperceptible movement, a facial muscle flexed near his eye and Ted saw it. Hope spilled forth.

"It's a drug, a new drug, a performance enhancement supplement. It's virtually undetectable. Only a few people in the world know about it. We're about to introduce it to pro-sports. We've already slipped it in on a few athletes. Their performance level peaked three-fold. Please, you have to listen."

The interrogator stood silent and he listened. He listened as Ted told him of his financial interest in the Portland Falcons and his connections to sports medicine. He listened as; Ted described his business partner and the amazing trek through the Brazilian rain forest. He listened as; Ted told of the astounding stamina the people of the Amazon exhibited to his partner. He listened as, Ted described the simple ingredients found in the forest and readily available as herbs, bark, minerals, and vitamins. And he listened as; Ted shared the one ingredient that bound and ignited the ingredients to enhance strength to superhuman strength.

Natural abilities become magnified. Stamina, range, and perception all thrived at peak performance and without violent outbursts or shrinking testicles. He listened and recorded every detail and when the interrogation was complete, he had all he needed.

Ted felt relief, great relief. So great was his relief, he was compelled to close his eyes and breathe deeply. A feeling of well-being flowed through him as he lay still. A smile flickered across his lips and lovely sleep enveloped him as his life's blood flowed unbeknownst to him through the tubes along the sides of the table.

CHAPTER 10

NEW BEGINNINGS

That was the third outfit Sarah had tried on in the last twenty minutes. She really was feeling like she was in high school again.

Elegant but not matronly, youthful but not overtly sexy, that's the look she was going for.

Why was she acting this way? Dating can't be this trying. It used to be fun, something to look forward to. Greg had made it so easy but then again so had Dan. Apparently, she was the problem. Sarah stared into the mirror, puckered her lips, pulled her hair up, flipped it back down, rolled her eyes and walked out of the room.

Dan was a few minutes early when he arrived to pick Sarah up for their date. She knew it was silly, but she felt excited and nervous. What if time had changed things? Sometimes memories are shaded, and reality can be harsh.

"Hi, you're early."

Sarah smiled as, Dan, stepped through the door.

"Hi, you look great."

"You always were sweet."

"Your dad sure didn't think so."

"That's because he said you always drove into the driveway way too fast."

"He put in a speed bump—in the driveway!" Dan's voice was incredulous, his brows high on his forehead.

"Yes, just for you. See, he did care."

Suddenly everything was easy and familiar as they laughed at her father's expense.

"Are you ready?"

"Yes, I think I am."

Sarah smiled to herself as she gathered her handbag and set the security system. She really was ready, ready to begin again.

Harrah's fine dining was just that, fine dining. When they arrived at the restaurant the Maître d' was elegantly dressed in coat tails. The host wore a tiny master wine tasters cup around his neck on a gold chain. The wine list was impressive to say the least and the ambiance was elegant and sophisticated.

Locals and tourists alike filled the candlelit room. Sarah and Dan sipped their wine and suddenly, Dan laughed.

"What?" Sarah smiled and waited.

"The last date we had you were sixteen and I was seventeen."

"And?"

"And this is the last place I would have been able to take

you to on a date."

"We were kids. Kids aren't supposed to afford this place."

"Hey, remember the new Mustang I bought?"

Sarah blushed because she did remember the new Mustang. She also remembered the old, abandoned racetrack. The racetrack was where they would spend their date nights talking about any and everything under the stars. The place where, if her parents hadn't moved her away, would have surely been the place and the man she would have lost her virginity to. oh… that Mustang.

"Whatever happened to that car?"

"I was seventeen!"

"Ahh ohh."

Sarah's eyes widened and they both burst into laughter.

"Wherever the car is I hope it holds as many good memories for its current owner as it does for me," Dan said.

Sarah blushed again and Dan smiled, knowing her memories were the same as his.

Salads arrived, and the hours slipped away as if Harrah's was a secluded racetrack and time kindly returned them to the moments they embraced.

CHAPTER 11

MORRISON INVESTIGATIONS

Dan sat at his desk once again perusing the financial s, which were bleak, bleak, and bleaker. He turned to the sports section and the Portland Falcon's took center court of the section.

Scott Rader dominated last night's game. He was unstoppable, and the headlines were calling the team the Portland Rader's. The sportswriter droned on and on as if, Rader, was the team in and of himself. According to the writer, Rader made every point alone and the other team seemed to be non-existent on the court.

Dan wondered how rough it was going to get on, Rader, with his teammates being virtually discounted in the papers. Being a phenom usually makes one a pariah on a team sport. Well at least until the endorsements start rolling in and then the guy is a rock star complete with groupies, good ole boys, and an entourage at his beck and call.

Scott Rader was as astounded as anyone else at his current

rise in stock. He had been performing at levels unbelievable not only to himself but flabbergasting to his team and adversaries alike. Scott had always pushed himself, had always strived to excel. His dedication to skill, diet, and workouts must finally be paying off.

Scott's performance was magic. He ran faster, jumped higher, shot straighter. Even his sight and depth perception seemed enhanced. Scott never tired on the court, his endurance levels were superhuman.

There was talk of an endorsement and his sports manager nearly vibrated with anticipation as he geared up for a once in a lifetime opportunity of money and fame to hit his client.

Behind the scenes, brass at the Portland Falcons were worried and holed up in sequestered meetings privy only to a select few. Sudden star ability, arising out of the blue usually meant one thing—enhancement of some sort. The team would take a hit, a huge blow if Rader was using.

"I want him tested! Use an alias, no one outside of this room is to know, got it?" the manager barked at Doc.

"Yea, yea I got it!" Doc was cock sure, Scott, would come up clean. He was sure because he tested Scott regularly as part of his health program.

Doc was methodical in his quest to perfect the performance of select athletes. Scott Rader being the first real athlete to excel under his new methods. And when his career rocketed, Doc would take the credit for Scott's new and improved abilities on court. After all, Doc had Scott on his own personalized regime of diet, exercise, herbs, and vitamins. The cocktail he prescribed for Scott was known only to him and a couple of other people. Even Scott didn't know exactly what he took. He trusted, Doc, and it was paying off.

Doc knew his stock would rise as well. Teams across the nation would be seeking to steal him away from the Falcons. Maybe he could go independent? Set up a huge private practice in New York or L.A., the sports industry would pay him millions to churn out champions like Rader. He would be a rock star in his field. He envisioned a private jet whisking him to exotic beaches where he would wine and dine with other worthy celebrities.

"Doc, Doc, now damn it!"

"On it," Doc fired back confidently, as he gathered his files the approved files on, Rader, and stuffed them into the briefcase. *His Eyes-only* files were encoded and not susceptible to spy-ware activity and there were spies everywhere in this industry.

Dan Morrison had spent too much time away from his main office in Portland. Fritz, the office manager, was very capable of keeping the three field agents busy on existing and on-going cases. But clients want to know that the PI in charge is on their case as well.

The clients and I mean each client feel their case is of the utmost importance. And if they thought Dan wasn't on top of their case, well, let's just say Morrison Investigations was not the only PI firm available to them.

Dan's office was on the sixth floor of a waterfront warehouse that had been renovated a few years back into office space. Ground floor boutique shops and eateries that served fresh seafood caught by local fisherman along the Columbia River.

The waterfront offered tourists and locals artistic flavor and the excitement of bustling street vendors, hawkers, and the occasional pickpocket. The space was great. Investors had done an exceptional job restoring the buildings and code required period design inside and out.

Four large rooms and a bath and a half belonged to the PI suite. Dan's office was large with an adjacent full bath. His view was of the barges, freighters, and boat traffic on the river below. When he first opened here, he was afraid the view would be a constant distraction from his work. Like most people, his work life became a distraction from the pleasures in life.

Even in Seaside, the beach house that had been in his family for three generations and offered panoramic views of the Pacific often went unnoticed by him when he was in work mode.

Fritz was at the massive desk in the entry of the suite when Dan walked in. He was carrying a file and a huge bubba keg sized cup, of dark Colombian roast, heavy on the cream, coffee. Sometimes the coffee tore his stomach up, so he went to blond rather than black. No way was he cutting down on the coffee.

Dan's vices were few but deeply embedded these days. The occasional double shot, wine with dinner a couple of times a week, no cigarettes, and since Sarah was back in his life, no more dates with other women.

Women had always been attracted to him with his tall muscular build, dark hair, and dark eyes above that strong angular jaw line. Dan looked dangerous and sexy as hell. Women young and not so young wanted to get up close and personal with his kind of danger.

"Ed at the Falcons sent a file over. It's on your desk."

Fritz stood behind the desk flipped a page on the field agent assignment book and ran his finger down the list to Gina's case load.

"Gina's flying out at noon. She'll be in Miami overnight maybe longer, depends on whether or not her mark screws up."

Dan set his file on Fritz's desk and held his hand out for the field agent assignment book.

"You see the game last night?" Dan asked Fritz.

"Yea, Rader tore…it…up. Man, he's going to be bigger than Magic, bigger than Shaq."

"Bigger than Shaq!" Dan cocked his brow at Fritz.

"You wanna put some green on it? I'm telling you he'll have an endorsement by this time next month. Then, every kid in America will be eating breakfast with Rader on his Wheaties box."

"Pass, I'm fine tuning my list of vices. Gambling is one I'm cutting back on."

"You might want to limit the coffee intake while you're at it." Fritz eyed Dan's Bubba keg of coffee.

"You might wanna get, Ed, on the phone for me and mind your own business when it comes to my caffeine fix."

Dan smiled at his keg as he tipped it to his mouth.

"Just a suggestion," Fritz muttered as he hit speed dial to, Ed's office at the Falcon's.

Dan wrapped the most pressing business up and was headed back to the coast by early afternoon.

***

Sarah was putting on the green next to the house when Dan pulled through the gate and spotted her. He cocked his brow in surprise at the sight of her. *Sarah golfed?* Why didn't he know this? Dan stopped the car next to the putting green and got out.

"Who's winning?" His smile was warm not condescending.

"I have another putter, a Ping, if you think that will help you?" her banter was equally warm.

"Do I hear a challenge? You're on, Lady!"

They played, they laughed, they swam in her pool and ordered take out.

Dan woke next to her on the sofa, the movie credits were rolling quietly on the screen. He turned the screen off with the remote and grabbed a blanket from the back of the sofa to cover her. Before he could spread the blanket over her, she turned over stretching long, her breasts tugging her sweater tight over them. Dan swallowed hard holding the blanket in midair.

"You're leaving?" Sarah squinted up smiling, waiting for a

response.

Dan stood, blanket in hand and said nothing.

"Dan."

"What?"

"You're leaving?"

"Um… yea, ahh yea I've gotta go. I've got work tomorrow. I… here let me cover you up."

Dan quickly spread the blanket over Sarah. Sarah flipped the blanket off her legs and stood up.

"What's wrong, you seem upset, did I do something?"

"No. Not at all! I just need to go that's all." Dan turned and strode toward the door.

"Stop!"

The command of her voice brought him up short and he turned, brow cocked and watched as she crossed to him her hands on her hips. He stood watching her and his breath caught as she reached out to touch him.

"What have I done?"

He simply stared at her saying nothing.

"Dan?"

Her voice was soft and quiet and when she said his name, it was like no other. The sound of his name on her lips made him weak. It made him want her so badly he didn't trust his resolve to respect her wishes to take things slowly, as he had promised. Just as he had promised her all those years ago in the Mustang, at the racetrack, under the stars.

"Dan, please."

Sarah's eyes glistened with the threat of tears and Dan's resolve vanished in the instant it took for him to gather her to him, his mouth crushing hers. Sarah froze for a moment before wrapping her arms around his neck, her fingers raking through his hair and pulling him into her body.

Her tongue shyly flicked across his lips and he lost it. Dan's mouth never stopped kissing her as he scooped her up and crossed the room pulling her down into his lap on the sofa.

The years were swept away by his touch only this time, Sarah was not that sixteen-year-old girl. This time she was unafraid to explore, to taste, to love.

Morning light shone on the sea-capped swells of the ocean below and still she was tangled beneath him. He kissed her slightly swollen lips and she responded with her hips pushing into him.

"Sarah, please," was all he could whisper.

She parted her lips against his mouth. He didn't have the heart to tell her he had no more to give. But he did and as his mouth gently nestled her neck, he made love to her one more time.

CHAPTER 12

RADER

Scott Rader was on fire, right up until the moment he dropped dead on the court. Fans and spectators around the globe froze in shock as broadcasters spread news and speculation. Vegas odds-makers were taking bets on verification of enhancement drugs in his system.

Everyone, especially the Falcon's owners were waiting with bated breath for the ME to disclose cause of death. Emergency meetings were held and Doc was quietly freaking out. His face was one of grief and shock while his mind was reeling with fear and hysteria.

What was the ME going to be able to piece together? Doc himself had run every test he could think of while Scott was alive and excelling. Every drug test was negative. Every stamina test was near perfect. What the hell happened? Scott was in perfect condition, no complaints, no pains, nothing…nothing was wrong!

The Falcon's owner picked up the phone and called

Morrison's Agency. Fritz called Dan in Seaside with a heads-up. The Falcon's had Dan's agency on retainer and used their services often. The agency had investigated various team members, adversaries, etc. for the owners. This was big. Dan's personal hands on were critical and discretion was of the utmost importance.

Dan's plane was ready at the private runway. A pilot himself, Dan usually flew alone, not this time. He pulled his pilot out of a pub before Bob could take a pull on his first round.

Bob was tall and thin with blond hair, and surely now, as he prepared the preflight checks and radioed in the flight plan. Dan scribbled notes while listening intently to the Falcon's owner's highly animated diatribe on the other end of the cell.

The Falcon's personal limo would be waiting for Dan in Portland. Dan prepared a plan of action in flight. He first and foremost wanted to calm his client and assure results ASAP. Barring natural causes, Dan's chief job was to find out what or who killed Scott Rader. Drugs were everyone's first bet and, Doc, was the first one on Dan's hit list.

Meetings were held non-stop at Falcon headquarters while the media was held at bay by security and reception recited the canned monologue sent over by legal.

Dan was eyed suspiciously by nearly everyone except the brass. Everyone knew he was there to dig, to examine, and to find truth while sifting through conjecture and everyone's lives. He was not welcomed with open arms and he felt the heat.

Around noon, Dan called Sarah.

"I'm in Portland and it looks like I'll be here in meetings for several more hours. I'm afraid we'll have to cancel our reservations for this evening. Sarah, I'm sorry."

"It's no problem, really. I'll probably call Janet or Cindy or just hang around here."

"Now, I really feel bad."

"What? Don't you dare feel bad! Work happens and I understand. Really, Dan, it's not a problem."

"When I get back in town I'll make it up to you, I promise."

"Oh really, what do you have in mind exactly?"

"I'll have to get back to you on that. I want to think about the possibilities before I sell myself short with a quick answer."

"Smart man, I like that."

"I've got to go I'll call you tonight."

"Bye, Dan."

Dan's lunch consisted of bitter coffee followed up with an energy drink from vending. Doc skipped lunch altogether as he meticulously layered handpicked files in orderly rows for Dan's perusal.

Doc had dealt with Dan before. When Dan's PI firm ran investigations on new team members coming on board, and other team members, or their owners. Never though had he dealt with him under these circumstances and not when, Doc, had so much to hide and so much to lose.

Dan's knock was harsh, and the rapping sound had Doc's, already frayed nerves jumping under his skin. Doc forced calm through a deep cleansing breath and reached for his office door.

"Dan, it's good to see you again even if it's under these terrible circumstances. Come in, I've pulled the files as you can see. I think it's everything you'll need. Let me know if there's anything else. Umm… here, sit, do you want anything, a coffee?"

"No. No, I'm good."

Dan had always liked Doc, even though his time with him had been limited in their past experiences together. He was truly fond of the guy. So why did Doc seem overly accommodating, almost skittish.

Then again, everyone here at the Falcon's was on edge. Snapping questions and answers back and forth at one another. The tension wasn't likely to change until the ME had some answers from autopsy.

The two men spent the greater part of the day poring over Scott's files. Dan grew weary of Scott's daily grind. Documented from the time he got out of bed till the time he dropped back in the sack. Doc kept track of the players' daily habits nearly down to the time of their bowel movements and that Dan did not want to know.

"Nutrition, exercise, supplements, you monitored their intake?" Dan questioned.

"Yes, that's part of my job here. Why?"

"Well, how do you monitor the players on their off time?"

he wondered.

"Each player is expected to keep a journal, sloppy notes really. Then I transcribe their notes weekly into their files."

"So, they could do whatever they want. Eat what they want, take what they want, and then jot down whatever the hell they want you to enter into their files, right? he speculated.

"Of course, of course they could and I'm sure they did."

Doc felt a sudden surge of relief and a moment of clarity. Self-medicating could be a very plausible conclusion, one that would relieve Doc of any responsibility.

He knew very well that the non-prescribed ingredients would be difficult at best to track. And even if they could be traced, they were not illegal. Except, of course for the one and final ingredient used to pull it altogether. The power behind the entire process could and would send him to hell figuratively and most likely—in reality.

Dan eyed, Doc, for a moment noting the gleam of perspiration on his upper lip and glanced back at the file he held in his hand. Dan looked up again.

"I need to see the video, the final five minutes again."

Dan had of course seen what the world had seen. Scott Rader's final jump shot had been undeniably high-flying and endorsement worthy—and then he crumpled. His body simply stopped mid-flight and crashed to the ground in a sprawling heap. Scott was gone instantly. Of course, the world didn't know it at that moment and not even the other players grasped the undeniable fact that Scott Rader was dead at their feet.

Dan took copies of Doc's files and video of the game back to his office. He was prepared to pore over their content through the evening and into the night if need be.

Tomorrow he was scheduled to interview Scott's girlfriend and a few of the team members. Scott's family was put on hold for a few days. They deserved some time to adjust before Dan showed up on their doorstep with questions that may be construed as insulting or derogatory to Scott's character. Dan had no desire to be punched in the face by an irate family member.

Dan was hungry, his stomach growled at the thought of food. The thought of food reminded him of his canceled dinner reservation with Sarah, and he sighed with resignation. Their evening out would have to wait longer than he had anticipated.

The remains of his dinner sat cold on his desk as Dan dialed Sarah's number and stretched his bare feet out across the dark mahogany wood. Her phone began to ring just as his foot tipped the beer bottle over, spilling its amber liquid across the files.

"Damn it to hell," Dan muttered into the cell as he mopped at the, Old Milwaukee, with a discarded sock.

"Excuse me," Sarah questioned back into his ear?

"No, I'm sorry. I've made a mess of the files here. I didn't know you had picked me up. Really, I'm sorry about that."

Sarah was laughing. "It's tough going there I take it?"

"Well, let's just say, I've never seen so many high rollers

on edge gathered in one place before. They have a lot riding on the outcome of the ME's report. The world is watching, and somebody's head will surely roll if toxicology proves enhancement use."

"Yes, they would be on edge, wouldn't they?"

"Yes, they would. Sarah, I need to be here for a while, and I don't know how long I'll need to stay."

"Hey, it's fine. Please don't worry about me, I'm good."

"Actually, I'd rather hoped you wanted me back. I'd hoped you missed me just a little bit."

"I'll tell you what, if I find myself desperately missing you, I'll jump in my car and race to see you in Portland."

"I'll tell you what, Sarah. I already miss you so why don't you jump in your car this weekend and stay at my place for a couple of days? I may be tied up during the days, but my nights will be yours I promise."

"Portland does have a lot to keep me busy during the day. I always did love the waterfront. Yes, I would love it but if you find that you need to work through the weekend please don't worry about me, I'll be fine on my own."

"I FIND that I need to see more of you, Sarah, and I hope you feel the same about me."

"Dan I'm coming to see you because I need to be with you…very much." The *very much* caught him off guard, happily off guard.

"Good night, Sarah, see you soon."

The next few days were a blur of interviews, fact checking, and missed appointments by a couple of Scott's teammates. Scott's girlfriend was by far the most intriguing aspect of the latest round of interviews. While she appeared to be grieving profusely for, Scott, she also had planned for all his furniture to be moved to a storage facility. To be fair, Dan didn't know what had belonged to Scott or to her.

Jolie was a 5'10", long legged, tiny waist, blond, with overflowing C cups. Jolie and Scott had lived together in the high-rise condo for nearly six months so… maybe she was entitled to the goods.

Dan managed to interview Jolie in and around the constant condolence phone calls and two unannounced visitors that showed up at the door with casserole dishes in hand.

Jolie seemed convinced that Scott's new and improved performance stunts on court were due to a combination of his strict daily regime of diet and exercise. Plus, his commitment to the team and of course…her.

"Jolie, I don't want to offend you but is there any possibility that, Scott, may have been taking performance drugs?"

"Why does everyone always assume a great athlete is using? Scott wouldn't do that, he wouldn't cheat. Scott was exceptional that's all. He was committed to the game…to me."

A new flood of tears began to flow, and Dan was hesitant to add any fuel to a potentially explosive situation, but he had to ask.

"Why were you putting all of Scott's things in storage? Why are you moving out of here so fast?" he asked.

The questions brought her up short. A long pause followed by a deep guttural wail that emanated from her abundant chest froze, Dan, in place. What the hell was he supposed to do now? He did nothing. He waited. He looked at his notes. He stared at the food congealing in the casseroles dishes and checked the time on his watch.

Finally, he patted Jolie on her shoulder and still said nothing. The sobbing continued with no sign of letting up. So, in frustration, Dan jumped up, quickly roamed the condo until he found a little half bath where he snatched the roll of toilet paper off the back of the toilet and tore off a streamer and demanded that she, "blow!"

The force of his demand and the toilet paper streamer one inch from her running nose brought her wracking sobs to an abrupt halt and a case of the hiccups. Dan used the time it took her to loudly blow her nose, to bring a glass of water to the table.

"Drink," he was on a roll!

Jolie seemed to respond to demands under duress.

"Now, tell me why you're moving and why you're so upset?"

"I. Don't. Have. A. Choice."

She enunciated each word as if Dan were a dolt that couldn't see what was clearly obvious to her.

More gently, Dan said, "why don't you have a choice,

Jolie?"

"Because the condo is leased in Doc's name and he wants me out…now!"

"Jolie, that doesn't make any sense. Why would the condo be leased to, Doc? Scott had plenty of money, why wouldn't he have his own place?"

"All I know is, Scott did everything Doc asked of him. Including moving into this condo. When I met Scott, he was already living here. It wasn't until I moved in that Scott told me that the condo was leased to Doc. Scott had to clear it with Doc, before I could even move in."

"Didn't you think that was strange?"

"Strange? It was freaking weird. But Scott said it was part of the bigger picture, the plan!"

"The plan, what was the plan?"

"To make, Scott, a super star. Don't you see, Doc demanded complete control of Scott's life? Doc controlled where he lived, the food he ate, the supplements he took, his exercise, entertainment, and…"

"And, what?"

"Me."

"You, what do you mean you?"

"Doc introduced me to Scott. Doc told me what Scott liked. What topics interested him, his favorite foods, movies, books, everything."

"Why would he do that? Why would you do that?"

Dan's head was reeling! The man he was so fond of was seriously damaged if this was true.

"I'm not proud of this. I… it's not the same as it was in the beginning." She said.

"What's not the same?"

"I love, Scott."

She said it so simply so factually that Dan knew it to be true. Whatever else she was, she was in love with, Scott, and Scott, was dead.

***

Dan snapped the phone shut in irritation, Ed, at the Falcon's had sent, Doc, to L.A. It seems Ed had a financial interest in an eighteen-year-old tennis hopeful. The kid had better look out because she won't know what hit her after, Doc, gets a hold of her. Next, he dialed the ME's office.

"You know I don't have toxicology back." The ME said.

"Wayne, I know you. You may not have toxicology back yet, but I know you have something to tell me."

"This isn't your garden variety case we're talking about here, Dan. I can't spill classified information of this magnitude."

"Wayne you've got to give me something. Just point me in the right direction, I'll go from there."

"Look, when the toxicology report comes back, I'll hold a press conference and give my findings. Until then I suggest you get, Doc, to show you this guy's family medical history information along with his current scans and blood work."

"I've seen his medical files. I didn't see anything that stood out and, Doc sure didn't point to anything out of the ordinary, so what are you getting at?"

"I've already said more than I should on a high-profile case, Dan."

"Hey, has anything you've ever told me come back to bite you, yet?"

"It's the, yet I'm worried about here," Wayne shot back!

"Gees, it's like pulling teeth with you Wayne, spit it out. I'll owe you big and you know you WILL eventually want to collect."

Dan waited out the long pause before the ME spoke.

"Have you ever heard of a twenty-three-year-old, non-smoking, healthy looking male, with no known medical afflictions dropping dead in mid-air of advanced, stage four, lung carcinoma?"

"Say again!"

"I said, Scott Rader, died of advanced stage 4 metastatic non-squamous, non- small, disseminated tumors in both of his lungs!"

"Dumb it down for me Wayne."

"His lungs were shriveled, porous, and covered in deadly cancerous lesions."

"How in the hell is that even possible, Wayne?"

"I don't know…yet, but I do know this, nothing about this entire case is normal. The state medical board is going to have something to say to Doc, about his findings or lack thereof."

"What do you mean?"

"I mean there is no way this kid had stage four lung cancer and, Doc, didn't know anything about it."

"Wayne, did you see this kid play the hoops?"

"Up until the moment he dropped."

"Then you tell me how he did it. How did Scott Rader do everything he did on court with black and shriveled lungs?"

"I don't know. He should have been bedridden given his condition. Bedridden, hell, he should have been in hospice at that point." Doc's voice was incredulous.

The rest of the week came and went just like the numerous interviews conducted by Dan personally. Doc wouldn't be back and available until Monday around noon. Dan wasn't looking forward to that confrontation. But confront him he would. Doc had a lot to answer for including the spy-ware apparatus, Dan found in Scott's condo the day Jolie moved out.

The day, Jolie had called Dan, to tell him that she had found a couple of Scott's older journals. She asked him if he wanted them. Of course, he wanted them. When he got to the condo everything but, Jolie, and the journals were already out of the building.

"Where are you going to live?"

Dan asked as Jolie, handed him the journals bound with a couple of wide rubber-bands.

"I have my own checking account and, Scott was so good

to me. He made sure I had money. I'm going to stay with my parents until I find a job. Then I guess I'll rent a little place somewhere. I don't really know right now it just doesn't seem to matter anymore I guess."

"Jolie, honestly, things will get better. It'll take time, but it will get better."

"Look, Dan, I've got to get out of here. I can't stand to be here without Scott."

She looked around the room and sighed.

"This place wasn't even our home; it was Doc's clinic. See you around."

With that, she turned and walked out the door without so much as a glance behind her.

Dan watched as she left and thought about what she had just said. *"'This place wasn't even our home; it was, Doc's clinic.'"* She was right, it was Doc's clinic. And, Doc, kept close in-depth records. It stood to reason that he wouldn't take for granted that, Scott would've simply towed the line. Doc would've seen to it that he towed the line.

Doc would've seen… Dan whirled around and scanned every surface, every wall, and the light fixtures. In the end, three cameras were hidden throughout the condo complete with flash drives designed for easy access and exchanges.

Dan knew he should take the memory sticks, sight unseen, to the authorities but who was he kidding? He took the sticks back to his office and plugged them into his laptop. The images he saw were of the final few days of Scott and Jolie's life together.

He watched as Scott lived his twenty-three-year-old life loud, laughing, and horny as hell. As far as he could tell, Scott didn't look sick, tired, and certainly not out of breath. He appeared to follow Doc's nutritional plan, no pizza deliveries, or alcohol, and not a cigarette in sight. Not even guests lit up in the condo.

I'm missing something here, Dan thought. He followed the plan. He followed Doc's plan to the letter.

"So where are the freaking supplements now?" Dan stated out loud.

He snatched up the cell and hit Jolie's number.

"Jolie, Dan here, where are the supplements?"

"What are you talking about?"

"Scott's supplements, the ones Doc gave him. Where are they?"

"In his locker or with the authorities I guess, why?"

"Jolie, this is important, why wouldn't there be a supply at the condo?"

"There were no extra supplements because, Doc, only gave him a few days' supply of supplements at a time. He said he monitored Scott so closely that he had to make slight adjustments in his doses every few days. Scott carried them with him always. Doc insisted."

"Doc insisted?"

"Yes, he insisted."

"Thanks, Jolie, are you doing ok?"

Dan couldn't tell her about the spy-ware or about him seeing their private lives together. The less she knew the safer she would be if there was anything to worry about.

"I'm getting there," she said.

CHAPTER 13

SARAH

It was Friday afternoon and she would be at his place by now. He had left instructions with the doorman to let her in the apartment and to give her the key. Thankfully, he had a full bath at the office to take a quick shower and brush his teeth before going home to her. It seemed like weeks since they were together and he didn't want either one of them to lose that incredible feeling of finally coming together.

He thought of that night as he showered. The moment when he knew she was ready to commit, and he didn't have to hold back any longer. He knew he treated her like fine china, as if she might shatter. He couldn't help himself, making love to her for the first time was more than he had hoped for that night. And he didn't want to scare her away with his need for her.

Now, she was in his apartment waiting for him to come home. Was he supposed to rush in sweep her off her feet or hold off? Maybe he should let her take the lead.

Dan let himself into his apartment with his other key and was instantly met with the aroma of something delicious cooking in the kitchen. He walked in and smiled at the sight of her behind the island pouring red wine into two glasses. She looked gorgeous with her hair down and shining under the light.

"Hi," was all he could manage.

"Hi," she said.

A slight blush flushed her cheekbones. Before he could reach for her, she said.

"Do you remember what I wanted from you when we dated in high school?"

He drew a blank and his mind was grasping for—anything to say. Then she smiled and lifted the collar of his dress shirt, *she was wearing his dress shirt*, to her face and breathed in deeply. It was so sexy he was literally stunned into silence for a moment.

"My T-shirt, you wanted one of my T-shirts to sleep in at night. You said all the girls were wearing their boyfriend's T-shirts to bed. I figured that was as close as I would ever get to being in your bed. I wanted to give them all to you."

"This isn't your T-shirt," she said as she came around the island. "But it does have your scent and I love wearing it."

"It's yours."

Dan pulled her into his arms, and she wrapped her arms around his neck pulling his mouth down over hers. His hands found nothing but soft skin beneath his shirt.

It came so soon, Monday morning, and she was gone.

Sarah and Seaside seemed a million miles away.

CHAPTER 14

DOC

Dan was waiting for him in the same office they had both used to pour over, Scot's, medical files and journals the week before. Doc was not surprised to see Dan waiting for him.

"What can I do for you today, Dan?"

"You can help me to understand the hold you had on Scot."

Doc was taken aback by the accusation in Dan's statement.

"What, exactly are you accusing me of?" Doc asked.

"You tell me because I don't understand the control you had and needed to have over that kid."

"What control, what are you talking about?"

Dan opened his fist and let the spy-ware cameras clatter to the desk.

"What the…"

Doc's face twisted in confusion as he picked up the cameras and examined them.

"You're going to try and tell me you didn't put these

cameras all over Scot's condo?"

"No… hell no, I didn't do that. What's wrong with you?" Doc dropped the cameras to the desk.

"Come on! You monitored every aspect of that kid's life including who he slept with. You're going to stand there and tell me you didn't plant these all over his apartment?"

Doc's hand went to his face rubbing fiercely as if trying to erase the guilt of his actions. The gravity of that guilt seemed to pull him down as he slumped into his office chair and covered his face with both hands.

"I may have gone overboard. No, I know that I went overboard with Scott. I knew he would be great. Historically great if, if only I could…"

"Could what? Make him a prisoner!"

"A prisoner, what the hell are you talking about?"

"Doc, nothing was real, Scott's life was what you demanded of him, that's prison. Even his girl was your choice."

"I only introduced Jolie to Scott; they did the rest."

"Bull shit! You hand fed her everything. What he liked, what he read, what he watched. Did you dictate their sex life as well?"

"Enough—damn it! I introduced her to him and yes, yes, I did hand feed her information about Scott, as you so adamantly pointed out. But I did it for him and for her."

"Do you expect me to believe that crap? How could it have possibly been in his best interest to control every aspect of his

Justifiable: Oregon

life?"

"Frankly, Dan, I'm getting freaking tired of your accusations when you obviously don't know what the hell you're talking about."

"Then by all means explain it to me. Because from where I'm sitting, you had a noose around that kid's neck long before he died."

Tears filled Doc's eyes and slid slowly down his cheeks, which embarrassed the hell out of him. He sniffed loudly and dragged his sleeve roughly across his eyes.

"I loved that boy like he was my own son! But I could see the handwriting on the wall. The fame, the money, and the more seasoned players taking him under their wings."

Distain crept across his face as he talked of the older players.

"They were all so ready to throw his career away. The all-night parties, the prostitutes they all shared, and I knew it was only a matter of time before worse would happen. So yes, I introduced him to Jolie, because I knew her parents. I'd watched her grow up and I knew she would be good for him. I'd only hoped that it would work out for them and it did, they were happy. Never and I mean never would I have put these, these…" Doc snatched the cameras off the desk and shook them in Dan's face, "in… his… condo."

The last three words spewed out slowly like air from a balloon with a pinprick.

Dan carefully put his hand over the cameras dangling precariously through Doc's fingers.

"Give them to me."

Dan pealed the cameras out of Doc's hand and put them back in his jacket pocket.

"I believe you, Doc. I believe you about the cameras and about, Jolie. But about the rest—you were over the line. I still want to know what was in those supplements he was taking. And I want samples as well."

"Well, you'll have to get in line because so does everyone else it seems. The cops took my supply into evidence."

"Did you check Scott's locker? Jolie said he took them everywhere he went. She said you adjusted the dose every few days or so."

"That's right, but everything from his locker is in evidence as well. I've got nothing left."

Doc failed to disclose the fact that he received shipments through Mexico with the push of a button on his cell. He failed to disclose the fact that he had far more serious legal issues hanging over his head than a few little spy-ware cameras set up to snoop on Scott and Jolie in their condo. So, who exactly was spying on, Scott and Jolie, and why?

"Who would do this? Why would anyone besides you and maybe the competition, monitor his life like that?"

Doc ignored Dan's sarcastic jab at him.

"What would the competition gain by getting video of life

in the condo?”

"Sounds like an interesting reality show but other than that I don’t know," Doc lied.

"What, EXACTLY, is in those supplements?”

Doc hesitated for a second studying, Dan’s face, gauging the implication behind the question.

"Those supplements are natural herbs, minerals, vitamins, and complex nutrients—that’s it.”

"Arsenic and pot are natural too, but I don’t want them in my morning coffee.”

Doc raised a condescending brow at, Dan.

"I can assure you there was no poison or illicit drugs being stirred up in a cauldron and pressed into my supplements.”

"Who manufactures the supplements for you?”

"Mexico, many pharmaceuticals are being produced in Mexico.”

"No shit!”

"I’m not talking about that kind of pharmaceuticals you idiot.”

Dan ignored Doc’s rancor.

"So, you get your vitamins, herbs, minerals, etc. from Mexico?”

"No, I get my ingredients from the US, India, Brazil, the UK, and Australia. I have those ingredients shipped to Mexico along with my revisions on dosage. Then the pharmaceutical manufacturer produces the supplements and ships them to me on demand, satisfied?"

"Not really. So, Doc, are you afraid of what they'll find pressed into those supplements when they run their tests on them?"

Doc smiled as friendly as he could muster.

"No, Dan, I'm not afraid of what they'll find."

Because Doc new that cremation destroyed all trace evidence of the human that once was.

CHAPTER 15

THE CARTEL

Garcia and Rodrigo had sat outside the condo and watched the last of the belongings being loaded into the moving van. They would wait until the woman was gone before taking their equipment out of the ceiling and walls of the condo that she had shared with the basketball player.

While they had waited, they also had videoed the movers and the tall dark-haired gringo that came in last.

Imagine their surprise when they broke in after the rooms were deserted and discovered their equipment had been lifted. However, their equipment also had the most recent memory sticks, making their job much more complicated to complete.

They'd have to find out who had their equipment and how much he or she knew about their cartel, if anything. Though it didn't much matter one way or the other. They didn't take chances and they didn't leave loose ends.

Garcia and Rodrigo watched as the gringo left the sports

center. They knew he was a PI and that he was being paid by the Falcon's.

Dan left the sports center and pressed Sarah's number. She answered on the third ring.

"Hey, you can't miss me already," Sarah said when she picked up.

"Right."

He smiled at the memory of her in his dress shirt, and of her out of his dress shirt.

"Well, I missed you as soon as I hit Sunset highway and realized how bored I was going to be on my own in Seaside."

"Come back."

"What? You can't be serious."

"Come back now, I mean it. We can watch old movies, walk the wharf, trade shirts…"

Sarah giggled; she loved his humor.

"Actually, I'm almost at the Signal. I forgot to tell you that I have an interview today."

"An interview?"

"Yes, an interview. Seaside's historical society is working in conjunction with the Seaside Signal, on a full-colored hardback book. It is to display the area's history as well as current points of interest. I'm interviewing for the photojournalist position."

"Wow, that's big. You know you have it in the bag."

"No, I do not know that. But thanks for the vote of confidence, I needed that."

"I'm hoping to see you this weekend. If I get to a holding place in the case, I'll head to the coast."

"I have a confession to make," she owned.

Dan stopped on the sidewalk and cocked his brow.

"A confession, what have you done now?"

"I stole something from your apartment."

"I gave you the dress shirt, remember?"

"Yea, well I stole a T-shirt too and I'm keeping it."

"Did you leave me my pants?"

"We'll talk about that in depth when you get here this weekend. Hey, I've got to go I just pulled into the parking lot, and I don't want to be late."

"See you soon, Sarah, and don't worry. The job's yours."

He loved that about her, her innocents. She had no idea that she was gorgeous, or incredibly smart, or the envy of nearly every woman, or wanted by men any place any time. He loved her.

CHAPTER 16

THE SIGNAL

Phil Waxman—The Editor in Chief—of the Seaside Signal could not believe his luck. He didn't know why a woman like, Sarah Knight, with her millions, would want the job as photojournalist for his small publication and he didn't really care. He just wanted her to sign on. Newspaper and advertisements sales would jump considerably because she was this small town's rock star and she didn't even know it.

"Let me know the moment Ms. Knight gets here, do not keep her waiting," Waxman instructed his assistant.

"Of course not," Mary nodded as if in complete agreement that Ms. Knight couldn't possibly be kept waiting.

Waxman had barely sat behind his desk when Mary opened his door and presented Sarah.

"Mr. Waxman, Sarah Knight," she said.

"Ms. Knight."

Waxman rose and thrust out his hand. Sarah smiled and

put her right hand in Waxman's. Waxman shook her hand with his right hand and patted her hand with his left.

"Sarah, please call me, Sarah," she said smiling.

"Well then, call me, Phil. Please, won't you have a seat?"

Mary rolled her eyes and closed the door behind her.

Phil and Sarah talked for a couple of hours discussing the photo project and her qualifications, as if he gave a damn about her education or her ambitions. If she could point a camera and click a button, she had the job as far as he was concerned.

Sarah carried the heavy information packet from the Signal and the Historical Society to the sofa in her living room, along with a glass of chardonnay.

Moments later the call button from the front gate crackled and a male voice said.

"Flower delivery."

Flower delivery, I'm not expecting any flowers, she thought. Sarah walked to the monitor and looked at the man in the delivery truck. Then she hit the buttons on the monitor to view the delivery van from other angles. She had seen the van in town parked in front of the flower shop before.

"Come on up."

She spoke into the monitor as she pushed the button that swung the front gate open for him to enter. Sarah stepped out onto the steps and waited for the driver to bring the bouquet to her. She had a ten-dollar bill tucked in her hand for his tip.

Only he didn't bring her a bouquet. He brought her four or

five bouquets in a gigantic basket that she recognized as the, one of a kind, baskets designed and woven by an artist living and working in Cannon Beach.

"Oh, my goodness, that's huge and incredible! Please, can you bring it in for me?"

"Yes ma'am, I can."

The guy was a boy really, with short hair under a ball cap bearing the flower shop logo. Sarah made room for the basket on the bar in the kitchen and the kid set it down.

"This is for you."

Sarah handed the bill to the kid, and he took it and nodded with a smile.

"Thank you, ma'am, enjoy the flowers."

"Oh, I will as soon as I know who they're from."

Sarah walked him to the door and when his van passed through the gate, she pressed the button to close it.

The card was small and tucked into the flowers. She pulled the card out of the bouquet as she buried her nose in a bloom and inhaled deeply, the scent of gardenia's. Which she loved by the way. She took the card to the sofa and opened it to read.

There was never any doubt. You'll do a fantastic job, Love Dan.

"Nosey PI, if he doesn't come here this weekend, I'll need to go to him," she mused.

She looked through the doorway to the basket of overflowing flowers.

The next morning, Sarah had her expensive camera equipment strew all over the bed and floor. She had pretty much been given free rein to choose her photo shoots with just a few stipulations regarding, must shoot targets.

Targets like Haystack Rock jutting out of the sea, Ecola State Park with its whale watching vistas and of course the wineries and local artists. There are so many people, places, and things of interest to shoot.

One point of interest that she was looking forward to shooting was Terrible Tilly. The lighthouse had always piqued her interest even as a teenager. Now that she had a view of it from her home, she looked forward to photographing it inside and out. She'd have to get permission from the owners of course but that shouldn't be a problem.

The caretaker would have to be contacted, and arrangements made to get out to the rock. Aerial shots of the lighthouse would be easy, but it was the inside that most intrigued her. Sarah had read in the information packet that Phil had given her that some of the earlier lighthouse keepers of the 1800's had literally gone mad.

Many of the keepers failed to make it to the end of their contract, they left the rock and never returned. Some reported seeing apparitions while others attacked their coworker. One keeper had ground up glass from light fixtures and mixed it into the food of another keeper. And of course, the man nearly died. She wanted to see for herself what could be so terrifying in that lighthouse as to drive one to murder.

CHAPTER 17

TILLY'S CARETAKER

Dr. Kerr knew the old man had little time left, his organs were shutting down, and he had no one with him. Not one person had come to see him through his illness.

Cirrhosis of the liver was an insidious disease brought on by years of hard drinking. The old man was pitifully thin and withered; he was a ghost of a man beneath the white sheet that covered his fragile frame.

Dr. Kerr sat with Samuel every evening and rarely did they speak. Speaking seemed painful to, Samuel. Dr. Kerr needed Samuel to know he was not alone. To know that someone cared for him and about him. And Samuel did know as, Dr. Kerr, held his hand as he passed from this life.

Arrangements were made to have Samuel s body cremated, and his ash spread upon the sea by the caretaker of the crematorium at the lighthouse.

The plain wooden box that the county provided was placed

in the long flat bottom boat with an outboard. And it carried the body to the lighthouse where the caretaker waited patiently. The boat bobbed on the water and the two men struggled to drag the box out of the boat and onto the low gurney.

Once the box was on the gurney, the boatmen were grateful when the caretaker assured them, that he could take it from there. The men quickly climbed back into the boat and pushed off the jagged rock landing and puttered back toward shore. The caretaker easily rolled the box up the walkway through the entry and into the furnace room.

The caretaker had packaged and shipped the last of the finely sifted powdery ash to the pharmaceutical manufacturer in Mexico the day before. Bone and teeth fragments left behind were placed in urns. They were properly labeled and laid to rest in the slot paid for by the relatives of the deceased.

Portland was where the caretaker shipped from. He packaged and labeled the containers carrying the ash as *food grade mineral composite.* He was careful, so careful to always wear the same clothing, the same concealing hat, and tinted glasses. There were endless mail drops in Portland for him to send his per-weighed and postage paid packages from.

The banker had explained to him the process that was in place to automatically be paid. The fees he was paid for the...*food grade mineral composites* shipped to the Mexican pharmaceutical manufacturer.

A specific set of ID numbers were shipped with the ash.

Once the ash was received, the manufacturing plant entered the shipments into their database and sent confirmation on to a routing terminal. Which automatically released payment to the offshore accounts using the ID numbers attached to each shipment.

Shipments came in from around the world, not that those crematoriums had any idea what the ash was used for. That information was exclusive to the caretaker and the cartel.

All offshore accounts except the caretakers belonged to the cartel. Crematoriums around the world were paid small fees to ship the ash of non-claimed remains to a hub in Mexico, *the cartel*, where they were re-packaged and sent to the manufacturing plant.

The cartel had discretely bought a few crematoriums here and there, the most important one being in Phoenix. Which is the kidnapping capital of the US, and by the hand of the cartel.

Cartel owned crematoriums shipped directly to the manufacturer bypassing the hub and large fees automatically entered their accounts. The caretaker followed the same procedure as the cartel owned crematoriums, but under their radar.

The banker had failed to disclose to the caretaker all he knew, all he had done, in those final moments of his life. He'd failed to tell him of the cartel's involvement; he'd failed to tell him of the worldwide industries and markets he had only just begun to sell to. Muti-billion-dollar industries, industries that created cosmetics, personal hygiene products and yes, the supplements for the sports industry that Doc was so proud of. He had failed to tell all of this to the caretaker just as he'd failed to tell Doc, of all that he had set in motion.

Poor, Doc, he thought he had found the secret of the fountain of youth. He'd wanted to play God and to handpick the chosen few who would receive the amazing benefits of the supplements. Those handpicked athletes, and he, would become famous and rich beyond their wildest dreams.

The banker, however, was a businessman. A dirty businessman and worse, a filthy pedophile. Like most pedophiles he let his twisted lust override his logic and therein was his fatal flaw.

The banker was too good a businessman. He was so worried about a paper trail leading back to him, he had set up every minuscule portion of the business to function on auto- pilot. Each transaction was setting off a chain of events, like domino's, to the next order of business like a well-oiled automated machine. The business was a machine that no longer needed the man.

The cartel, like most vermin, soiled where they ate. They only knew that there was finally a market for their brutal slayings. Their main stay is drugs and where there are drugs there is death. There is death because they kill each other and each others families. There is death because drug use always brings death in various ways. Now, there is death because there is a quickly growing market for the dead themselves.

No, the cartel was not yet aware of the muti-billion dollar deals the banker had set in motion, they were however aware of the supplements being shipped to, Doc, in the U S. And they were very aware of the new market for the devastation that they left in their wake.

CHAPTER 18

JACKMAN

Marcus Jackman sat in his stateroom aboard Duplicity. He went over the files of the businessmen that would soon be boarding the ship. Businessmen he would have to regale with amusing stories and anecdotes, most of which, were taken from previous men who had enjoyed the pleasures of Duplicity—before their departure to the rock.

Marcus always told the story of the young newlywed couple honeymooning on an amazing tropical island in the Caribbean.

The bride was beautiful, breathtaking in fact. It didn't matter to traffickers that she was not a virgin, virgins were a separate class of stock, a younger class of stock.

This young woman fit the profile of what numerous buyers wanted and would bring about a huge price in a bidding war. Once she was separated from her new husband, she could be whisked away by plane or another ship. Which is exactly what happened to her.

Marcus kept a photograph of the young bride, to show the men who boarded Duplicity. He knew, even if they preferred children, they would appreciate her beauty and the quality of the merchandise offered.

The photograph of the young woman was passed from hand to hand of all the men who boarded Duplicity. Very much the same way she had probably been passed from man to man since her taking, several years ago. Until she was killed, or died, or quite possibly took her own life, though he had no personal knowledge of her death.

He knew the chance of her being alive was very slim. And if she were still alive, she had been used up and pawned off to some filthy brothel that caters to working class men.

He told his guests of the brokers placed around the world. Brokers that lie in wait for the right young woman or the right child. Brokers who find, track, and take the merchandise to holding points until the merchandise can be bought and shipped to various destinations around the globe.

Marcus always looked for a glimmer of recognition in the eyes of all those men. Hoping eventually, one would remember her and entertain the others with tales of his passion and lust with the young woman.

That was the day he waited for. The day when all of this would be worth subjecting himself to. That would be the day he would learn what happened to his wife, five years, eight months,

Justifiable: Oregon

and three days ago.

CHAPTER 19

FOLLOWED

While Sarah waited on permission to photograph the inside of the lighthouse, she took her gear to Cannon Beach. The weather was clear, a little breezy, but the fog had burned off and the day was bright. And she was anxious to get started on her project.

Thankfully, she remembered how rocky the base of Haystack was, so she wore cross trainers and sweat socks, as well as jeans and a sweater over, Dan's T-shirt.

Cannon Beach Cafe was beachfront on Hemlock and had good access close to Haystack and was available to the public. She smiled as she remembered and stepped over the tiny runoff stream that ran through the sand to the ocean, along the side of the cafe.

She loved the memory she had of riding a horse named Comanche and galloping through the surf on her way to Haystack rock. Comanche loved running through the surf, he loved to run period. Sometimes he was difficult to control like the time he threw her into the hard-wet sand.

Photo-ops were abundant and there was no shortage of perfect shots along the Oregon coast. Sarah happily took shot after shot as she took her time meandering toward the rock.

Children were climbing all around the base. Climbing the rock itself was a federal offence, the rock represented a bird sanctuary for the gulls and yet nearly every year someone would attempt the climb regardless of the fine or arrest. Helicopter rescue would be sent, and the climber would get fifteen minutes of local fame and years of debt along with a record.

Tiny tide pools held wonderful creatures that didn't seem to mind a close-up with the camera. One crevice was narrow but quite deep with a tiny squid near the bottom. Sarah took her time and shot it from several angles. These photos would make great filler pieces in and around the text of the book.

A couple in their fifties strolled together, arms circled around one another s waist, and they stopped to ask Sarah what she was doing. Once she explained, she asked if she could photograph them by the rock. The couple was so excited to be included in her work, and they told her they were celebrating their thirty-year anniversary by coming back to where their life together had begun.

Thirty years ago, they had married in Buxton, Oregon. About fifty or so miles down Sunset Highway. Cannon Beach and Seaside were where they had honeymooned. They told her of the many vacations abroad they had enjoyed together over the years but that coming back here to the coast was the most special, the place closest to their hearts.

Sarah watched as they left the rock, arms still supporting one another, and she wondered if she would ever have what they seemed to possess. A passion for life, a passion for the sea, and a passion for each other. Maybe one day she will have all those things as well.

Later that evening, Sarah thought about the couple she had met on the beach. The beginning of an idea came to her, and she quickly started making notations in her assignment book.

The book should bring more to the readers than beautiful Oregon coast photos, it should tell the story of some of those people that have been touched by its vast magnificence. She wanted to tell those love stories through photos and text. The love story of the couple she had met and photographed would have a special place in the book, she would see to that.

***

Dan threw a small bag of his things together. He had everything he needed at the beach house, but he always took a bag out of habit. He never knew when it would come in handy.

The case was on going and twisted in knotted confusion, but he needed a break. He needed to step back just a little, to refocus and see the big picture. He was missing something, something that would bring everything into focus. Yes, a break was what he needed to gain perspective. He needed Sarah.

Sunset highway was a good drive and gave him time to think things through. Dan worked the case through in his mind trying to unravel the knots. Who had set up the spy-ware and why? What was there to gain by spying on Scott's life like that? Obviously, his career was skyrocketing, and he stood to reach the pinnacle very rapidly.

Could diet, exercise, and the right mix of supplements really bring such amazing results? Natural talent played a huge role of course but most guys in pro-sports have natural ability. Couple that with hard endless hours of work spent perfecting their skill could make any of them stand out.

Would the marketing industry stoop to those types of spying levels? Many super star athlete gained a huge endorsement only to have their life scrutinized under a microscope.

Many pro-athlete didn't need a microscope for all to spot the low life trash their personal life had become. The fame, money, and glitz made it so easy to fall. And when an athlete did fall, the marketing industry bailed hard and fast.

Would marketing decide to gain some insight, before the world could know of an athlete's fall from grace? *Not likely*, Dan thought as he tried to picture a corporate CEO giving the go ahead to some shady character with a fist full of cameras. Besides, Scott's life was hardly a din of iniquity. Not like the pre-Jolie days had become anyway. Scott's life had been videoed but by who?

The car came up on, Dan, fast and out of nowhere. Careening sharply to the left and around him.

"What the hell!"

Dan swerved and braked slightly as the idiot sped past him. The curves on portions of the 101 were nothing but cliffs over airspace with rocky surf below.

"Probably a college kid," Dan muttered.

Most college kids didn't drive a black Escalade like that one with tinted windows, that nearly pushed him into the Northern Coastal Mountains looming at his right.

The Escalade sat to the left of a large pine in the parking lot of Elderberry Inn as Dan passed. Noting it, he watched in the rear-view mirror, it did not move while he had it in sight.

Dan recovered and resumed his thoughts on the case.

Scott's watchers might be a rival sports team, a team that wanted to know the secret to Scott's recent and vast improvements. Dan ran through his list of possible spies and other aspects of the case.

The cameras were being tracked by Dan's associates, if that was even possible. The equipment was high dollar and state of the art. Sometimes that meant it was difficult if not impossible to trace. The people that used this type of sophisticated technology stayed in the shadows and didn't leave breadcrumbs for guys like Dan to follow.

Dan pulled into his usual stop along the highway. The place, *Stayleys*, had become a bit run down over the years. Still, he always filled his bubba keg with the great coffee, it had chicory brewed with the fresh ground beans and he couldn't resist the temptation.

Next stop was a winery that had a label he knew Sarah liked, and he was looking forward to an evening alone with her. He planned on a side trip to Cannon Beach before he went to Sarah's house. Dan wanted to pick up some haystack bread, Tillamook cheese, the unbelievable honey infused dried beef, and Mo's clam chowder, none of which was elegant but it sure was great.

He left Mo's diner and got back on the 101 headed to Seaside when he caught a glimpse of the black Escalade. It was eased behind one of the art galleries that showcased local artists' work like that of the late, Dallas McKennon, of TV and film fame.

Who the hell were these guys, he thought? They had to be tailing him because of the case, probably because of the equipment in his possession. The illegally obtained equipment in his possession. Dan wasn't about to lead them strait to Sarah's house, even though they may already know about her. He decided to call his friend at the cop shop in Seaside.

Billy and his partner, Zane, were waiting for them behind the cannon that marked the turn from Seaside to Cannon Beach. Just as Dan passed the cannon, Billy waited with his lights off until the Escalade passed him. Billy slipped behind the Cadillac with Arizona plates and hit the lights and siren. Dan drove straight to Sarah's house while, Billy and Zane, detained the guys in the Escalade.

Sarah opened the gate just after the call from Dan, she

closed the gate once he was inside.

"What's wrong, Dan?"

Sarah was outside on the steps when Dan reached her.

"Let's go inside and I'll explain everything."

Dan ushered her inside the house before taking her in his arms.

"I wanted this weekend to be just about you and me. No work, no worries, but it looks like I may have brought my work home with me."

Sarah listened as Dan explained the minor parts of the case that he felt her safe in knowing about. He explained the danger that at times skirted his line of work. And he explained how he would fully understand if she wanted to distance herself from him for the time being.

Then, Dan listened as Sarah explained a few things to him. Dan listened as she once again explained her anger at being kept in the dark about her father's escapades that brought the FBI into their lives, which inevitably separated her from, Dan, in the first place.

She explained to him that she was not only a woman fully capable of taking care of herself, but she was also a woman who wouldn't distance herself from this situation nor him. Then, Sarah showed, Dan, throughout the evening just how much she wouldn't distance herself from him.

Sometime around two am hunger pulled them apart and Dan remembered the picnic of sorts he had brought with him. He

118

walked to his car while Sarah pulled his T-shirt over her head and raked her fingers through her hair.

Mo's clam chowder was so good re-heated. Crusty haystack bread wrapped around Tillamook cheese and dipped in the chowder was beyond words. They ate in silence for a while. Dan bit into a fat little honey beef strip and licked his lips. Sarah sipped wine and watched as, Dan, listened intently to a song on the radio.

He loved this song, she remembered. He would turn the radio up, long ago in the Mustang when it played. Quietly she watched him and remembered how much she had wanted to let go and lose herself in him at that abandoned racetrack all those years ago.

Dan knew she was being quiet purposefully so he could enjoy the music just as she used to do on their dates in high school. Without a word, he reached for her.

***

Dan was drinking the coffee he had brewed when Sarah came into the kitchen. He had the cell to his ear as he smiled at her freshly washed hair clinging to her neck and he mouthed.

"Hey gorgeous." He whispered.

She felt pretty good, beautiful in fact. Because he made her feel beautiful in the way he treated her, valued her, loved her. Thoughts of last night lingered and she caught herself looking at his broad chest and the button on his jeans. Dan caught her looking as well and a deep blush rose in her cheeks.

"I've got to go Billy. Thanks for the help, I owe you one."

Dan caught her hand as he snapped the cell shut and set it on the counter.

"Girl," he breathed into her ear making her tremble, "you're going to be the end of me."

***

Billy had told, Dan, of the two men in the black Cadillac Escalade. Both were Hispanic with Arizona driver's licenses. Billy ran a check on them, but nothing came up. Not even a speeding ticket.

There wasn't anything Billy could do without it looking like racial profiling. Considering, Dan had asked Billy not to question them about tailing him. However, Dan now had the names and addresses of both men and so did the police.

Garcia and Rodrigo drove the thirty miles or so to Astoria, located at the mouth of the Columbia River. They didn't want to have their Escalade flagged by the local police and it would be after being stopped by the cops the night before.

They would rent a compact and nose around Seaside. But if they were stopped again, the cops in that town would be all over them with questions. They already had their fake names and licenses. The most damning information the cops had on them was the fact that they did have ties to Arizona and Arizona has unwanted ties to the drug cartels.

***

Dan took Sarah out to lunch at Lil Bayou near the center

of town where they enjoyed some Cajun seafood while Sarah shared her work project with him and bounced a few ideas off him.

She was on to something with her idea of personalizing the book with locals and tourists' personal experiences with the coastal region. He was proud of Sarah. She was intelligent and used her intelligence in a creative way. Sarah never let her money define who she was or what she did.

After a leisurely lunch, they drove to Ecola State Park. Sarah took her camera with her where she shot film from the many vantage points. Together they talked with several tourists and a few locals that Dan knew.

One tourist couple was on their honeymoon and during their conversation asked Sarah how long she and Dan had been together. Before Sarah could answer, Dan spoke up.

"I've loved her since high school."

They waved as the honeymooners walked away hand in hand and as Sarah took Dan's hand, she looked into his eyes and whispered.

"You were my first love and now my last."

Tears blanketed her eyelashes as he pulled her into his chest because he didn't want her to see the emotion he was feeling.

Neither one regretted the lives they had lived without each other. They were simply happy to have found each other again and they were greedy for every moment they could spend together.

The rest of the day was gone in a flash, and they found themselves at Dan's family beach house. She had been inside only once before while in high school. He had stopped by his house to pick something up before taking her home.

Dan's bedroom at the time had been a small room just off the living room. He would call her at night from his bedroom, and they would talk for hours. She would imagine him lying on his bed and she wondered what it would be like to lie there with him. Sarah looked in the small bedroom as, Dan came behind her wrapping his arms around her waist.

"What is it, love?"

Sarah turned in his arms to face him.

"I always wanted to know what it would feel like to be here in your bed."

"There's no satisfying you, is there?"

Dan squeezed her tight lifting her off her feet.

***

Sunday rain drizzled outside, and fog hazed the view of the beach. Sarah stood on deck of the ship shaped lanai that skirted the front of Dan's beach house. It was unique, a bit whimsical and utterly charming.

The cottage next door had a widow's walk jutting out from the upstairs deck and Sarah waved to the woman standing at the end of the walkway and she waved back with a smile.

Later that morning they had breakfast at the Pig and Pancake on Broadway. The potato pancakes with fresh applesauce were good but Sarah loved the fresh vegetable omelet with Tillamook cheese and hash browns. Dan devoured pancakes and coffee, lots of coffee. He winked at Sarah as he raised his cup to her.

"I have to keep my energy levels up with you around, lady!"

Sarah smiled at Dan, as he stuffed another fork full of pancakes into his mouth.

The dining room was full of locals with their cells or newspapers. And tourists with their pamphlets of attractions though the true attraction needed no pamphlet to find. The sea was due west.

Dan had not yet had time to go into the police station to look at the copies of the driver's license that Billy had photocopied with the equipment in his cruiser. So, the two Hispanic men sitting to the left and slightly behind them hadn't yet provoked any alarms.

Dan listened as Sarah talked about her project and upcoming events that she wanted them to take part in. Dan made a comment here and there only partially listening while he paid attention to the two men. He had caught them glance their way several times and he was now on alert.

Dan was always aware of his surroundings, an occupational hazard that had served him well on more than one occasion with past cases. Just to be careful he decided to put some evasive tactics to good use, tactics that Sarah might not be suspicious of.

"Are you ready to go?" Dan asked, rising as he spoke, not giving her much of a choice. "How about a walk to the promenade?" He added as he took cash from his wallet and laid it on the table.

They left the car parked in front of the restaurant as they walked up Broadway toward the beach. What looked like meandering toward the promenade after breakfast was an opportunity to see if they were being followed. Window shopping was a perfect way to watch passersby or to catch someone watching you.

Their slow walk and talk that, Dan, kept on point with Sarah's work project, took about thirty minutes up one side of Broadway. Sarah looked up at Dan, noting how quiet and aloof he had suddenly become. He only half-listened when she spoke, and he kept stopping to look in shop windows though most of the shops were tourist traps with the same old, same old souvenirs.

He was scanning the street again as they started down the other side of Broadway toward the car. Once again, Dan stopped in front of a souvenir shop, across the street he saw the men he had been watching for.

"I want to grab something in here, do you mind?"

Dan asked as he took her by the elbow and ushered her into the gift shop that carried newspapers and magazines. The shop was long and narrow; it also had a door to a side street. A side street they could use in an emergency.

That was the second time in thirty minutes that he had asked her while leading her at the same time, and she didn't like it. Something was up and she wanted to know what it was.

Dan picked up a couple of newspapers with front-page articles covering the death of, Scott Rader, and the inquiry into his possible drug use. The cashier bagged the papers as, Dan, scanned his debit card.

He could see the two men in his peripheral vision. They were now in an isle that carried various trinkets for children. He had two choices, leave with Sarah and risk a confrontation with them that would put her in danger. Or he could call Billy, so he could bring them into the station if these guys were indeed the two from the black Escalade.

"Dan." Sarah said.

"What?" he didn't even look at her.

"What's wrong?"

"What do you mean?"

Sarah just looked at him willing him to look at her before she spoke, but he didn't. Sarah took a few steps away from, Dan, trying to figure what was going on here. The cell rang and Dan put it to his ear and walked the few steps to where Sarah stood.

"I was just about to call you, buddy."

Billy caught the tone in Dan's voice.

"I take it you have a tail?"

"Sarah and I are doing a little shopping at, Doogan's, why don't you join us?"

"I'm just around the corner and I have a few questions for our Arizona tourists."

"Glad to hear it."

"Where are they now?"

"Kids section, left of the front door." Dan's voice low.

Sarah couldn't make out the words Dan spoke into the phone. She just knew something was wrong.

"Stay put we're walking in now."

Dan watched as Billy and Zane entered the shop from the side door and headed toward the front of the shop. He kept his hand at the small of Sarah's back, ready to put her on the floor if need be.

Zane was in the isle with the Hispanic men, but he didn't approach them. Dan caught his eye and, Zane, shook his head in the negative. These guys weren't the two from the Escalade.

Sarah watched as Dan's stance visibly relaxed; she watched the Hispanic men take a few trinkets to check out and she watched the cops pretend to shop the kiddy isle.

"Ready to go?" Dan inquired as he attempted to move her toward the front door.

"What is going on?" Sarah planted her feet, demanding an answer.

"Nothing, did you want to get something?"

This ridiculous attempt to misdirect her was demeaning and she'd had enough.

"Fine," she said crisply, "let's go!"

Dan trailed behind her as she walked at a fast clip to the front door. He nodded his thanks to Billy and Zane on his way out. He needed to talk to them as soon as possible and that meant he would have to find a way to leave Sarah at her house where she had security. Frankly, he felt given her mood that he would have no trouble accomplishing his goal.

The two from the Escalade were watching from the compact they had rented. They knew where Dan lived, where Sarah lived, they had what they needed here. It was time to head to Portland to Morrison's office and his apartment.

There was no point in risking a confrontation with the local cops. It was obvious the PI was here for a weekend with the woman. It was also obvious he had no information on the supplements…yet. They'd keep tabs on the PI and the woman; she was good leverage if they needed it.

The walk to the car was quick and quiet except for the street noise and the tourists they weaved in and around on the sidewalk. Dan used the remote to unlock the car doors, but Sarah jerked her door open before Dan could open it for her. He walked around the rear of the car and braced himself for the gale force storm that was about to hit him.

"What was all that about, Dan?"

"What are you talking about?"

Dan knew he wasn't going to get away with this, but his goal was to get her back to her house where it was secure. He stared straight faced at her pursed lips and raised eyebrows. He didn't dare smile, so he opted for the, *what did I do wrong look.*

"You must think I'm incredibly stupid."

"No, Sarah…I"

"Save it, Dan, I want to go home. I have work to do."

The ride to her house was painfully silent. What had started out as a great weekend had ended in irritated silence coming from the passenger side of the car. The security gate was closed of course when he pulled up to it.

"You may think you're protecting me in some way but let me assure you, I can take care of myself, and I have a right to know if there is a problem."

Sarah waited for Dan to respond, he didn't. He pushed the window button instead.

"What's the code?" he quietly asked.

Unbelievable, she thought. "731…"

"I can't believe you! You were just going to give up your security code, because I asked for it. And I'm supposed to believe you can take care of yourself?"

"I've given up more important things to you, Dan, than my security code!"

"Don't change the subject, Sarah!"

"You're crazy!"

Sarah yanked the latch free on the seat buckle and climbed across Dan's lap, hung out the window, and punched in the code on the security panel, opening the gate. She ground her knee into his lap with purpose as she flung herself back into her seat and out the door.

He watched as she hit a button on the control panel and marched through the gate as it began to close behind her.

"Damn," he muttered.

He had no idea how to fix this, but he couldn't think about that right now. He needed to talk to Billy; he may even need a doctor for his groin.

Sarah stormed through the house to her bedroom. She snatched the door open to the bedside table and took out the small safe, placed it on the bed, and put her palm against the reader. She could hear the locks tumble as it acknowledged her print. When it opened, she pulled out the Glock and picked up the bedside phone. He answered on the second ring.

"Ben, I need your help."

By the time the phone conversation ended, Ben had a rough idea of what was going on, and he had a few phone calls he would make to confirm it. Sarah had overheard, Dan, say something about Phoenix during a phone conversation. Couple that with his paranoia over the two Latino men in the souvenir shop and, Ben, had a pretty good idea the drug Cartel weighed into it somehow.

"Sarah," he'd warned, "Sounds like you've gotten in over your head."

"I haven't gotten myself into anything, Ben. This is about Dan's case with the Falcon's and with Scott Rader's death."

"Sarah, the Cartel doesn't waste time assigning blame,

they kidnap, and they murder—period. How long has it been since you've trained with a professional?"

"It's been over a year."

"I know someone in Portland, Greg knew him in special ops."

***

Dan pulled into the police station and met up with Zane and Billy.

"We haven't seen the Escalade since we stopped them the other night, but we got suspicious of their ID's and ran a check in Arizona as well as on the Escalade."

"What'd you find?"

"Nothing really," Zane said. "That's the funny thing. We got a sterilized version of the usual information we get on a run down."

Billy shifted back on his left foot as if he were bracing himself.

"Don't you see, Dan, these guys are not who their ID's say they are. The Escalade can't be traced to a dealership. It's registered to the name on the driver's license but that's where it ends. The Cadillac's new, one owner, the dealership name should show up, but it doesn't and that's a problem."

"What are you thinking?"

"I'm thinking what the hell kind of case are you on that has ties to the Mexican drug cartel in Phoenix? I'm thinking, what have you got yourself into and what have you gotten, Sarah into?"

Dan was thinking the same thing.

"Look, Sarah doesn't know anything about this, and I want to keep it that way as long as I can."

"Do you think that's the best way to go? What if they come after her and she has no warning? That's not right, Dan."

"It'd be worse to drag her into it. I'm going back to Portland. They'll follow me there and I can keep her out of it."

"What if she comes to Portland?"

"Trust me that's not likely." Dan stated, brow raised.

"Billy and I can keep an eye on her, but we can't sit on her 24/7."

"I appreciate it, Zane, but just so you know, she's working on a project that has her all over the county and talking to every person she meets."

"Well, that's just great isn't it!"

The look of exasperation on Zane's face moved, Dan, toward the door.

Billy and Zane were good at their jobs and Dan would never intentionally insult them, but he would get a field agent on Sarah, just to be safe. Zane was right, they couldn't guard her 24/7 but his agents could and would.

***

Sarah received a call from Ben's contact in Portland the next day. After a brief discussion and his condolences regarding Greg's death, they made plans to meet at Sarah's house the following day.

Sarah used the remaining time prepping the lower level of her house for combat. This guy had been special ops…*black ops* and may still be active on a specialized basis, he wouldn't take it easy on her.

Bright and early the next morning the security system signaled a visitor at the gate. Sarah was having coffee at the bar. She was ready and had been expecting, Mr. Hunter, she wasn't expecting two cops to be standing beside him at the gate though. Sarah immediately recognized the two cops as Dan's friends and she was instantly angry. *What, she couldn't have visitors now without Dan's approval?*

"Good morning officers, what seems to be the problem?"

Sarah used a friendly tone as she spoke into the speaker while opening the security gate.

"Good morning, Ma'am, do you know this man?"

"Well yes I do," she lied, "Didn't he tell you about our meeting this morning?"

"He mentioned he was a friend of your—umm—your deceased husband."

"That's correct officer. Would you gentleman like to come up as well, I have fresh coffee?"

Sarah knew they would decline her invitation.

"No thank you, Ma'am, we'll be getting back on patrol. But if you need anything, don't hesitate to call 911 and we'll be right here."

"Of course. Thank you, officers, for being so…helpful."

Sarah watched while the cops allowed Mr. Hunter's car access through the gate. Sarah closed the gate behind his car and stepped out to greet her guest.

Jake was tall, rugged, and had the body of someone serious about martial arts. His sandy colored hair was pulled back into a tight rubber band and his blue eyes crinkled when he smiled.

"Sarah, Greg told me you were gorgeous. I thought he was exaggerating at the time."

"If I'm flattered will you take it easy on me?"

"Not a chance. I respected Greg too much for that."

"Well then, I'm ready if you are. Sorry about the cops."

"Don't be, be grateful. Ben filled me in on what he has learned so far. He's using his contacts to do some digging. I put some feelers out as well. We should get some answers real soon and by the way, the cops aren't the only two watching out for you."

"Oh, no, I really do appreciate your help."

"I'm not talking about me or, Ben, there's someone outside the gate up on the hill with a pair of field glasses watching the house. The cops are fully aware of them, so it looks like your friend the PI has one of his people staked out as well."

"Now I'm really pissed off," she said.

"Great, let's put that energy to good use."

By the time Jake left that evening, Sarah needed a hot shower and several cold compresses for the bruises all over her body. Jake didn't lie; he did not take it easy on her.

"Get up, Sarah, this isn't a tennis lesson."

She was so sick of hearing him say that; she wanted to cram a tennis racket down his throat if he had said it one more time.

***

"Ben its, Jake, I've put her through hell. She's banged up, but trust me, Greg did right with her training. She was a little rusty, but her training came back to her with a vengeance. Hell, I need an ice pack. What'd you find out?"

***

Dan had just gotten a report from Zane, right after the one from his own field agent in Seaside. Jake Hunter was well known in Portland, his face hung over the interstate staring down into the cars with piercing blue eyes. His billboards made men want to sign up with his studio, they made women just want to be near him.

Dan tapped his closed cell mildly on the table while he tried to put the pieces together. His agent had said she couldn't see Sarah or Hunter through the field glasses in any of the rooms on the main level of the house. They didn't leave the house, not even to eat out and it was late in the evening when Hunter left.

The agent said he had looked disheveled as did, Sarah, when she walked him to his car. Dan would be furious except for the fact that he knew Sarah. He knew there was far more going on than met the eye here. Plus, his agent said Hunter shook Sarah's hand before he left the property.

People who have had an all-day tryst do not shake hands when they part. She was a mystery and just full of surprises. He wondered if she was still too pissed off to talk to him. Checking Hunter out seemed less risky. And he could be at his studio in twenty minutes if he wanted a face to face.

Dan pulled into a parking space at Hunter's Dojo; it was crowded and what he really wanted was to see him in action. Parents and visitors were sitting on a stage overlooking the floor space and mats used by the students.

Master Hunter or Sensei as the students called him were sparring with an advanced adult student and, Dan, had to admit he was impressed. When the class was over, Dan kept his seat while the others collected their children and filed out of the Dojo.

Hunter knew who Dan was and walked to the stage gauging his mood. Hunter nodded an acknowledgement.

"Mr. Morrison, what can I do for you today? I doubt you're here for lessons."

"No, no lessons today."

Dan sensed no animosity and he wasn't surprised that Hunter knew who he was.

"I am curious though about your recent visit to Seaside. More to the point, your time spent with Sarah."

"Why don't you ask Sarah?"

"I could do that, but I think you know she's a bit annoyed with me at the moment so why don't we talk about it?"

A smile spread across, Hunters face.

"She may be annoyed with you, but she kicked the crap out of me though I must say I left her pretty bruised up."

"Sarah—kicked the crap out of you?"

"Maybe you should be grateful she's just annoyed."

Hunter wondered what else Morrison didn't know about Sarah.

"Why don't you tell me what's going on? Why are you making personal house calls and how do you know Sarah?"

"I think the pertinent question is why Sarah's involvement with you should bring her into contact with a Mexican drug cartel?"

Hunter could see that question cut to the quick and he almost regretted asking it.

"How do you know about that?"

"I make it my business to know these things when they involve my best friend's widow."

Dan knew Hunter was right, he had no right putting Sarah in danger and the cartel was very involved in his case.

"You knew her husband?"

"We served together in special forces. He made sure she was safe; he taught her to protect herself. Sometimes having money brings the crazies to your door and he didn't want her to be vulnerable."

"You're saying she can take care of herself?"

"Not against bullets, friend, the cartel is serious about their business."

"So, Sarah knows about the cartel? I wanted to keep her free of this that's why I came back to Portland."

"Greg had loyal friends, which means, Sarah has loyal friends. Sarah will do better when she has all the facts Mr. Morrison, which is why we had you checked out when you re-entered her life."

"Sarah had you check me out?"

"Not exactly, I said we had you checked out. We, having been Greg's friends therefore Sarah's friends. I doubt she would approve all our methods."

"What happened to her knowing all the facts?"

"Our facts will keep her alive. Your facts have put her at an extreme disadvantage. We level the playing field."

"You're… going to take care of the cartel for me?"

"Hardly, we're going to quietly remove the danger around, Sarah."

Hunter's eyes were less friendly, and Dan knew he'd just been warned.

"Anything else I can help you with Mr. Morrison?"

"Yea, there is."

Dan wasn't stupid or overly egotistical, he was very aware of the depths that the cartels sunk to, to protect their flow of drugs into the US. He would gladly take the backup if it meant keeping Sarah protected. Besides, he had no delusions about taking on ex-special ops.

CHAPTER 20

THE LIGHTHOUSE

The caretaker had known this day would come. He was prepared and ready to handle the inconvenience of a photo shoot inside the lighthouse. The owners had made it clear that he was to cooperate with this project. And he wasn't about to send up any red flags by objecting, not with his operations inside the lighthouse. Let alone the lucrative sideline he had stumbled across.

The last of the tools of the trade he used to intimidate and interrogate the subjects, were locked in one of the rooms off the main floor. He'd simply tell the woman it was his private quarters and preferred not to have it included in the tour. He'd memorized the stories of *Terrible Tilly* from the internet and felt prepared to answer any questions the woman may ask.

His associates were not scheduled to arrive for a few days, and the next authorized cremation would take place in two days. Even so, he had called his associates with the news of this unexpected turn of events, and they had agreed it was better to cooperate amiably so they could return to their work quickly and quietly.

Marcus thought about the conversation he had with the caretaker, and he wondered how much longer the lighthouse would be available to them. The crematorium had been unique and ideal to their work. The owners were business-people that rarely came to the rock to check on the new caretaker.

Once the interrogations were concluded, the caretaker could easily dispose of the traffickers with no trace whatsoever. Places like Terrible Tilly were rare and losing the convenience of its usefulness would be a serious loss to the mission.

Still, allowances must be made and if the Historical Society wanted to film it then they would simply comply. He would, however, monitor the situation and anyone who ever stepped foot on the rock.

***

Sarah had kept herself busy with her work project. Filming vistas high above the sea and the sea level sandy dunes of Gearhart were a favorite of hers. Dan had first taken her to the dunes in high school, later she had enjoyed walks through the dunes on her own. Interviews with tourists and locals had been interesting and she had many quotes and photos to sort through.

Dan had a small Cessna that would be perfect for taking aerial shots including shots of the lighthouse. Unfortunately, she hadn't spoken with Dan since Sunday's fiasco at the front gate.

He had called her house as well as her cell, but she hadn't

picked up or returned the calls. Sarah wasn't intending to be childish or petulant she simply wanted him to take her seriously, to treat her as an equal and to be included and trusted.

Sarah didn't really mind the tail Dan had placed on her. The agent Dan sent and the cops she'd spot here and there were not intrusive as she went about her work. Hunter had told her it was smart and safer to accept the bodyguards and she had agreed. They made her safer and freer to do her work. There had been no sign of the two men from the tourist shop on Sunday, and she thought her guards must surely have been getting bored by now.

The hell with it, Sarah thought as she dialed Dan's cell.

"Sarah, hi, how are you?" his voice was guarded, waiting to gauge her mood.

"I'm good, and busy with the project. How about you, how's your case going?"

Dan felt relief, her voice was just as hesitant as he felt, and it seemed the worst of their argument may be over.

"I'm good and as for the case, well, let's just say it's taking some interesting turns. The ME will announce his findings in the next day or so and…"

"And you can't tell me anymore about it."

Sarah knew he couldn't talk to her about specifics on an ongoing case, that she understood.

"Sarah, listen, I didn't handle things right. I should have explained what I could to you and included you when you became involved."

"You've been talking to, Hunter, haven't you?"

Sarah knew he wouldn't be able to resist checking, Hunter out.

"Are you tailing me, Sarah?"

"Turnabout's fair play isn't it?" she said.

A smile spread across her face as she took note of the long pause before he let out a sigh of resignation.

"I know you can take care of yourself but go with the safety measures for me, okay. If not for me do it for the sake of the book."

"For the sake of the book…give me a break. I'll do it because it's smart, I'll do it because I think it's a good idea, I'll do it for you."

"I want to see you."

"Come to the coast," she said.

"I will but first my team is setting a little trap for our Latino friends."

"Do I need to know?"

"Yes, Sarah, you do but not because it will endanger you. You need to know because I trust you."

Dan explained his plan in some detail and if it worked, the two from the black Escalade would be taken out of the equation, for a while anyway.

***

So much hinged on the ME's report and drug enhancement would bring Doc to his knees. Doc already had a known connection to Mexico's pharmaceutical industry. Making the leap from a Mexican pharmaceutical manufacturer to the cartel drug trade wasn't much of a jump. Proving that connection though was another matter.

That evening, Dan ate a TV dinner while NBC news played. He half listened as he read the scroll at the bottom of the screen. *Rhianna Ryan, promising tennis star, dead at age eighteen.*

"What the hell!"

Dan flipped through the channels of news until finally a FOX news anchor covered the details of the death.

"Tonight, Los Angeles mourns the loss of one of their own. Tennis's rising star, eighteen-year-old, Rhianna Ryan. Ryan died on the court today during a match with celebrated Wimbledon great, Sylvia Warren, while millions of fans around the world watched in shock. There's no word yet on cause of death, a spokesperson for the coroner's office says it could take several weeks before a determination is made.

Meanwhile, the sports world waits again for answers into the deaths of two young, seemingly healthy sports figures. Scott Rader of the Portland Falcons died recently during a game as well, leaving sports fans around the world stunned."

Dan picked up the phone and called, Doc's, private cell number, it went straight to voice mail.

"Doc this is Dan Morrison, call me as soon as you get this."

Two athletes, both under Doc's tutelage for optimum health and performance are dead. *How many more are on his program*, Dan wondered?

CHAPTER 21

KARMA

Doc's phone sat unanswered on the floor next to the foot of his wife, Barbara. Doc was terrified as he stared at the intruders towering over them.

Both men wore identical black head to toe tactical gear. Their faces were covered, and they wore Kevlar helmets, raid shirts over body armor, BDU pants, and boots. They carried AR-15 rifles with aim point sights, and each had a side arm strapped to their thigh. They looked like S.W.A.T. except they weren't there to negotiate a hostage release.

Barbara was shaking so badly she was nearly convulsing on the floor next to her husband in fear.

"Please, tell me what you want. I'll do anything, please let my wife go."

The gunmen pointed their rifles for a moment before one handed his rifle to the other and pulled, Doc, to his feet.

"Get the files, Doctor, all of the files on, Scott Rader."

The English was good but not even close to masking the heavy Spanish accent.

"Yes, of course, please don't hurt us, I'll get you everything."

One intruder stayed with Doc's wife while the other escorted him into his home office. Doc's hands shook as he unlocked the cabinet and pulled Rader's file, he handed it to the man.

"Now the real file please, Doctor."

Doc had no intention of trying to lie or fend off these intruders. Besides, it was best if they did steal all his files. Rhianna Ryan's death along with, Scott Rader's, was linked to him. He was the common thread that tied the two deaths together and he knew his career was over. Soon the other athletes on his regime may drop dead as well and the files would send him to prison.

"Of course, they're on disc right here." Doc eagerly unlocked another drawer and handed the man the discs. He wanted them gone along with the men scaring the hell out of him and his wife.

"Have a seat."

Rodrigo put, Doc, firmly in the office chair.

"Now Doctor, you will tell me all the athletes you have been giving the supplements to, yes?"

"Of course, anything you want but there are only five."

"I want their files and discs as well," the intruder said.

"Take them all, please just leave us alone! Leave us alone!"

Doc was close to losing it as he buried his face in his hands praying the men would leave now.

They didn't, Rodrigo pulled the small untraceable 22 pistol from a side pocket of his pants and fired a single shot to the right temple as Doc sat in his chair.

Barbara's scream was cut off as Garcia crammed a gag into her mouth and held her down while Rodrigo set the stage in the other room. Doc and his wife would be found tomorrow, an apparent murder/suicide following the deaths of his star clients.

Many assumptions would be made by the press, none of which would be tied to the cartel. Rodrigo quickly pressed Doc's dead fingers to the handle and trigger of the 22, gathered the files and discs, and joined Garcia.

Barbara knew she was dead though she struggled violently to claw at their skin, but it was useless. The bullet to her brain stilled her struggles and the two men quickly placed the gun near Doc's body as if it simply fell from his hand when he ended his own life.

***

Dan was at his desk at the agency when the cops arrived. They had rarely worked with Dan, as his cases mostly revolved around sports figures and the wealthy who were amid expensive nasty divorces.

Fritz buzzed Dan's office.

"Yea, have you located Doc?"

"No not yet, but the police are here to see you."

"The police, send them in." Dan said.

Dan was curious. This had to be about, Rader, maybe even the spy-ware he'd confiscated from the condo. Doc may have spilled his guts to them about his little visit to the sports center.

Fritz opened the door and stood aside to let the cops file in.

"Officers, what can I do for you? Please, have a seat."

Dan motioned to the chairs opposite his desk. He could hear their gear rustle and squeak as they took their seats.

"Mr. Morrison, what is your relationship to Doctor Jason Bennet and his wife, Barbara Bennet?"

The cop waited pen poised to take notations.

Dan was totally confused. What could Doc's wife possibly have to do with the case?

"I don't understand officer. I work with Doc from time to time but his wife; I've never actually met her." Dan waited for an explanation.

The cops stared back for a second then glanced at each other as if deciding what they would disclose to the PI.

"We found a message from you on the Doctor's cell. You sounded agitated, Mr. Morrison. Do you care to explain your agitation?"

"I needed to speak with, Doc, about Scott Rader's death. I'm investigating the death on behalf of the Falcon's. I still need to talk to, Doc, and why do you have his cell phone?"

"Mr. Morrison, where were you last night?"

"You're kidding right? You're telling me, Doc, is dead that he was murdered?"

Dan was stunned as he waited for a response from the cop asking the questions.

"I'm not telling you anything, Mr. Morrison. I'm asking where you were last night from 9:00 to midnight?"

The cop was trying to control the situation, taking on an authoritative tone in his voice.

"Here, gentleman, right here until 2:00 am."

Dan pushed a button on his phone and Fritz answered immediately.

"Yes."

"Fritz, grab last night's security tape and bring it in here, please."

"ok."

Dan chose to adopt a steely exterior until the cops were satisfied. There were plenty of ways to find out what was going on without the cops. He rarely used the cops in an investigation anyway. He'd have more information in twenty-four hours than they would have even with their head start.

Fritz brought in the tape and played it for the cops. It showed video of the inside of the office, after hours. The office employed this security measure as a safeguard to the sensitive nature of the cases the agency dealt with.

Dan could be seen with his bubba keg going to and from

the coffee maker in the break room. Fritz raised a brow and smirked at Dan. Dan knew what he was thinking, *finally, a good reason for drinking all that caffeine, an alibi for the cops.* The cops seemed satisfied but refrained from disclosing any information. Fritz showed them out while Dan called Hunter.

"Give me a couple of hours and I'll have some answers. I understand Sarah's giving your cops in Seaside quite the workout, hiking all over the county."

"Sounds about right, don't tell me, you have someone watching her too?" Dan wasn't surprised.

"I don't give up my trade secrets, brother. I can tell you there's been no sign of the Escalade or the two men."

"Yea, that's the report I've been getting three times a day."

"I'm impressed, three times a day. Does Sarah know she's being sat on by your people?"

"She's aware."

"I'll be in touch as soon as I know something," Hunter said.

Hunter knew if the cartel killed the Doctor and his wife then chances were good they would go after, Dan and Sarah, to make a point. He and his associates would have little trouble finding them if they were in Portland.

***

Dan called Wayne at the ME's office.

"Wayne, it's Dan, I need some information."

"Let me guess, Dr. and Mrs. Bennett."

Wayne knew the evidence he had just bagged would be extremely volatile once released. He also knew once the police had wind of this evidence all hell would break loose and the media frenzy would go viral.

"I know that edge in your voice, what have you got?"

Dan listened as Wayne explained the evidence he had found under Mrs. Bennett nails, microfibers from an ACU cover used on Kevlar helmets, standardized issue among the police department. S.W.A.T. used this type of gear and the backlash from a public scandal of this magnitude was the last thing the police department would want.

***

It had taken thirty-three minutes for Hunter to gather the intelligence he needed to confirm the two men with the black Escalade were in Portland. Given another hour, his contacts would have them under surveillance and he'd keep them within reach.

***

News of the supposed murder/suicide had leaked to the press and film crews were in abundance around the police station. The commissioner prepared a statement with very limited time for questions from the media.

Banks of microphones were spread across the makeshift staging area in front of the police station, but most film crews had their microphones on poles hovering near the podium.

The commissioner, the police chief, and the two detectives assigned to the case were all front and center. Commissioner

Abrams stepped forward and all but the street noise quieted down and waited for Abrams to begin speaking.

"Good morning. Before I begin I would like to introduce the Chief of Police, Chief Glen Michaels the lead Detective on the case, Robert Elmes, and Detective William Perry. Please hold your questions until I give my statement then you may direct your questions to these gentlemen."

Abrams cleared his throat.

"This morning at approximately 9:15, Dr. and Mrs. Jason Bennett were found dead in their home, and the scene may appear to be a possible murder/suicide. No note or letter was found and a full investigation into these deaths is being conducted at this time. Please be brief with your questions as time is limited."

The onslaught of questions nearly all pertained to the recent deaths of Scott Rader and Rhianna Ryan. The officials fielded the questions as best they could without giving away too much information. When in fact, they had very little information to give out.

The most damning question asked in every conceivable way by most reporters from all the stations was, *is Dr. Jason Bennett responsible for the deaths of Scott Rader and Rhianna Ryan?*

Commissioner Abrams concluded the news conference abruptly, as intended, and the various news teams resumed speculation as they performed for their own cameras.

***

Rodrigo and Garcia had watched the news conference along with the rest of the world and were less than satisfied. And so was the rest of the world, but for different reasons.

The Commissioner left an air of doubt in the public's mind as to the murder/suicide theory. The men they answered to in Phoenix would not like that. Now the deaths of the PI and his woman would be much more difficult to camouflage as accidental.

The men made their calls up the food chain and were instructed to return to Sonora 180 miles from Phoenix, over the Mexican border. They had all they could get their hands on at this point, the files and discs as well as the few earlier flash drives from the basketball players' condo. That would help to smooth over their botched job with the Doctor and his wife.

Their instructions had been to leave no doubt of a murder/suicide and to send the PI and the woman over a cliff, high above the Pacific. Killing Americans within their own border was not something the cartel took lightly. Drawing that kind of unwanted attention to their trade was normally too big a risk.

It took less than fifteen minutes for Garcia and Rodrigo to gather the few possessions they brought with them from Nogales, Sonora.

***

Hunter had given the green light to his associates' moments after he had hung up with Morrison. The fibers off the cover of the Kevlar helmet under Barbara Bennett's nails sealed the deal for Hunter. He'd seen this type of kill before, and he knew the risk to Greg's widow was real and already too close.

Morrison had no way of knowing that the men and the Escalade were about to disappear off the face of the earth. He didn't need to know, and Hunter didn't need his input or any ethical misgivings he might have.

Hunter had owed Greg since the Gulf war and there had never been an opportunity to repay the debt not that Greg had even understood Hunter's need for it. Then the opportunities died with, Greg, or so he had thought.

Morrison would be told the intelligence showed the men had moved back over the border. Hunter would allow the evidence from the crime scene at the Bennett's to run its course in whatever direction it took. Saving the reputation of local cops was not on his agenda.

The team worked in silent unison just as they had in the Gulf and in all the, for hire, missions since. The men knew this one was for, Greg, there was no paycheck to collect, and they were good with that. Neither Greg nor his widow would ever know the debt was repaid and that was good with them too.

It took all of fifteen seconds for the team to take down the two men without so much as a grunt, another thirty to load them and their gear into the van and sixty seconds to drive the Escalade into the semi standing by.

The warehouse they used was twenty minutes over the

bridge into Vancouver and no one saw or heard a thing as the team wrapped it up by disposing of everything but the files, discs, and flash drives, which were sent to Hunters private mail drop.

***

Twenty minutes outside of Nogales, *number nineteen on the state departments list of most dangerous cities in Mexico*, an Israeli mercenary tactical team trained member of the Kaibiles Cartel. Simple street thugs from the slums of Mexico's drug trade were recruited by cartel members, taken to training camps like this one and taught by some of the world's most lethal belligerents.

Warring cartels were upping their game in their fight for the trafficking routes into the US... and the nearly 70% of the foreign drug trade that flows into the states.

Fifty billion annually in drug money will hire as many mercenaries as there are cartel members and they're good at training kids. Kids with no one and nothing, not even enough food to eat, who are all too willing to join the fight. Hell, even white bread American kids might join up if they knew they would get to use military assault rifles and grenade launchers.

The Mexican cartels knew that killing each other even on American soil would not garner much outrage among US citizens. Most citizens would be glad they were killing each other off; it was the collateral damage in the US that had Americans anxious and hostile.

For the most part the cartels were not looking for undue attention and drawing down on Americans in general was a foolish and fast trip to hell for them to take. When cornered, however, they would kill anyone that got in their way including US law enforcement, military, and citizens. So, when Americans encroached on their drug trade, they would swiftly put an end to them as well.

***

Two days later the ME in Portland released his findings into the death of, Scott Rader, toxicology showed no known evidence of illegal drug use. Rader's death was listed as natural causes associated with advanced stage 4 carcinoma affecting both lungs, as the world and sports fans everywhere scratched their heads in disbelief.

The Los Angeles ME's office had yet to release the findings into the death of, Rhianna Ryan, but Dan felt sure the findings would be like those of Scott Rader.

Dan had mixed emotions of relief and concern when, Hunter called to tell him that his sources had reliable intelligence that the two men in the Escalade were back in Mexico and not likely to return.

Dan knew the two had murdered Doc and his wife. He knew Doc had to have files on the athletes at his home. Doc was always too anal with his record keeping not to have additional files on hand. In fact, he felt sure the legitimate files had been in the Bennett's home. And the two men that killed them, had left with the files.

Dan had wanted to question Hunter, to press him for more

information but Hunter wasn't one you could press with an effective outcome. Hunter was hands on, Dan knew that, and it seemed unlikely the two men slipped through the fingers of his team.

Instead, Dan laid it out for him. He told him what he did know, and he told him what he thought he knew. More athletes would die if those files were lost or in the hands of someone who didn't give a damn if they did die. Dan had no way of knowing if he had appealed to Hunters sense of decency, or morality, or even if he possessed those qualities. He was, however, relieved and grateful that Hunter had chosen to protect Sarah, even if it was out of the loyalty he had felt for Greg.

It was time to go home.

***

A collective sigh of relief could be heard from the Falcon's camp with the release of the ME's report. The death of Bennett and his wife faded from the spotlight as soon as the ME's report on Rader's death hit the media. Dan had filed his report with Ed at Falcon headquarters, though he wasn't sure if Ed had bothered to read it. The Falcon's had a business to run and Scott Rader was no longer a part of that business.

CHAPTER 22

TRUST

Sarah had greeted Dan the night he made it back to Seaside. He had called her from the road, and they stayed up late into the night while he filled her in on the closing of the case that he knew was still wide open with unanswered questions.

Without Doc's files the case was stalled, and the Falcons had no desire to rock the boat now that they were off the hook. Dan had no client, no files, and no leads at this point.

The only thing he held back from telling her was the fact that Hunter knew a great deal more than he was willing to tell. Dan had no desire to put Sarah in the position of choosing between him and a sense of loyalty for her dead husband's best friend.

***

Morning sun streamed through the white gauzy drapes and woke Dan before Sarah, so he made a pot of coffee and turned the flat screen on in the kitchen. He listened as one of the anchors for

Good Morning America delivered news while he poured milk into his first cup.

In a strange turn of events, three seemingly unrelated disappearances involving three highly visible businessmen occurred on the same day.

Pictures of three older men appeared on the screen with captions under each stating their names and positions and the cities they disappeared from. The anchor reporting the story continued:

"Ted Anderson, a Banker in Fresno, California was last seen boarding a Delta flight to the Grand Cayman Islands, though customs have no record of Mr. Anderson entering their country. Mr. Anderson's disappearance is most disturbing since he was scheduled to undergo a round of chemotherapy upon his return, which he missed. Mr. Anderson has advanced lung cancer, and it is imperative that he receive treatment.

Silicon Valley, .com executive, Frank Wilson boarded a United Airlines flight to Hong Kong and never cleared customs as well.

The third man to disappear was Hollywood producer Roman Caulfield who, like the other men, boarded a flight. This one to Cannes on Air France. Again, customs in France have no record of Caulfield entering their country."

The anchor told of no known affiliations connecting the men to one another but that the airlines have records of the men boarding the flights as scheduled.

"It seems the mystery begins for each of these men, on foreign soil. Could this be the work of Al Qaida using another form of terrorism aimed at our most influential Americans?"

The morning news show moved on to the next item involving Arizona's immigration laws and the impending lawsuits from the US Government.

***

Sarah came into the kitchen and wrapped her arms around him from behind. Dan took her hand and pulled her around to face him.

"What do you want to do today, you name it."

A mischievous look of anticipation lit up her face.

"I want to go to Terrible Tilly."

"You're kidding, right?"

A look of shock and awe pained his face. Sarah laughed outright at the sight of his expression.

"It's ok. We don't have to go today. I can go another time by myself. I intended to go before you came back earlier than I expected."

"No, I said you name it, so we'll go.

Dan arranged for a boatman to take them out to the lighthouse.

***

The surf was choppy, and the small boat bounced and bobbed its way at an angle toward the lighthouse. Sarah had taken an anti-nausea pill before leaving the house. But poor Dan chose not to. He wasn't fully motion sick, but his stomach was a bit queasy by the time they got to the rock.

The caretaker watched them on closed circuit monitors and took one last look around, he was ready. The oven was cold and loomed ominously in the background. The ash had been meticulously cleaned from the surface and the dust that seemed to settle everywhere had been wiped as well.

The pounding of the surf hitting the rock was deafening and the wind cut right through to the bone as the three made their way up the ramp that was meant for heavy caskets being rolled into the crematorium.

The boatman was having second thoughts though it was too late for that. He was going to get an education and tour of the crematorium whether he wanted one or not.

The caretaker adopted a smile and genial manner as he opened the door to greet his guests. Sarah was quick to warmly shake his hand as she introduced Dan and the boatman.

John Garrett had used this alias for years now and it had served him well. However, should there ever be a need, his identity along with the appropriate documents were available at a moment's notice and the ever-growing offshore bank account was his ace in the hole.

John performed beautifully for the trio even the boatman was engaged in the lighthearted conversation. Sarah took numerous shots within the lighthouse and graciously accepted the privacy factor of the one room, John, asked her not to shoot.

The actual Fresnel lens in the lantern room had been smashed in a horrific storm in 1934 and had never been replaced.

The money shot for Sarah had been taken from inside the tower as she stood on a table and stretched as far as she could from a window opening. With Dan hanging on to her legs like a safety chain.

Photos outside were taken by, Sarah, while, John, chatted it up with Dan and the boatman. Deep sea fishing being the topic of choice. John shook their hands and clapped the boatman on the back for good measure as they prepared for their return to shore. Even the boatman had an entertaining afternoon.

The trip back seemed less unsettling to Dan's stomach, and he found himself craving seafood after the sport fishing stories the men had one-upped each other with. They thanked the boatman as Dan gave him a bonus for his good sportsmanship and walked to the car.

"How about some chowder and clams at, Norma's?" Dan's stomach growled in anticipation. They had skipped breakfast and lunch; plus a cool beer was calling his name. An early dinner at Norma's would be less crowded than usual.

"That sounds good plus I need a favor I've been meaning to ask you for."

"What, another favor? What do you call the trip to the lighthouse?"

"I think I did the favor by giving you an opportunity to swap fish stories."

"Woman, every word was gospel that fish was huge, I swear! It took everything I had just to haul it in the boat."

"Uh huh, I'm sure it was."

"I can't believe you're going to stand there and disparage my good name like that."

"Come on, you're hungry and cranky, let's go eat."

Norma's was busy but there wasn't a line to the street like there would be in about an hour or so. They ordered a couple of beers on tap and people watched for a moment or two.

"okay, what's the favor you're after?"

Dan asked after he'd eaten half of his food and ordered a second beer.

"I need you to fly over some landmarks so that I can photograph them for the book."

"I don't know, what with fuel prices being what they are you may not be able to afford me."

"You don't say."

"I'm willing to negotiate with you though, what have you got?" Dan was enjoying himself.

"I have tickets to the opera in Portland next month, and I can't wait for you to take me."

Sarah kept her expression sincere as she gazed into his horrified face.

"Next month... ummm, next month is one of my busiest times. I'm not sure I can."

Dan watched the slow smile spread across her face as she

watched him try to stumble his way out of an evening at the opera.

"You are a cruel woman, Sarah Knight."

Yea, he was whipped, and he didn't care.

The flight was great the next day. Dan took his time and seemed to enjoy the photo shoot as much as she did. He even took her to places she normally wouldn't have thought to include but the locals would appreciate those shots even more than tourists.

One such place was an old fish hatchery that had not been used in years. It was nestled in a lush emerald, green sea of forest and had a waterfall with a clear water pool at the base that begged to be swam in.

Dan was quite the photographer himself and had, years ago, taken an incredible photo of the bridge from Astoria, Oregon to Chinook, Washington. The bridge was shrouded in fog with glimpses of the bridge showing through the morning sunlight. All too quickly the flight ended, and the real work had to begin.

Dan had a few cases pending and he needed to meet with his people at the agency in Portland. He helped Sarah put her gear into the car trunk before preparing for his flight to Portland. Sarah came around the car and put her arms around his waist her face laid against his chest, and he kissed the top of her head.

"I'll see you tonight. I'll bring takeout."

"Thank you for today. I loved it. Oh, and the offer stands, the tickets to the opera are available at any time."

Dan groaned and leaned down to kiss her goodbye.

"I'll see you tonight."

Sarah drove a short distance to her house and opened the doors to the tri-level decks. The breeze coming in off the ocean fluttered drapes and brought the scent of the sea indoors. It was wonderful.

The sound of an engine faltering caught her attention, and she rushed out to the upper deck. Instantly she was overwhelmed by the sight of Dan's plane as he flew over the sea and tipped his wings to her, she waved back. A lump caught in her throat at the simple gesture that seemed so meaningful to her.

The intentional stalling of the plane always sounded frightening but was part of the pilot training. She watched as the plane banked left and resumed its course to Portland, as it disappeared over her house a strange sense of loneliness engulfed her.

"He'll be back in a few hours," she said out loud.

It was time to get busy printing out the new film and sorting through the mountain of photos. Once she made a few choices she could begin the text of the book, something she could lose herself in. Dan's photo of the bridge for sure was going in the book. It would be a wonderful surprise for him. The waterfall amidst the sea of green was the next choice she made.

***

Gina was back from Miami when Dan got to the office. Their client would be devastated when she saw the file, Gina had prepared for her. The husband's infidelity lay out in full color across the conference desk.

They hated the next part, the part where the spouse came to view the file. Gina always put the least graphic photos in the front of the file so that the client could choose when to stop looking as their world fell apart in front of them.

"The Falcon case, is it closed?"

Gina was making conversation as she organized the file pages spread before her.

"Yes and no, Ed wants it closed and forgotten but my best guess is the case has a few more twists."

"How so?" she asked.

Gina stopped and looked up as Dan took a drink from his keg.

"Doc may be dead, but he still has athletes out there that are taking those supplements. When Rhianna Ryan's cause of death is announced we'll know more…maybe. Rader's cause of death may say natural causes but I'm telling you, nothing about his death was natural."

"Do the cops know about the cartel's involvement?"

"What cartel? Those guys are long gone and there's no evidence that they were even here let alone involved with Doc."

"So is the case open or closed?"

"We have no client willing to pay to keep the case open, Gina."

"So, it's open."

"Hell yes, it's open. My bet is, it's just getting started."

Gina finished the file and tapped the edge on top on the

desk.

"Do you want to sit in while I ruin this woman's life?"

"Let's keep her humiliation to a minimum, she doesn't need an audience. I'll be available if she wants to see me though."

Dan checked in with the other field agents and scheduled a meeting for new assignments and final procedures with wrapped cases. Fritz handed him a check that had arrived that morning. Dan looked at the zeros on the check and wondered what in the hell, Ed, was up to.

"Did you call Ed about this?"

"No, I figured you were doing additional work I wasn't aware of. Do you want me to call him now?"

"No, I'll do it. Don't bank this check until I get back with you."

Dan couldn't reach Ed, but the accountant told him Ed had personally sent the figures over for disbursement. Dan would have liked to bank the check as a generous bonus, but he had the distinct feeling it was a *shut up and go away check* and that he wouldn't do.

The flight back to Seaside was completely socked in. Dan had to rely on the plane's instrument panel in the cockpit, and he hoped the runway lights in Seaside were up and running because on occasion, they're not.

Once, he needed to land the plane and he was low on fuel, but the lights were out leaving the runway pitch dark. Luckily, the guy who owned the motor home park next to the runway heard him as he made a few passes over the park and saw that the lights were out. In no time at all numerous motor homes lined the runway with their headlights lighting the field for him. Dan sent the guy a fifth of Jack Daniel's.

The lights were on as he brought the plane down on the runway and hooked up the tie downs to the plane adjacent to the field.

"Do you want Chinese or Italian?" Dan asked when Sarah answered the phone.

"I'm not sure, what is your ethnic heritage?"

"What?"

"I want you right here, all night."

"Oh, trust me that can be arranged."

"Bring it then."

CHAPTER 23

DUPLICITY

Duplicity dropped anchor a mile or so west of the lighthouse. The sea was choppy causing the ship a slight rocking motion. Which lulled its passengers in their drug-induced sleep.

Let them drift dreamily between the silky linens as they enjoy the brutality of the nightmares they've brought their victims. Because tomorrow morning as each woke, they would find themselves facing judgment day whether they were ready for it or not.

CHAPTER 24

ON JACKMAN'S RADAR

Morning found, Sarah and Dan, wrapped together too comfortable to begin the day. Unlike the night before, the sky was clear and the day bright.

"Sarah, I'm starving. Let's get dressed and go eat at the Pig and Pancake."

"You know what happened the last time we ate there."

"Sarah, I promise, if anyone comes after us, I'll get behind you this time. You can kick their asses just like you did Hunter's. I'll even hold your purse while you do it but I'm so hungry, let's go."

"I knew it!" Sarah rose up on her elbows and glared down at Dan. "You did go and confront, Hunter."

"Fine, we don't have to go to the Pig and Pancake. The Pig and Pancake seem to be the driving force behind our disagreements."

"I'll give you a driving force, Dan Morrison."

Sarah flipped agilely into a straddling position pinning him to the bed. Before she could do more damage, they were both laughing and rolling about the bed.

Breakfast was not at the restaurant it was in the kitchen. They drank coffee made with fresh ground beans while sautéing onions and mushrooms in clarified butter for the omelets. Tiny biscuits baked in the convection oven, and homemade pear butter was warmed for the pancakes.

"Do you want to fly again today," Dan asked in between bites? "Where did you get this pear butter, it's great, we need to get more?"

"It is good but I'm not sure I can get anymore because I sort of threw whatever I thought sounded good into the pot when I made it. Thanks though."

"You are full of surprises, aren't you?"

Dan studied her face for a moment before leaning in to kiss her cheek.

"You're like this beautiful, brilliant, ninja butt kicking, photojournalist—covered in pear butter."

Dan used his finger to brush away a single drop from her lip.

"I love you. You know that don't you. I've always loved you, Dan."

"Come here baby."

Dan rose from his chair taking Sarah by the hand as he led

her out onto the deck.

"Where are we going?"

Dan led her to the telescope.

"I'll show you something."

Sarah watched as he scanned the beach for a moment.

"There, look right there."

Sarah looked through the scope.

"It's your house. Why am I looking at your house?"

Dan pulled her into him, wrapping his arms around her waist.

"The first time I ever saw you, you were right there on the beach, in front of my house. I couldn't get you out of my mind especially while you dated, Chuck, what the hell were you thinking by the way?"

"I dated him for about ten minutes and then it was you."

"You'll always have me. That's never going to change. I love you, Sarah, always."

Morning turned to afternoon and Dan grew restless in the house.

"How about that flight we were going to take, do you still want to go?"

"I'll get my camera."

Sarah was back and ready to go before Dan had his shoes on. This time they flew over the surf and out to sea.

"Do you want me to teach you to fly or do you fly the chopper for Hunter's team in your spare time?"

"Very funny, Dan, I've only had two lessons so long ago I'm afraid I don't remember any of the instructions. So yes, I would love to learn to fly."

Dan banked right, turning the plane toward the mainland.

"Take the yoke."

"Now?"

"Why not, now's as good a time as any, it'll be okay."

Sarah took the yoke and remembered to keep the wings steady and level to the horizon on the plane's instrument panel as she flew above the water.

"Hey there's a big yacht down there, it's gorgeous. I need to photograph it; can you take the plane?"

"Got it," Dan said as he took the controls.

Sarah shot the yacht from many angles as, Dan, crisscrossed above the ship. They could see personnel striding about the upper deck, and one stopped to point to the plane. When she had finished the shoot, they landed back at the airport and made plans for the evening.

***

Mr. Jackman had been informed of the photographer and the plane flying circles around them. He was not overly concerned because the yacht had been photographed nearly everywhere it docked. The ship drew attention and that in itself was part of its cover.

The guests were sleeping in their staterooms and oblivious to their circumstances.

Still, the planes identification off the tail was useful and finding out exactly who the owner was wouldn't be difficult. Yes, he felt secure in transporting his guests to the lighthouse that evening after dark.

***

The caretaker was ready. After the photographer and the other two had concluded their business with the lighthouse, he had once again set the stage for interrogation. Delivery was scheduled for tonight and he needed new inventory to ship to Mexico.

The two tonight, coupled with the two recent authorized cremations would be ready to send in a day or two. However, news of that Doctor and his wife's death had been unsettling. Though he was very certain they had known nothing of him or his shipments to Mexico.

What a lucrative break it had been to interrogate that banker. Since the disappearance of all three men had been so easily explained away by speculation and the constant threat of terrorism. He toyed with the idea of others that might deserve a similar end to their deadly sins.

CHAPTER 25

RHIANNA RYAN

The news Dan had been waiting for finally hit the airwaves. *In the sports world, the Medical Examiner in Los Angeles, California released his findings today into the death of, Rhianna Ryan. The eighteen-year-old Tennis hopeful died of cirrhosis of the liver and the toxicology report listed no illegal drug use.*

The news commentator went on to speculate on the surprising results of the cause of death, and the networks medical spokesperson spoke in circles as well. In the end, no rational explanation was given, and Rhianna Ryan's measly fifteen minutes of fame came post-mortem.

Dan couldn't wrap his head around the concept that an eighteen-year-old athletic tennis pro could suddenly die of cirrhosis of the liver with no previously known symptoms.

This was a similar situation with a different disease as, Scott Rader. Diseases that are highly unusual in people so young with no history of tobacco or alcohol use. There was an answer, but he had nowhere to look for it and no one would be willing to dig any deeper.

Dan called Fritz.

"Get any information you can on the Ryan girl. Bribe someone if you can in the ME's office in L.A. but add the information to the Rader file. I'll pick it up later."

"I'll take care of it, anything else?"

"Yea, but I'll handle it myself, bye." Dan called Hunter's cell.

"Mr. Morrison, what can I do for you today?"

"I want your take on the deaths of, Scott Rader and Rhianna Ryan."

Hunter knew Dan wouldn't leave well enough alone.

"I don't have an opinion on either one, why?"

Dan spent the next five minutes connecting the dots for Hunter. Which Hunter was already familiarized with especially since he had Doc's files, discs, and flash drives, as well as the cell he confiscated from the two cartel members his team intercepted and neutralized.

"There's no way those two kids died of natural causes. Come on, Hunter, cirrhosis of the liver, in an eighteen-year-old girl who never drank a day in her life."

"Yes, that's unusual but what can be done at this point? What do you hope to accomplish by keeping this stirred up?"

"I hope to keep other athletes, other kids from dying."

"Well, your doctor friend is dead so I don't see how you

will get more information on his client list. You could leak your theory to the media. Surely any clients he may still have out there will stop taking the supplements and that should take care of the problem."

"You know as well as I do that, Doc had to have had associates, someone who could get more supplements. Listen, can I get back with you, I need to check something out?"

"No problem, I'll be around."

Doc had said something about shipments. Dan wracked his brain to remember Doc's exact quote. *The pharmaceutical manufacturer produces the supplements and ships them to me on demand, satisfied?* Dan couldn't simply call Mexico for a new shipment. The world knew, Doc was dead. The few supplements taken into evidence, if any, were in police lock up. Doc changed the formula frequently to meet his requirements for the athletes. What the hell, he called Fritz.

"Fritz, get me a list of the pharmaceutical manufacturers in Mexico along with phone numbers please."

"No problem. We are talking about the legal ones, aren't we?"

"Who knows, legal, illegal they may be one and the same."

While he waited on the information Fritz was gathering, Dan ran previous conversations and facts through his head. Toxicology had come up empty on both athletes. Even if Dan had the supplements there was nothing coming up on the tox screen. Still, he wanted a sample so people he trusted could break it down for him. Fritz texted the information to Dan's cell, and Dan began the tedious task of calling Mexico's manufactures.

Between the language barrier, company policies, and a ream of red tape he learned that each client had an encoded set of Pin numbers. The numbers had to be punched in along with routing numbers that directed their instructions to the manufacturer.

Without those numbers, Dan didn't see how he would be able to get his hands on a new shipment of supplements. Dan assumed Doc's cell was in the police evidence room with everything else. That cell was the key to Doc's encoded Pin number and his routing instructions to the manufacturer. Now…he could use a leak at the Portland Police Department.

***

Hunter thought about his team and the work they did for pay. What they were willing to do for pay verses what they were willing to do for conviction. Men like them existed out of necessity for a government or a dictatorship, it didn't really seem to matter anymore.

No country was exempt from tyrants and extremists. Terrorism is a worldwide plague, as is the effects of genocide and drugs. Hunter's team was one of many black ops teams that didn't exist in any case file yet was sent to equalize situations for the weak and exploited. They're the non-existent teams that level the playing field in war torn areas of desolation and hopelessness.

The last thing Hunter's team did for conviction brought

him to this introspective crap. He didn't need this. The team came first, before tennis stars, and basketball players, even before Greg's widow, and even Greg would understand that. The men, his men, would decide the risks they were willing to take in the name of conviction.

CHAPTER 26

EZEQUIEL

The Kaibiles Drug lord, Ignacio Ezequiel, speculated on the disappearance of Garcia and Rodrigo. Had the men suspected he might kill them for bringing attention to his drug trade—maybe? Maybe they decided to take what they had and break free from his control. Either way they had taken with them the information he required to embed himself into the pro-sports world. Mexico's soccer team for one, as well as the Mexican up and coming Olympic teams.

Ezequiel meant to have that pass into pro-sports and Garcia and Rodrigo had done the one thing no member of his cartel had ever dared to do. They had made it impossible for him not to track them down and bring them back to Nogales. A ritual killing in front of the rest of his cartel would be an effective deterrent, one that would keep others from following suit. Otherwise, his choke hold would be gone along with his business. Ezequiel would send some of his best men to Portland, they would either find the men or find the reason for their missing in action

Justifiable: Oregon

status.

CHAPTER 27

REFUSE

The yacht sailed at night, cleansed of refuse and ready to entice the next wealthy man on the list. The list was long and held some of the worlds prized "WHO'S WHO" names in business and on Wall Street. Foreign dignitaries, oil Sheikh's, as well as those who did business with them, peppered the list of names also.

Duplicity didn't discriminate, anyone who traded in human trafficking was welcome to enjoy the luxurious privileges that the ship had to offer.

There was no shortage of human refuse that lies in wait to prey upon the weak, the vulnerable, and the innocent. No segment of society was more innocent than children. Around the world at any given moment, there are those that buy and sell children into the sex trade as if they were buying and selling pork bellies.

The market was huge and the younger the child the higher the price. Every day, parents can be seen begging for the safe return of their children. But often, their children are already sold, defiled, or dead.

Young women are targeted, kidnapped, and traded like baseball cards and when they are used up, they are killed and dumped like garbage. Over eight million young women and children annually are stolen and sold worldwide. The animals that lay waste to these children have no mercy and they will not stop…ever.

The caretaker knew these facts and understood and accepted his role with a certain amount of pride.

The new role he took did bother him and he had no idea that the supplements would cause harm let alone death. The banker had said nothing about side-effects, and he had no way of knowing the human ash played a role in those side-effects or if some other ingredient was the defective agent. What he did know was his associates would not hesitate in treating him like one of their guests aboard Duplicity if they knew of his sideline.

John, as he was known, wondered if the money was worth the risk. Could he ever break away from his role as the caretaker and if he could, would he be allowed to simply vanish to live out his life?

CHAPTER 28

TARGETED

Sarah was deep into the text of the book. She knew she had better write while Dan was in Portland because while he was here, she couldn't seem to get anything done.

Photos were spread out all over the floor and tables, she had chosen a couple dozen or so and numbered the backs according to order of importance. Next, she indexed them and had begun the text for each photo…when the siren on her alarm system began its ear-piercing scream.

Sarah froze for a moment before it registered with her that there was an intruder warning. Then she was up and running for the Glock safe, the phone was ringing and all she could think of was getting to the gun.

Sliding through the bedroom door, Sarah rolled across the bed landing in a squatting position beside the table. The Glock was in her hands in less than twenty seconds. The incessant ringing of the phone and the screaming of the alarm had her adrenaline pumping so hard her breath was coming in short, ragged gasps.

Then, she could almost hear Greg's voice calming her like when he had trained her to move, to act instead of reacting. Deliberate tactics for plausible circumstances was what he called the training. Sarah grabbed the phone and moved into the master bathroom locking the door before she moved into the deep stone steam shower.

"I need help!" Sarah stated into the phone the moment she pressed the answer button.

"Mrs. Knight, this is the police we are at the gate; where are you?"

"I'm in the bathroom on the main floor."

"Do you know where the intruder is?"

"No, I can't hear anything over the siren, I can barely hear you!"

"Stay where you are, Mrs. Knight, and give me the emergency over-ride code, now."

Sarah gave him the over-ride code, and in seconds the siren was shut off, and she could hear movement a lot of movement in the house. Then they were beating on the door.

"Mrs. Knight, it's the police, are you all right?"

"Yes, yes I'm fine!"

"Open the door, Mrs. Knight, we need to see you."

Sarah had enough sense to remember that she had better not open the door with a gun in her hand. She laid it down in the shower and went to open the door.

The next hour was spent with cops filing in and out of her

house and scouting the grounds as well as moving the tram to and from the beach. Dan had been called, she suspected by Billy, and he tried to sooth her over the phone through the commotion. The thing was she was fine.

Once she remembered the in-depth training, Greg had insisted she learn, she went into autopilot. Get to safety first. Do not engage an intruder unless you have no other options. If no other options exist, shoot them. If you have no weapon to shoot them with, kick the crap out of them and take their eyes out with your thumbs.

Greg had shown her how to use the heel of her hand and to ram with enough force to drive facial bone into the brain of an intruder. He had shown her how to get an attacker off her no matter which hold he used on her. Every bit of the training had rushed back to her as soon as she tuned into Greg's voice.

Sarah shared none of this with Dan, though he needed to reassure her, and she let him, for him. Billy and Zane hung around long after the rest of the cops left. Sarah made coffee and snacks while they admired her Glock and asked her questions about Greg and Boston. Sarah knew she was being babysat until Dan arrived, and she was fine with that.

Even Greg had needed to feel like he was her protector and he had been. Greg taught her well, she could easily take Zane and Billy, probably together, in hand-to-hand combat. However, she knew that Greg would want someone to watch out for her as well. Next time, if there was a next time she wouldn't freak, not even for a moment.

Dan arrived in no time and he all but checked her over like one would with a small child who had taken a spill off a bike.

"I'm fine, really, nothing happened."

"Except that someone tried to break in!"

Dan's face was a mixture of worry and anger.

"Billy, show me where they tried to get in."

All three followed, Billy, outside to the ocean side of the house.

"Here let me show you, it's under the decks, the window to the laundry room has been jimmied."

"Looks like he used a crowbar maybe."

"Yea, that's what we figured. We got no prints and the concrete doesn't have any shoe prints either."

Billy had shown all of this to Sarah before Dan arrived, but she wanted to know if Billy had any more to add now that Dan was there.

"Where did he come in at on the grounds?"

"We think he came over the fence from the ledge over here."

The ledge was high above the fence, and someone would need a running start to make the leap from the ledge to clear the fence. Also, the guy would have to be able to tuck and roll because the drop from that ledge was a good ten feet.

"How did he get off the property?"

"He could have gone over the fence anywhere once the

alarm went off because it wouldn't have mattered. We checked for damage, but we didn't find any. He could have climbed down the cliff, but I doubt it because he'd have run a risk of being seen from the beach."

Dan and Billy walked the perimeter of the grounds discussing flaws in the security system while Zane kept Sarah occupied inside the house. Finally, Zane and Billy left, and the house seemed eerily quiet.

"You did good, Sarah, you did really well. Billy said you had locked yourself in the bathroom …with a Glock. He also said you held it together."

"Well, he didn't see the hyperventilating part before the cavalry arrived."

Dan had her in his arms holding her, kissing the top of her head.

"Sarah, can I see the Glock?"

"Yes, Dan, you can see the Glock."

***

Sergio Leyva was long gone. He was long gone before the cops had an opportunity to respond to the alarm. It was just a test anyway. The system would have to be disabled if they intended to get into the house. They could, however, simply wait until she left her property. They could get inside the house once they had her. The PI would give up everything he had on the sports doctor once they had her.

Ezequiel had been clear. Find Garcia and Rodrigo or find

the doctor's files and discs. There was no sign of or lead to the missing men and for all they knew the PI had their men and the missing information that Ezequiel wanted.

Leyva had been sent to Seaside on his own, his job was to see how difficult it would be to take the woman. Outside the gates of her house, it would not be difficult he reported to the men in Portland.

***

That night, Dan was still wired over the attempted break in and wanted to know if Sarah could defend herself one on one. Hunter had said she could, but he may have overstated his ability to train her for all Dan knew.

"Really, Sarah, I need to know you can handle yourself. I can't be here all the time, and I don't want to be worried constantly when I'm not."

"Dan you're asking me to deliberately hurt you. I don't want to do that. Besides, I know Hunter told you I can take care of myself."

"Hunter thinks way too much of his own skills and he may have exaggerated yours, just a little."

"Really, I have exaggerated skills!"

Sarah stepped into, Dan, flipping him over her shoulder and onto the hard floor of the lower level of the house. With one swift move she flipped him to his stomach pulling his wrists to his butt while she straddled his legs, pinning him down.

Dan couldn't flip over to his back with his arms stretched

behind him to his butt nor could he use his legs to throw her off because she had his legs pinned beneath the length of her body. His back was arched, and his head hung back painfully.

"Do you want to tap out?"

"Sure, let go of my wrists and I'll tap out."

If she eased up just for a second, he could be on top of her.

"So, you think I'm stupid on top of having exaggerated skills. I can do this all day, Dan, can you?"

"Sarah, you are so hot right now. Let me go."

"Say the words, Dan."

"I love you."

"Say the words, Dan."

Dan struggled a bit more, and he was getting short of breath with his back arched and his head pulled so far back.

"Fine, I'm tapping out…"

"I don't know, Dan, sounds phony to me. I don't want to get tricked I could get hurt."

"Sarah, really, I'm tapping out."

Sarah thought about it for a moment longer then she released and spun away from his body simultaneously and sprung to her feet in a crouched position waiting.

"Come on, Dan, you're not hurt. You just want a chance to get me."

"I wanted to get you right here on the floor a few minutes ago, but I don't think I can anymore."

She wasn't buying it.

"Fine, I'll wait right over here until you get up."

Dan rolled to his back and sat up. His brow was cocked, and a grin tugged at his lips. Without taking his eyes off her, he slowly rose to his feet and rolled his shoulders and neck loosening the kinks she had put in them.

"Now let's see if you can go one on one without blind-siding a guy."

Sarah cupped her hand palm up and bent her fingers twice.

"Bring it," she whispered.

Dan charged and almost had her just before he hit the wall.

"Had enough?" Sarah panted.

"Please!"

Dan whipped around and dove for her legs.

Sarah dove sideways into a roll and jumped to her feet about the same time he did.

"If this is your idea of foreplay, Sarah, I have to tell you, you're going to have to do most of the work tonight."

"You can quit anytime; this was your idea not mine."

"Yea, like I can quit now. I'd be laughed out of town."

Dan lunged into a side sweep his right foot grazing her leg as she leaped to the right, not giving him a chance to back sweep. She circled him trying to anticipate his next move.

"You're good, I'll give you that, but what will you do if the guy has a knife or a gun?"

"I won't go down without a fight that's the best I can do, Dan, the same as you. If you've had enough, I would love a steam shower… with you."

"You're such a cheater, Sarah."

***

Hunter called Dan's cell bright and early the next morning.

"Thought you might want to know, some men from the Kaibiles cartel out of Sonora are in town. Three of them, they're staking out the last place the guys in the Escalade were seen."

"How long have they been in town?"

"A couple of days, why?"

"Because someone tried to break into Sarah's house yesterday, the security alarm ran him off."

"How's she doing?"

"She handled it better than I did when I heard the news. I never should have pulled my agent off her."

"Don't second guess it brother, it doesn't help."

"By the way, she kicked my butt too."

"Do I want to know?"

"I had to be sure she could take care of herself, she can, but I'm still putting someone back on security."

"Yea, I would too. When will you be back in your office?"

"You know what they're after don't you, Hunter. They want Doc's files. Apparently the two didn't make it back to Sonora with the files, maybe they didn't leave with the files, or maybe they didn't leave at all."

"That's a lot of maybe's brother. I think the Kaibiles think you have the files and I think they'll use, Sarah, to get to you."

"I'll stay with Sarah for a couple of days, talk her into letting an agent ghost her, then I'll head to Portland."

"I'll let you know if they move your way but watch your back anyway."

"I always do."

Hunter closed the cell. He needed Dan out of the way for a little longer and who better to protect Greg's widow than Dan.

The team knew killing these three would bring ten more; those ten dead would bring a hundred and so on. No, they needed something a little more sophisticated to get rid of these jokers. If he needed more time, he'd tell Dan they lost sight of the Mexicans, Dan would go into lock down with, Sarah, even if he had to tie her down.

***

Dan called Fritz at the office and filled him in on the cartel involvement with the Rader case. Fritz was to inform the field agents to watch their backs ASAP. Dan went so far as to suggest the agents move their families into relatives' homes for a while, just to be safe.

Fritz would make sure the office safety measures were implemented to the letter. A break in would most likely occur at night after hours and the more he thought about it, an idea began to form, an idea that just might get the Kaibiles scum out of their lives. Dan made one more phone call to Billy, then he went back to the bedroom where Sarah was waiting for him.

"What now?" She was sitting in the middle of the bed a

worried look on her face.

"I'm staying for a while, a couple of days at least."

"Why, what's happened?"

"Well as I see it you have two choices here, me or an agent from my office. Now I like to think I have more to offer you in the way of personalized care, but you make the call."

"Dan it's obviously in your nature to run a con on me and it's in my nature to call you on it so let's just cut to the chase here. What is going on?"

"Three cartel members are in Portland; Hunter has them under surveillance. One of them may have been the guy that tried to break in here. Hunter will watch them, and I'll watch you. Satisfied?" Dan held his hands out in resignation.

Sarah pulled the covers down and stood on the bed. Slowly she walked to the end and wrapped her arms around Dan's neck.

"Do you remember that thing you did in the steam shower last night, well, I was satisfied then."

Dan cupped his hands under her butt as she wrapped her legs around his waist and walked to the steam shower.

"You really don't know how to play fair, do you?"

Mid-afternoon found them both antsy to get out of the house.

"Let's go to the beach we can take the tram. I really want a caramel apple twist and coffee from the bakery," Sarah suggested.

"Hang on."

Dan pulled the cell out of his pocket and hit speed dial to Hunter.

"Morrison, what's going on?"

"We're getting restless here."

"Ahh, well we have the three under watch so go out, just know there is no guarantee that only three came to Oregon."

The tram inched down the cable lines as Dan held her from behind, watching the tourists and anyone that looked at them which was plenty. The tram to the beach was probably the only one within fifty miles, so it drew attention.

Sarah pocketed the key when it stopped in the sand and they walked up the beach toward the promenade. As usual, the bakery had a line but being in the middle of a crowd gave them a sense of security and as Dan watched the people, Sarah watched him.

"What," Dan asked when he noticed her watching him.

"You take good care of me."

"Yea, like you need it. My neck still hurts."

Sarah couldn't help smiling at the image she had of him arched like a pretzel.

"If it weren't for me you could be taking care of your business and your friends at the office."

Dan paused and looked down at her. He didn't say anything as he studied her face for a moment. Then he simply bent his head and whispered in her ear as a single tear slid down her cheek.

***

Mr. Jackman wondered why a PI from Portland would be photographing Duplicity from the air. Jackman and his team had gone over every detail, every moment to see if there had been a mistake that would bring an investigator into their mission. He knew no mistake had been made. The team didn't jump the gun, they took their time, they made sure. No one had ever boarded Duplicity as a guest who wasn't one hundred percent guilty of crimes against women and children.

That didn't mean a guest didn't have friends or family that wouldn't hire a PI firm to find them. Nevertheless, Jackman wouldn't jump the gun with Mr. Morrison either. Facts would be checked and re-checked before a determination was made on what to do about the PI.

Obviously, there was no urgency or evidence because they had no visit from port authority or the coast guard. The lighthouse's only visitor's outside of authorized cremation personnel was a photojournalist, Mr. Morrison, and the boatman that delivered them to the rock.

Morrison may have used the photojournalist as a ruse to investigate. The woman may not even know she's being used. She was indeed a journalist with a legitimate job that took her to the lighthouse. Jackman had her checked out as well.

Wealthy widow seeing divorced PI, no red flags there. The nearly non-paying job she took with the Signal seemed odd to him but maybe she was bored or maybe it was more of a hobby.

Regardless, his team would perform a private investigation into Dan Morrison's motives with Duplicity.

***

Later that night, Sarah felt restless and bored, the breeze coming off the water also brought in patches of fog. Sarah scanned the water through the telescope; there was nothing to see so she decided to look at Dan's beach house again. He wasn't there so it wasn't technically snooping, plus he wouldn't mind if she did snoop.

Dan was getting takeout for them and this time it was Chinese. The house was whimsical and reminded her of some of the houses on Nantucket Island. She loved thinking of him as a little boy playing on the beach, building sandcastles, or heaven forbid investigating the neighbors.

A little to the north and she could see into the living room, even the family photos on the wall. To the south, his dads' study. Now, Dan's office and... *Hey, he's there, she thought.* He moved around the desk to the files. She wanted to call him, to see him answer her call while she watched, so she pulled her phone out of her pocket and hit number one.

Smiling she watched through the telescope. Dan didn't even look up from the file cabinet because when his phone rang, it rang from the kitchen, her kitchen. *Shoot, he forgot his phone.*

"Hey baby, why are you calling me on the phone?"

"Dan?"

"What's wrong, Sarah?" Dan was already out on the deck

looking at her as she was pointing to the beach.

"Your house, someone's in your house! I thought it was you!"

Sarah moved out of his way while he focused the telescope.

"He's in your office at the file cabinet. I'm calling the cops!"

"Tell them I'm on my way to the house; tell them I'll meet them there."

Dan was out the door before she could put up a fight that she would have lost anyway. She reported Dan's message and resumed her position at the telescope and saw the man put files into a small carry-on type bag and leave the house by the deck, ocean side. He was heading north toward the promenade when she called Dan's cell and told him. The man disappeared from her sight into the fog, as it rolled in from the sea.

Dan parked on Broadway and ran the short distance to the promenade and down the steps to the beach. The fog was patchy but very thick in areas and swirled around, Dan, as he searched the base of the stone wall that supported the promenade. Dan stopped and held his breath listening for the sound of footsteps or breathing. The only noise was the sound of the surf distorted by the fog. Still, he searched, sometimes simply feeling the space around him blanketed by the thick air. The search was useless, and he decided to head to his house to meet up with the cops.

Sarah waited anxiously for word from him. She didn't call

him again because she wouldn't distract him when he could be in danger. Watching his house kept her occupied, then she saw Dan and the cops enter from the street side. She could see the lights turn on as they went from room to room. The office was where they gathered and Dan looked toward her house and waved, knowing she would be watching him.

The guy with the fingerprint kit was working the file cabinet and desk while, Dan and Billy, went out the way the man had left. The man could be anywhere at this point; she didn't have a description except that she thought he was Dan at first. Billy and Dan walked toward the promenade the same direction the man had gone. Sarah jumped when her cell rang near her hand.

"Hello."

"Hey, it's me, I'm on my way back so please don't pull out your Glock."

"Did they get him?"

"No but he got a lot of files, there's no way to pin down exactly which file he was after because he took an assortment. The main office has duplicates but it'll take a while to cross match what he took. Hey, I'll be there in a minute do you need anything?"

"Just you."

"I'm already there."

***

The cartel needed to be dealt with in such a way that made them think it was their choice to leave the area. They needed a win in the way that suited them best. Dan had thought about this a great deal after the attempted break-in at Sarah's, and then the actual break in at the beach house. His plan was workable but needed input from the kind of help offered by special forces.

Hunter's team had been informed and given the choice to opt out, as always. As always, they agreed to make the impossible possible. Each team member was a specialist in one way or another. Even Hunter wasn't keyed in to all the individual resources the men had at their disposal, some things were better kept under wraps. The *eyes-only attitude* kept the pissing matches to a minimum among the men, so missions were successful.

Both Dan and Sarah flew to Portland to meet with Hunter's team. They were a team now even though Dan struggled with the concept of her being in the middle of a conflict especially with the cartel. Tucking her away somewhere wasn't a viable option. Plus, she wouldn't put up with it and when he was away from her, he worried about her safety and the distraction was dangerous.

CHAPTER 29

HUNTER'S TEAM

The Dojo was not where they met. Too many parents and kids popping in, even after hours was a risk. There was a small building in a run-down section of town, three blocks off waterfront that the team kept leased. A floor below street level housed their equipment, kept ready for use at a moment's notice.

They met in the street-level-parking garage connected to the building and entered through the west side. Furniture was sparse. The office had a few dented fold-out chairs, a couple of metal desks, and old tables with ancient office equipment sitting here and there.

Dan cocked his brow and began to worry. There wasn't a viable piece of equipment installed anywhere. This wasn't even a pretense of a working office. What the hell was this place? Hunter and the other men watched them take in the trashed office space and waited for a response.

Sarah spoke first.

"So, where's the real office?"

Hunter turned and led them to an equally ancient elevator that squealed and wheezed them to the next floor down. This floor didn't look any better as they were led to a row of doors lining a hallway. Hunter opened a door and walked in ahead of the rest flipping the light switch on. They walked to the middle of the room because that was the only space available to stand.

Frankly, it looked like NASA had a going out of business sale and these guys were the only bidders. Equipment lined stainless steel shelving around the perimeter of the room with enough flat screens on the walls to put Best Buy to shame.

"ok, now I'm impressed."

Dan moved toward a flat screen monitoring a live feed in what looked like Afghanistan.

"Afghanistan?"

Dan pointed incredulously at the monitor, but the screen had already gone to black as one of the men tapped a keyboard and ignored his interest.

"Need-to-know brother, and you don't."

Dan accepted the point-blank rejection with humility. These guys had what he needed so he checked his ego at the door.

The next few hours were laid out according to each man's field of expertise. Sarah got the first real look into the world Greg had been a part of yet never spoke about. Part of her felt as if, Greg, had shut her out of an important piece of his life and that stung. Strange that she would be deeply involved in this part of his world now, now that he was gone and she herself was at risk.

Three or four days at most and they would have everything they needed in place to send the cartel back where they came from. Their best guess was it would take several months to a year for the cartel to realize the intelligence they had from Doc's files, and discs, were useless notes and harmless formulas. When they did figure it out, they would have no one to blame but Doc, and they had already murdered him and his wife.

Dan was breathing easier with a confirmed plan of attack hammered out. So, he and Sarah prepared to leave the building. Hunter took the elevator up with them and both men noticed a slight and somber change in Sarah's demeanor.

"Just so you know," Hunter directed to Sarah, "Greg let this go."

"This?"

"The life we lead. From time to time, every man you met today has regretted not making the same choice Greg made, for a woman he loved. Greg never regretted his choice, not once."

Without shame, Sarah let the tears fall and Dan watched as Sarah walked to Hunter and wrapped her arms around his waist. Hunter roughly hugged her and patted her head before disengaging himself, clearly uncomfortable with the show of affection.

"Thank you, Jake, how did you know?"

Sarah wiped her eyes and looked up at him.

"Really… Sarah?"

"Sorry, no offence intended. Your observation skills are

truly unmatched."

She couldn't help laughing at his indignant expression.

Without ceremony, Hunter said his goodbye and shut and locked the door behind them.

Dan took her hand pulling her into him.

"I'm sorry I didn't even think about how this might affect you."

"Don't be sorry. Most women, if their lucky, have only one man who truly loved them in their lifetime. I have you again and I couldn't ask for more than that."

The flight back to the coast was quiet and uneventful, each in their private thoughts. Hers reflective of her life with Greg, and the happiness they had shared. Greg had loved her and in a way was still watching over her through the very men he had depended on to watch his back. These men who had cared for Greg like a brother had accepted her and her relationship with Dan. They made no judgments against either one of them they just stepped up... for Greg. Tears slid down her cheeks again.

Dan noticed but said nothing. She had a right to her memories, to her loyalty to Greg. He loved her and he knew she loved him but was it enough to withstand this larger than life, ghost of a man that she could still depend on through his friends and brothers.

"I loved, Greg, I'll never deny it. Having said that I want to say something about you and me."

Dan waited, not knowing what to expect.

"You are the reason I came back to Seaside, even though I had no way of knowing if you were married, in love, or if you had forgotten about me. You, Dan, are the reason I feel loved again. You are the reason I hope again, and you are the only reason I love again."

Dan took her hand and held it to his lips for a moment.

"Forget you? That's not possible. I love you Sarah, I always have."

Sarah woke to find Dan was not beside her. She found him outside at the telescope.

"Are you ok?"

"I'm fine, I just couldn't sleep. Why are you awake?"

"I reached for you and you weren't there."

Sarah had deliberately put on one of Dan's T-shirts before going out to find him. She walked over to where he was sitting and sat in his lap with her arm around his neck.

Dan had wanted to make love to her when they got home but he didn't want her to feel obligated to prove she loved him; he wanted her to make the first move.

Hours seemed like minutes and night slipped into day and, Dan, no longer doubted her commitment to him. Sarah loved him, she was a part of him, one with him. Yet Dan couldn't help but feel Sarah was holding something back. A part of her he couldn't touch, he couldn't reach. He was willing to wait and maybe someday she would be ready to share all of who she was with him.

CHAPTER 30

THE SET-UP

Three days later, Hunter called. "Meet me at the Dojo, everything's set up," Then he hung up.

"He doesn't like to waste words, does he?" Sarah mused after Dan told her what he'd said.

"Nope, he sure doesn't. Come on we have a break-in to stage."

Sarah drove them to the small airport while Dan made several calls, using the disposable phones he'd paid cash for.

Fritz and the others at his agency as well as Hunter and his team were not taking chances. Anyone could remotely activate the microphone of a mobile phone whether the phone was in use or not. Eavesdropping into lives and homes are a given with cell phones, which is why their personal cells went without the batteries as well, out of habit.

The cartel was certainly savvy enough to employ the world tracker technique using the cell phone towers and GPS systems to pinpoint anyone anywhere, who has their phone on them if the battery was in the cell.

Everyone was in place and briefed in their assigned role.

Dan flew as he and Sarah ran through the plan pointing out every conceivable backfire and a contingency strategy to rectify it. By the time they reached the Dojo the parking lot was empty. Hunter was at the door waiting to let them in.

The files were prepared and appeared to be identical to the filing system Doc had used at the Falcons. Discs had been altered and filed in marked sleeves as were the ones Doc had prepared. The one thing Hunters team had not altered or shown to Morrison, was the flash drives from Rader's condo. The flash drives were nothing but daily life with Rader and his girlfriend. Hell, from what he saw, Rader had no idea what he was taking. He just did whatever, Doc, told him to do. The poor guy simply trusted Doc, like any twenty-three-year-old would.

Hunter had made duplicates of the flash drives and would plant them with the phony records for the Mexicans to find. Once the cartel had the records, they would most likely be back in Sonora thinking they had won. Neither they nor Morrison would ever know or care what happened to the two from the black Escalade.

It would take a great deal of time, money, and investigating around the world for the cartel to finally unravel the elaborate web they had weaved since they took their two men down. The last three days were spent establishing worldwide connections, a trail of proof to spur them on and keep them tied up indefinitely.

First and foremost, Hunter backed his team and the first two Mexicans were never going to surface.

It didn't take long for the three Mexicans to take the bait and break-in just as it had been planned. Dan reported the break-in as pre-arranged and filed his reports with the police. The police wanted to know if Dan had a security system installed and he assured them he did. Together they discovered the security override of a highly technical nature as Dan preformed his rehearsed act for the cops.

Dan proposed the possibility that one of his client's wealthy spouses must have broken in to steal incriminating evidence in a divorce settlement. This scenario was then leaked to the press as a bonus to add to the files and discs the cartel took back to Sonora with them.

CHAPTER 31

THE PRODUCT

The caretaker was running out of product; authorized cremations were far and few between. Duplicity hadn't arranged another drop since the night the PI and the woman had flown over the ship taking photos. Mr. Jackman had them both checked out to the point of breaking into the PI's beach house and lifting his files.

Morrison's agency in Portland was heavily secured, and their man had reported unusual activity in and around the agency, so they simply watched and waited. The investigation had turned up nothing to lead them to believe the PI was on a case involving any of the pedophiles they had neutralized at the rock or anywhere else.

Still, the caretaker needed product, and he had thought long and hard about the possibilities available to him. He was in a situation with three possible outcomes, and he needed to find a solution soon, because his future was at stake.

First, he could choose to continue as the caretaker, always living his life between the rock and the few times he was able to break away to enjoy his pursuits. Pursuits like travel, theater, and fine wines shared time to time with women he would meet along the way.

Being the caretaker had its rewards. He knew he was contributing to make the world a better place for children to grow up. Every filthy pedophile removed from this earth was a blessing in his mind and he felt privileged to be the hand that put them down.

His work was his own personal therapy. Helping to ease if not erase the black memories of his own childhood at the hands of a mother that used him like a checkbook to pay all those men for her crack habit.

Second, he could resign as the caretaker, simply walk away from his responsibilities and live out his life in a middle-class way. The money he had established in his offshore accounts could last if he lived modestly, he was still young enough though that his current cash flow would eventually have to be supplemented to survive old age.

Third, he could spend the next few years doing his good works as the caretaker and… as a freelancer, building his retirement and ridding the world of a few other monsters and leeches that suck the life out of society in general.

Travel, fine wines, and beautiful women like the photojournalist who visited the rock do not come cheap. They are never part of a modest middle-class lifestyle. He was not meant to live a modest middle-class life. The very life he lived as the caretaker raised his status, his value in this world to his way of thinking.

Really, what choice was there for him to make? He'd known it all along. He had simply needed to weigh his options for his own peace of mind. Deep down, he'd known it the moment he'd read the front page of the Seaside Signal the night before.

An early morning raid by the Seaside Police Department busted a methamphetamine ring the SPD had been investigating for months. Along with four people of interest in the case, three children under the age of five, were taken into care by protective services.

The article had gone on to discuss the war on drugs, and the fine job law enforcement was doing to combat the ever-growing problem within our country and at our borders.

Bull shit! John thought. I'll bet those kids have been used in ways no one will ever know about or ever bother to find out about. John fumed at the way the article dismissed the kids as if they were nothing more than additional paraphernalia confiscated at the meth house.

In fact, he was pretty sure the mother would get them back if she could pass a piss test three months in a row. He knew how the judges were, determined to keep the family intact even if it meant some kids didn't make it. There was no culpability for a judge that makes a call that destroys a child. Maybe there should be…hell yes, there should be.

John needed to calm down. He hated feeling out of control

and the article had him feeling out of control. His role as the caretaker gave him the control he craved. The caretaker, controlled life and death…and HE ALWAYS controlled their deaths!

John couldn't stay on the rock another moment. His frustration over the article that had triggered memories of his childhood left him edgy and angry. He would get off the rock for a couple of days. His associates could reach him by phone if they needed to.

John sped around the curves of the coastal highway; he was headed to Lincoln City first, then on to Brandon to play one of the top championship courses. Modest middle-class people didn't play championship golf courses.

CHAPTER 32

RAGE

The next weekend, Sarah dressed for dinner while Dan was at his beach house. No fingerprints were found in or around the house and the man that had stolen his files vanished in the fog that night.

Fritz had cross-checked the files from the Portland office and none of it made any sense to Dan or Hunters team. The stolen files were across the board alphabetically with no lead to the target file. The cartel probably thought they were being covert, and that Dan had no idea they had ordered the hit on, Doc and his wife.

Tonight was not the night to sort it out. Tonight was a night to breathe easier and to enjoy an evening without threat.

The Partee Room was wonderful as usual. They sipped their mixed drinks and watched late evening duffers on the course. Men in parrot-colored pants and shirts played at dusk while their wives probably scrap-booked or sipped wine with one another.

Their steaks were rare and came perfect to the table. Sarah had Dan's full attention, no searching the faces of other dinner guests tonight. No being holed up behind her security system, it was great. They had just ordered coffee when Josh and Melinda came to their table.

"Hey, you two, we haven't seen you in quite a while. What's been going on?"

"Josh." Dan stuck his hand out to shake Josh's. "Sit down, have you eaten yet?"

"Yes, we ate earlier. We're here for a drink before we go home to free the babysitter."

Melinda sat by the window over the first tee, Josh sat across from Dan.

"We just saw that new film, the one with all the old action heroes. It was great except you could almost smell the Ben-gay and Viagra in the theater." Josh laughed at his own joke while Melinda rolled her eyes.

"Well?"

Melinda looked meaningfully at Sarah. Sarah smiled innocently.

"Well, what?"

"Where have you two been or should I ask what have you two been doing?"

Deep crimson flushed, Sarah's face because she didn't expect Melinda to be so direct. Plus, the memory of her and Dan on the deck a few nights back flashed through her mind.

Dan averted his eyes and smiled around the rim of the coffee cup he drank from, the other two laughed out right. Sarah was mortified and she had a horrifying thought, what if they had a telescope and a view of her deck?

The rest of the evening was spent talking about Sarah's work project or the tourists that frequented the beach sports shop.

"Why don't you come to the sand-sail race we're sponsoring next weekend? I'll bet you'll get some great shots for your book."

"I'll take the photographs, but I don't have the final pick on which photos are in the book."

"No problem, come anyway," Melinda coaxed.

"There's a lot going on in the area what with the sand-sail races and the sandcastle building in Cannon Beach at the end of the month. I'm going to have enough photos for two or three books."

The evening ended when Melinda got a call from their sitter. Dan paid the check and they walked out into the cool night with a soft mist falling around them.

"My house or yours, where would you like to stay tonight?"

Dan asked as he backed the car out of the parking spot in front of the golf course.

"Well, if we stay at my house we won't be repeating the deck scene from the other night, I can assure you."

Dan tried not to laugh but he knew that was why she had turned bright red when Melinda had asked what they had been up to.

"It's not funny!"

"You're right, it's not funny."

"Stop laughing! I'm so embarrassed."

"Sarah, how could they know about the other night?"

"How did I know about the break in at your house while it was happening?"

"I see your point, but they do live along the beach not up on the cliff like you. I doubt they can see the top deck even with a telescope, and if they did, they're just jealous."

"You're not helping."

Morning found them snuggled deep in the down comforter. Sarah rose first and made fresh coffee. She was going to drink hers on the deck, but rain kept her inside. So, she took a huge mug back to Dan's bed for him along with a copy of the Signal. He preferred the feel of the paper copy over technology.

The Bureau of Tourism has reported a decline in complaints regarding panhandling in Seaside recently. The paper went on to report on the apparent decline in homeless people taking advantage of the local shelter as of late and to whether the homeless moved on or became employed. Panhandling was always a problem in a tourist area.

Even vacationing college kids on break would panhandle in Seaside, hoping to drum-up enough change to buy the next beer. Most tourists expected the panhandlers to hound them; others reported them and apparently the cops were cracking down on the practice.

***

The smoke from the furnace in Terrible Tilly had dispersed by morning light. A few more hours of cooling, sifting, and packaging, and the caretaker would have a new shipment of *food grade minerals* to send to Mexico.

Last night had not been a mistake; the caretaker had done the job he was meant to do. Rape is EXACTLY why their mission exists.

He'd been very selective regarding the homeless, choosing only those he had personally seen as abusive to the others. Volunteering on occasion and helping at the shelter had given him an insight into the nature of some of the local homeless people. Some simple fell on hard times. Some had given up period, but a few were angry at the world, and were going to make others pay and they did.

Last night though had been unexpected. Happening on those two little bastards on the beach like that was foreordained, it had to be. The girl was down, face down in the sand and drunk, anyone could tell she was drunk. She'd probably wandered away from her friends and passed out on the beach.

One was still unzipped and trying to tuck his shirt in while the other had just finished having a turn at the girl. Both were laughing and joking about having the best summer break. They didn't even acknowledge the girl. They viewed her as just another shot of Tequila in their wild escapade at the beach.

He hated them, hated what they were. Those kinds of animals always took and never cared what they left behind, broken and sometimes damaged beyond repair…people. People who may have excelled in this world, yet, often become that which took from them, abusers themselves.

John followed the two. They were laughing and staggering down the beach, planning to meet up with their other friends back at the cheap motel they all shared, like cockroaches. He waited until they had exited the beach access and was close to his car. John used the remote to open the trunk of his car, the guys jumped when the trunk popped open beside them.

"What the hell, man." One said as the other laughed and pointed at him.

"You were scared shitless, you wimp."

Both were laughing and shoving each other as, John, stepped to the rear of his car.

"Bro, where'd you come from?" The taller one asked John.

"Hell," John answered as he tasered one after the other and dumped them in the trunk.

He'd lost it, he knew that he had. The control he thought he had mastered. The two were strapped to the gurneys, eyes bugging out, the adrenaline had burned the alcohol from their systems. They gasped air, dragging it in around the rags stuffed in their mouths as they sobbed and railed against the restraints.

The caretaker had not bothered to set up the mirrors he was so fond of. Why should he when they would clearly be able to watch what was happening to the other. He had cranked the head of the gurneys and faced them about ten feet apart as he set the stage in the lighthouse. All his instruments were laid out on rolling carts and ready for use. The tubes had been attached and led to the drains—he was ready.

"Shhh… shhh…" he quieted them.

Something he never did, this was different though; this time he had seen what they had done. He had seen first-hand what a waste they were, and he was unwavering.

"I need you to be very quiet," he nearly whispered to them.

The tall one railed harder against his restraints, bellowing behind the gag with rage. The caretaker took no offence. He knew how to get his attention, and he was going to enjoy it he thought, as he took a long scalpel from the tray and walked to the gurney.

"I told you to be quiet."

He spoke calmly never raising his voice.

"You don't listen, you don't follow the rules, now things are going to be very difficult for you."

The caretaker held the scalpel inches from the face of his subject as he spoke.

Cutting the pants off the tall one as he struggled had left a few bleeding cuts and gouges on his pelvis and legs but that was to be expected, at least he had his full attention now.

"Next time I tell you to be still I bet you will, won't you?"

"Please, please."

The words gurgled around the gag of the tall one.

"Please, please. Please don't, please stop," John mocked!

"How many times have you two heard that, would you estimate?

Please, enlighten me because I've seen only the one rape, on the beach tonight."

The shorter one quietly cried while the taller one raised his head to look at the blood running down his legs. They looked at each other. Sheer terror resonated through that look as they both turned to look at the caretaker.

John turned to the shorter one.

"If you're calm you won't bleed when I cut your pants off."

The shorter one whimpered as John walked to him and cut the front of his cut-offs free, exposing his genitals like he had done to the other guy.

"See, not a single nick... let's get started, shall we?"

***

Seaside was buzzing. A college girl been had raped on the beach with at least two DNA samples present from the rape kit and two college guys were missing. The police were certainly suspicious of the implications. The girl admitted to being drunk. She knew she had gone to the beach, but the rest were just bits and pieces she was unsure of.

When she woke on the beach, her clothes were torn away, and she was bruised and battered. She had used her cell phone to call one of her friends to come and help her. The friend convinced her to go to the hospital and that's when the police got involved.

Now two young men from OSU were missing and their parents were in Seaside nailing up posters all over town.

Lawyers for the parents of the missing men advised the parents not to submit anything that may contain a DNA sample to the police. Even a DNA sample from the parents could link their sons to the rape of the girl. The parents of course swore their sons would never be party to a rape and that their sons were victims not rapists.

The detectives on the squad spent their time going door to door canvassing the entirety of Seaside. Because no one remembered seeing the two men after they walked out of one of the pubs off the promenade, just as no one saw the girl or the rape.

Smiling faces of the two clean-cut looking college men stared out at the passersby from nearly every business and light pole. Businesses were afraid to take them down for fear of losing summer trade.

However, everyone was suspicious of the parent's refusal to submit DNA. The rape victim was long gone. Her parents had come to take her back to her home in Eastern Oregon, where she would endure years of therapy and berate herself for allowing herself to become a victim of rape. Because that's what so many rape victims do, they unjustly blamed themselves for the despicable actions of others.

Two weeks into the disappearance of the two men, the parents of one of them came into Morrison's Portland office and asked for him directly. Dan happened to be in the office that week and indeed met with them.

"Please, have a seat, Mr. and Mrs. Richards. I'm very

sorry to meet under these circumstances. Have you heard anything new?"

"No, that's why we're here Mr. Morrison. We hoped you would be able to help us. The police seem less than eager to pursue any real investigation and our son is missing; he is the victim here."

Mrs. Richardson spoke while Mr. Richardson stared at his hands.

"Mrs. Richardson, I know your scared and I can't even imagine being in your shoes with a missing child. Having said that I must ask you why you chose not to clear your son's name in the rape of that girl?"

Dan watched Mr. Richardson's reaction to his question. Mr. Richardson was not indignant he was... anguished.

"You mean, why didn't we give the police DNA samples?"

"Yes, Mrs. Richardson. Why didn't you just give the samples?"

Mrs. Richardson simply stared at Dan. It was her husband that finally whispered.

"Because we can't be sure he didn't rape that girl."

Tears streamed down his face and Mrs. Richardson was slowly shaking her head in defiance of what she knew to be true.

"I need to know where my son is. Can you understand that Mr. Morrison?"

Mrs. Richardson raised her chin, as she looked Dan in the

eye.

"Yes, I can, but you need to understand something about me. If I investigate this case and it leads me to your son and if I find out that he raped that girl, I will turn him in."

"I need to know where my son is, if he could, he would have contacted us. I need—we need to know even if—he's dead."

"I'll investigate for you; I'll do everything I can to find your son for you."

The next hour was spent gathering all the information he could from the parents. Dan had lists of Mark Richardson's friends, his professors, enemies, girlfriends, and exes. Dan especially wanted information on Allan Wood, Woody, as he was known by his friends.

Mark and Woody drank together, they partied, and vacationed together, and they may have raped together. One thing was for sure; they disappeared together.

Later, when Dan had an opportunity to speak with Mr. Richardson alone, he intended to find out all he could about Mark's apparently aggressive side toward women. Mrs. Richardson, he feared, may be one of those mothers who cover for their son's regardless of how despicable the son may be.

Dan returned to Seaside and stopped in at the cop shop to talk to Zane or Billy about the Richardson case. Billy was in an interview room with a local small-time pusher. He was interrogating the little creep hoping to find a lead in the disappearance of the two men. Some of the other kids from OSU suggested the two often enjoyed a little recreational use of an assortment of drugs.

"Did he see the guys, Zane?"

"You know I can't answer that Dan." Zane spoke the right words while his head bobbed yes, once.

Dan knew this little low-life dealer may at least give him something to work on. Possibly a direction to head in…here in Seaside where they went missing.

He wanted to work the case here before he left to interview some of Mark Richardson's friends and most definitely his ex-girlfriends. Exes often dramatized poor behavior in a relationship. But Dan wanted to find out if the guy had gotten rough or even raped a date. He'd start with phone calls and if he found anything promising he would meet with them in person.

First though, he'd catch up with the dealer when Billy was done with him.

"What's the guy's name?" Dan asked Zane.

"Pete, his name is Pete Houser. He lives on Tenth Street in that little tenant dump."

Pete didn't head towards Tenth when he left the Police Station; he headed toward the promenade and the pub he frequented. He needed to make a few bucks, and he always made a few bucks at the pub.

Dan had left the station before Billy had finished with Pete, so tailing his sorry little ass was no big deal. How did this guy get away with anything? Billy must leave him out of jail so he can get information from time to time on more critical issues.

Dan sat in the back booth and watched. It didn't take five minutes before some guy approached Pete. They didn't even go to the men's room to make the exchange. Dan used his cell phone to video the drug sale.

The bartender was busy cleaning and prepping so he saw nothing, probably by choice anyway. Dan slid out of the booth and made his way to the bar.

"I'll take a Bud on tap please."

The bartender nodded and got a glass out of the freezer and filled it. Dan handed him a five and waved off the change.

"Buy you a beer?" Dan offered Pete, as he turned back toward his booth.

"Sure, but that ain't part of the payment for anything I got."

"No problem."

Dan turned to the bartender.

"Another beer please." He requested as he set another five on the bar.

Dan picked up Pete's beer and took it to his booth with Pete, following along after him. They sat and Pete took a drink.

"What are you looking for? Cause I can get it."

Dan pulled out his cell and showed the deal he had just videoed to Pete.

"Damn man, I just left the cops."

Pete was squirming and whined like a five-year-old caught

lifting a candy bar.

"Relax, I don't want you arrested. I want some answers to my questions."

"Who are you? I've seen you with the cops before but you ain't one of em?"

Dan ignored his question and put a photo of Mark Richardson on the table in front of Pete.

"What did he buy off of you?"

Pete looked at the photo and shoved it back across the table.

"Nothing, he bought nothing... it was the other guy. The short one, he bought some weed that's all, just some weed."

"Thank you Pete. Now if you answer truthfully on this next question, I'll erase the video right in front of you."

Dan slid the photo of the girl to Pete's side of the table.

"What happened to her?"

"I didn't do it! It wasn't me, no way! I'm a lot of things but I ain't no rapist!"

"I believe you Pete. Really, I do, but I also believe you know something about it, and you need to tell me now."

"Look all I saw was the two guys on the beach with the girl. She was wasted; I mean on the ground out of it. She didn't even know they were on her like that."

"You saw the rape?"

Pete nodded his head once and looked up at Dan.

"You watched those guys rape that girl?"

Dan wanted to spit in his face and kick his teeth down his throat.

"Yea, I saw."

Dan was incredulous. This pig didn't even grasp what a piece of garbage he was. Pete had the opportunity to stop the rape and did nothing but watch. It took all that Dan had to control his voice, to act friendly.

"Then what did they do Pete?"

"They walked down the beach toward the head."

"Toward Tillamook Head?"

"Yea, now erase it, you said you would."

Pete looked at Dan, like he'd been a model citizen answering all his questions.

"One more question first. Did anyone else see that girl get raped that night?"

"I don't know if he saw or not, but some guy appeared out of nowhere walking the same way those guys left. That's it, no more questions, erase it now!"

"Listen up you piece of crap, you'll answer any question I have now or later because erasing this video won't save you from me smashing your stupid face in, got it!"

Dan was off his seat and leaning across the table hissing into Pete's punk-ass face.

"Got it, geez! Back off, what's your problem?" Pete knew the guy wanted to hit him; he could feel it.

Before Dan sat back down, he whispered.

"You're going to tell me what the guy looked like and then you're going to tell me how you're any different from the two sons-of-bitches that raped that girl."

In the end, the description Pete gave of the man on the beach was as generic as it gets. Even if Pete's description had been remotely distinct, the guy was probably a tourist that was long gone. Either way, Dan's options were a long shot, but he would try anyway.

A meeting had to be set up with Mr. Richardson. Dan had to tell him the truth whether he'd believe it or not. He knew deep down; Mr. Richardson already knew what his son was.

Dan had always wanted a child until something like this happened. He couldn't imagine which would be worse, having a missing child or fathering a rapist.

Billy and Zane didn't think Pete would be a very credible witness in a case against the two men in a rape trial. But his story gave them probable cause to request a search warrant from the prosecutor in the jurisdiction of OSU's campus.

The search provided plenty of DNA samples to test against the rape kit samples.

Billy also got a search warrant for Pete's DNA as well. So, they could exclude him or bury him if he was guilty of raping that girl after the two missing men had.

Photos of the missing men disappeared from storefronts and telephone poles as soon as the local prosecutor announced DNA testing confirmed the two had indeed raped the college student on the beach the night they went missing.

Frankly, no one cared anymore if they were found let alone found dead, no one except their parents of course. Dan had run newspaper, radio, and television ads billed to Mark's parents, searching for any information leading to the phantom man on the beach that night. Nothing surfaced, not even when both sets of parents offered a reward leading to the whereabouts of their sons.

Dan had interviewed family and friends of Mark Richardson, as well as professors and co-workers. The rape of the young woman on the beach was not a once in a lifetime grievous mistake. Mark Richardson had a history of violence against females in general, including his own mother. It seems he sent his mother to the hospital with a broken arm when he was fifteen. The mother swore it had been an accident of falling down the staircase, but relatives believed otherwise.

Most of their relatives avoided that branch of the family because their daughters had reported abusive behavior including Mark, grabbing at their breasts when he got angry.

One father proudly admitted to punching Mark in the mouth when Mark was seventeen for grabbing his daughter. That was the last time they had ever seen Mark or his parents.

What made Dan sick was the fact that, Mrs. Richardson knew damn well what her son was and continued to cover for him at the expense of every female he met.

Dan didn't pretend to know to what lengths a parent would go to protect their child in a case like this. He did know he would not have ignored the psychological damage; Mark Richardson had exhibited from an early age on.

***

The caretaker had watched every news story, had read the coverage in the newspapers and listened to the radio, nowhere did any of them even come close to describing him. He was relieved and grateful enough and would be wise enough to never lose control like that again.

The rape and sodomy of the girl on the beach had triggered a rage in him that he thought had been buried long ago. He couldn't ever let go like that again. But strangely enough the rage he had felt burned out the moment those two rapists were ash.

CHAPTER 33

SANDCASTLES

Summer in Seaside resumed for the new batch of tourists and the locals. The sandcastle contest in Cannon Beach was gearing up, and tourists poured into the tiny little town.

The guest judges were a collage of artists and celebrity personalities, Most judges were part-time locals with summerhouses at the beach. The most notable judge serving was a seventy-something, most famous for her reoccurring role on a daytime drama.

Previous judges that had served were Adam West, Dallas McKennon, and Tab Hunter, along with a smattering of lesser-known film and TV stars that had frequently visited the area through the years.

Film crews were back or maybe they had never left since the two rapists had disappeared. Most everyone assumed they had run and gone into hiding. Regardless, that story was history and the local businesses were grateful.

Getting into a restaurant was impossible without a long wait. Coffee and pastry at the bakery, forget it, Sarah drank coffee at home. Dan's bubba keg was not welcome anywhere for refills because his refills took the whole pot.

Walking the beach and promenade was an, at your own risk venture because the crowds were everywhere, and children were wild on their skateboards and roller-blades.

Josh and Melinda were beside themselves with sales and rentals of beach crafts and bicycles. Couples on tandem bicycles rode along the bike trail adjacent to the promenade.

Seaside and Cannon Beach were raking in their years' worth of money off the summer trade business, before school started the day after Labor Day. The rest of the year would be mostly mediocre sales from the locals and conventions that came to the coast.

Sarah no longer took the tram to the beach during this busy time. The last time she did she came back to find the beach patrol pulling six teenaged boys off the top of the tram. Apparently, they thought it was a beach ride and got bored waiting for the operator to return. Later the same six kids were seen base jumping off the highest point of Tillamook Head. Bets were being taken on whether they would make it through the week alive.

Dan had wrapped up a few pending cases and had been in Portland for a while, which was good because Sarah was able to write the text on most of the book while he was gone.

They planned to drive to Cannon Beach for the sandcastle contest. The judging wasn't going to happen for a couple of days, but the contestants were there in droves setting their stage and cording off protected areas for their artistry to begin.

Sarah suggested they check with Josh and Melinda, to see if they could rent scooters or motorcycles because parking in Cannon Beach would be impossible at best with a car. Josh told Dan, his stock was rented out with a waiting list as long as his arm, but they could borrow his personal motorcycle for the day.

The fifteen-mile ride down the coast would have taken an hour if they had not been able to weave through traffic on the bike. Parking was easy because it could be parked nearly anywhere, and they were able to get close to the beach and close to Haystack Rock.

They didn't even try to go into any of the shops or restaurants even though Dan wanted a coffee. The wait would have been ridiculous. The beach was crowded but that was part of the draw. Watching people interact, watching parents run after kids, and watching the artists was highly entertaining.

A commotion was erupting on the beach, north of the corded off area where the first of the sandcastles were being formed. Horses from the rental stables had left the designated trail and their riders were attempting to ride through the sandcastle building area. Sure enough, the riders were the same six teens that had climbed Sarah's tram. The same six that had base jumped from Tillamook Head and now, the six that were on foot because the beach patrol and the police took the horses and sent them back to the stables with the trail guide. Sarah and Dan could see the police giving the teens what appeared to be a stern warning and the commotion was over.

Venders on the beach did a brisk business selling food and drinks. One vender had a pump-up canister and was selling sunscreen at fifty cents a squirt. Dan waved him off when he approached them. He did buy a couple of diet cokes that they sipped as they admired the beginnings of some awesome sandcastles.

The dragon slayer standing on top of the slain dragon was Sarah's personal favorite, though she noticed mermaids seemed to be Dan's preference. It was amazing how quickly the artists formed the bases of their art and then came back in and built up the finer points of their designs.

The day went quickly yet the crowd on the beach never seemed to thin out until late afternoon. Around three-thirty, Sarah asked Dan if he wanted to try and get a table in a restaurant. Dan flipped his phone open and called the restaurant with a perfect view of Haystack Rock.

"They'll hold a table for us for ten minutes, so we need to hurry."

They walked into the restaurant with a couple of minutes to spare. The table was front row center of the view of Haystack with the sandcastle competition spread before them. The waitress warned them that service would be slow as they were getting ready for the onslaught of dinner guests to start in about an hour.

"No problem, we need the break."

Dan smiled appreciatively at the woman as she scribbled

on her order pad while Dan ordered a draft after, Sarah, ordered one for herself along with a plate of calamari which was always great here. Once their dinner orders were taken, they settled back to enjoy the scene on the beach.

The funny thing about Haystack was the rock was so huge around, complete with a cave at its base that when the tide was out people could climb completely around the base to the ocean side. However, when the tide was in, people that were on the ocean side of the rock could be swept off the rock by the pounding surf.

Those who chose to illegally climb Haystack usually do so from the ocean side because they can't be seen trying to get to the top before being caught by the police or the Coast Guard.

The bird sanctuary on top of the rock was completely covered in seagull waste causing the rock to be extremely slippery and nearly impossible to maintain a hand or foothold.

So naturally, here during the sandcastle contest the Coast Guard had to be called to rescue the same obnoxious six teenage boys as they clung to the side of Haystack two-thirds of the way up.

News crews filmed as rescue plucked them one by one from their perches and deposited them into the hands of waiting police. They were cuffed and placed in the rear of squad cars on the beach.

Sarah and Dan had front row seats for the entire dinner show and weren't surprised to see what looked like some of the boy's parents, arguing with the police. Apparently, one father annoyed an officer to the point that the cop cuffed him as well and sent him along with his son to lock up. The film crews got that too.

"You know, those kids' antics are the perfect infomercial for birth control use," Dan noted.

"Maybe even abstinence," Sarah suggested as she sipped her beer.

Dan nodded. The crowd on the beach applauded as the police drove away with the teens and a father in the squad cars.

After dinner, they strolled down the length of the sandcastle area admiring the entries and the incredible jaw-dropping sunset. The ride back to Sarah's house was a little breezy with a mist falling but it was all good.

The day had been exceptional except for the fact that Sarah had deliberately not brought her camera equipment because they were on the bike and she had no way of keeping it safe.

The photos of the helicopter rescue would have been fantastic. Though the Historical Society wouldn't have wanted to have photos of tourist being cuffed and hauled off, in their book. Still, she would have liked to have had the photos for herself.

After a shower, Sarah snuggled up to Dan on the sofa and closed her eyes.

"You weren't really serious about that abstinence thing, were you?" Dan's voice was hopeful.

Sarah opened her eyes and leaned across him.

"I think I can chance it. Besides, no child of ours would

ever act like that."

Dan leaned down to kiss her. He didn't know what to think of her statement.

"We should probably spend a great deal of time practicing first though," he said.

"I thought we had been but if you need more practice, I can arrange it." Sarah got up and pulled him to his feet. "Come on, I'll give you a full body massage you'll never forget."

***

The next morning, Dan dropped Sarah, as close to the beach as he could before he drove to find a parking spot. She had her equipment with her and it was cumbersome, but she was fine as she readjusted the straps over her shoulder.

"Here, let me help."

Sarah jumped when the man first spoke, as he took some of the equipment from her arm. It took only a second for Sarah to remember his name.

"John, thanks, how have you been?"

John smiled; he had forgotten how truly lovely she was.

"I'm good; looks like you're here for more book entries."

John held up the hand-full of straps he had managed to pull off her shoulder.

"Yes, but I sure missed an opportunity yesterday."

"How's that?" he inquired.

"Six kids tried to climb the rock and had to get rescued. Dan and I were watching from the restaurant, but I didn't have my equipment."

"Dan, is he here with you today?"

"Yes, that is if he can find parking that isn't all the way back in Seaside."

John was disappointed. He would have liked to spend some time with this woman without that damn PI tagging along. He knew the two dated each other, but they weren't married. She should know there were other options even in a small town like Seaside.

"Where would you like to start?"

"Really, are you sure?"

John turned on his heel. "Come on Sarah, I'm your caddy today."

He couldn't look at her without wanting to touch her. Forty-five minutes passed while he admired Sarah as she worked.

It took that long for Dan to make it back from parking the car. He was surprised to see John acting as Sarah's pack mule, that was his job.

"John, how's it going?" Dan held his hand out for John to shake.

"I can't complain, are you doing okay?" John shook his hand; he was good at small talk.

Sarah was shooting a photo of JAWS coming out of the sand complete with a leg in its mouth and hadn't even noticed that Dan was back. Dan wasn't offended; Sarah was focused on her work. The men watched her work for a few minutes. She engaged everyone around her because she had a way about her that naturally drew people in and made them feel important.

Dan did notice the way John watched Sarah, and he knew what that meant. John would like a shot at her which meant Dan may have to take a shot at him. Dan was proud of Sarah, and the fact that men were jealous of him.

The crowd's favorite castle turned out to be an actual castle with Excalibur protruding from a sand rock at its base. It was huge and very ornate, Sarah noticed as she shot it from numerous angles.

When she finished shooting, she saw Dan watching John watch her and it amused her just a bit, because honestly, why Dan would be intimidated was beyond her.

John was attractive, slightly younger than Dan, and probably younger than her. There was something, off putting, about him that she couldn't quite figure out. It didn't make any difference because she had no romantic interest in John, she simply appreciated his help.

"Hi," she smiled up at Dan, "is the car in the next county?"

"Not quite, I found Mike and Cindy on the way back and I got sidetracked."

Only an idiot would get sidetracked from a woman like, Sarah, John thought. John smiled at Dan, as he took the camera back from, Sarah, and replaced the lens cap. *John wished he'd get sidetracked for the rest of the day.*

Dan had offered to take over for John but, John seemed

pretty determined to hang in there throughout the rest of the afternoon. By late afternoon, Sarah could see that Dan was getting restless, so she asked him if he wanted to call it a day.

She had so many photos anyway. He did, and the drive back to Seaside would take an hour or so, on top of the hike to the car.

Sarah thanked John for all his help, and she truly meant it, as she shook his hand while they said their goodbyes.

Conversation on the ride back to Seaside had turned to John.

"You can't be serious. John is harmless, I think he's lonely being trapped at the lighthouse for days at a time."

"Oh, he's lonely alright. He's looking for companionship, why do you think he followed you around all day?"

"Dan, he was being nice, that's all."

"Was he being nice when he was staring at your butt while you took photos?"

"You're jealous, why are you jealous?"

"Get real, I'm not jealous. I just think you need to be careful of who you're nice to. I'll bet he thinks he's got a chance with you, that's all I'm saying."

"Hey, I doubt we'll run into him for a while but in case we do, I'll let you be friendly to him."

"Why do I have to be friendly to him?"

"There's no pleasing you, is there?"

Sarah was laughing, as she took her shoes off and rubbed her feet.

"I'll give you a massage when we get home." Dan offered

genially.

***

John didn't go to the lighthouse that night. He wondered if they were sleeping together. Of course they were sleeping together, unless the PI was gay. It didn't matter, he'd learned long ago, nothing lasts forever.

CHAPTER 34

THE ROCK

Jackman had spent a great deal of time investigating Morrison and the woman. Nothing pointed to any interest in Duplicity or the lighthouse. Morrison's files were directly related to sports figures, mostly for the Falcon's with an occasional look into some other pro-sports stars background.

Divorces were also a sizable part of Morrison's investigations. The rich were trying to screw the rich out of half the assets. In none of the stolen files did he come across a single name of anyone that had been aboard Duplicity or the rock. Mr. Jackman felt it was time to resume business as usual. He put a call in to John.

"I'll be ready, Mr. Jackman." John assured him.

A week would give, John, a bit of a break and he needed it. Mr. Jackman wouldn't be bringing Duplicity back if he had any idea of his recent…lapse in judgment. John was lucky and he knew it. A week gave him the time he needed to arrange another chance meeting with Sarah, maybe next time the PI would be busy somewhere else. Maybe he could see to it that the PI was busy somewhere else.

***

The proofs were ready for a preliminary viewing and Sarah had a meeting with the Historical Society at 10:00 am. The text was nearly complete and there was plenty of time for revisions, though she knew they would be minimal. Sarah was looking forward to getting their feedback. Dan was impressed but she wondered if he'd be impressed even if the work had been amateur, she hoped not.

The jacket cover gave her the most problems, it had to pop, it had to draw the eye amidst a sea of other hardcovers vying for attention on the shelves of Book-A- Million, Barnes & Noble, and other chain stores. Not to mention Amazon sales.

Dan had left for Portland that morning, so she had the house to herself, and she was dressing for her meeting when the phone rang.

"Hello," she answered.

"Hi Sarah," the voice was friendly.

"Hi." She didn't recognize the voice.

"It's, John, how are you?"

"Oh, John, I'm good. How are you?" Sarah was at a loss of what to say.

"Did you get your photos developed yet?"

"I did, they're great and thanks again for your help."

What does he want? She thought.

"I was happy to help. I'd like to take you to lunch today."

"John, I'd like to but I'm about to meet with some people about my book project. And I don't have any idea how long the meeting will run. Could we make it another day?"

Dan was right, now what was she supposed to do? Sarah wondered.

"Sure, no worries, I'll call you soon. You take care of yourself Sarah."

"Thank you John, you too, bye."

This was not good, but she was running late, and she'd have to deal with John later.

John watched from his car as Sarah left her property and the gate closed behind her. He wanted to know if she was a liar. And he wanted to know if her meeting would run through a simple lunch.

Dan called, Sarah, around 1:00. He wanted to know how her meeting had gone.

"Long and boring and frankly they want too many of the expected photos."

"Expected photos?"

"You know, sea shots or rock formations jutting out of the water, the shots that every other coffee table book of coastal living has in it. I wanted this book to be different. What about your work is there anything new there?"

"I have a face to face with, Ed, tomorrow. Personally, I think he wants me to slide back into the old arrangement with the team. He'll hand me a new player to run a background check on and he'll think the whole disaster with, Doc, is behind us."

"Will you continue to work with the Falcons?"

"I'll leave that to, Ed. I intend to set the record straight as I see it. The problem is I have no proof of cartel involvement in Doc's supplement sideline. I have no proof that the cartel killed Doc and his wife. The fact that the police truly believe in the murder/suicide scenario or are using that scenario to hide the fiber evidence found at the scene doesn't help any. What are your plans for the next few days?"

"I'm going to complete the book layout and text. I want to hand it in to the Society by the end of the week. I'm also completing the layout that I feel would be more appealing and then we'll see which they choose."

"That sounds risky, what if they choose the one you don't?"

"My ego can take it besides it's their money, their choice. I simply want them to think outside the box, to view the area from a different perspective, that's all."

"Well either way, the book is still personalized with your style and your words so it's a win/win for them and anyone who buys the book."

"I love your support, but I think you may be biased just a bit."

"I am, but that doesn't change the facts. Listen, I've got to go but I'll see you sometime Saturday afternoon. We'll go out. Do you want to call, Melinda and Josh, to see if they can join us?"

"Sure, I'm looking forward to it. I love you, Dan."

"I love you too, baby."

***

John had waited in *Brewed Awakenings*, the coffee shop across the street from the Signal. Sarah had taken a thin leather document satchel into the meeting. *Good, she wasn't lying, he thought, and he was pleased.* John was pleased that she hadn't made up some phony meeting just to avoid him.

He had waited for over two hours for her to come out of the building. Approaching her on the street after she had declined his offer seemed needy and that certainly was not his disposition. This woman was different from most of the other women he knew. Even the women he met on his getaways were not women he would spend more time with than an evening or two.

John got bored easily with the shallow conversations he had to engage in and the constant ego stroking he seemed to have to do just to get mediocre sex in return. John often wondered if a woman existed that could hold his interest in conversation let alone bed. He wondered if Sarah would be different. He wanted to give her a chance. He wanted to see if she was different. The fact that she didn't lie to him was promising.

***

Getting into the bakery was easier than it had been recently though there was still a bit of a wait. This time, Sarah chose a new creation, a blueberry cream cheese tart made with fresh pomegranate. Sarah knew she was going to pay for this treat, but she didn't care.

Sarah pulled up to the gate at her house and punched in the

code as she waited for Melinda to pick up the phone.

"Hi Melinda, it's Sarah, what are you up to?"

Melinda was taking a breather for the first time since the sandcastle contest had begun even though the tourists were still lingering through the week.

"Dan and I want you and Josh to go out to dinner with us Saturday night, can you make it?"

"Absolutely, I'll get a babysitter lined up." Melinda was delighted with the invitation.

"That's great! I need a night out after wrapping up the book for the committee. Why don't you come over here for a drink before dinner, how about 6:00?"

"Wonderful, we need some down time too. I've got to go get the kids now, but I'm looking forward to an evening out. We'll see you Saturday, bye."

Sarah pulled through the gate and watched as it began to close behind her. She was restless and needed some exercise especially after that tart from Sugar Mamma's. Mamma ought to be slapped for creating all those sugary treats. *Maybe I should be slapped for eating them,* Sarah thought as she contemplated taking the tram down to the beach.

The beach crowd had thinned out, and those six obnoxious kids were gone. The beach it was, Sarah changed and grabbed the key to the tram.

John could see glimpses of the house, beach side, as he climbed the ground adjacent to her house. He was always careful to stay behind the trees. He watched as she walked to the tram and started it on the slow ride down.

A chance meeting on the beach was perfect. Maybe she would ask him to ride back up with her for a coffee. John took his time making his way back to the car. There was no hurry because she always spent an hour or two on the beach when she went.

Sure enough, an hour and fifteen minutes later, John saw Sarah walking back at a fast clip. Her shoes were off, and she let the cold-water lap at her feet. He admired the way the sunlight brought the red and gold highlights out in her hair.

She was stunning and her graceful body was something else he admired about her. John wondered what it would feel like, being with her for the first time. Hopefully he will be in control, take his time, she would probably like that.

"Sarah, hi, how'd that meeting go?" he stepped in front of her, his hand shading his eyes from the sun.

"John, what are you doing here?" she was taken back by his sudden appearance.

"The same as you, getting some fresh air and a little exercise. I saw you walking back at a pretty fast pace, looks like exercise to me."

He was smiling trying to be charming, but it bothered him that she questioned his presence on the beach.

"How was your meeting?" he asked.

"It was long and boring just as I knew it would be."

Sarah was wondering where all this was going. She didn't

know if she should continue walking or make small talk. Letting him think he had a chance with her was not a good idea.

"It was nice to see you again John, but I have a lot of work to do before I wrap up the final layout on the book by Friday."

"Yet, you took a long walk on the beach. You must need a break to clear your mind. How about a coffee? We could even have it at your house if you like."

John waited, trying to read her face. She was contemplating it, he could tell.

Sarah contemplated the appropriate way to politely let him know she was not interested in him.

"John I can't really, I…"

John held his hand up to silence her excuses.

"No problem," John's show of attitude was accepting and relaxed. "I probably need to get back to work too. By the way, I forgot to tell you, I found some old photos of the lighthouse and some of the keepers also. They were tucked back in a drawer of an old desk in my private quarters."

"You're kidding. I'd love to see them sometime."

"I thought you may even want to incorporate them into your book somewhere."

Sarah thought about it for a moment, it was a great idea.

"John, when are you going to be back in Seaside?"

"Not until this weekend, why?"

John knew why, she needed those photos before this weekend. He knew she would come to the lighthouse—he was counting on it. He also knew a storm would be rolling in by morning. He was counting on that too.

"Would it be alright if I came to the lighthouse to get them?" Sarah asked.

"When?"

John waited while she weighed her options.

"I'll need to hire a boat."

"Don't do that, I'll take you out to Tilly. We'll get the photos and I'll have you back before dark, "John smiled benignly.

"I should get my handbag and my camera."

"You can if you want but you did take a hundred photos while you were out there. As for your handbag, there's nothing to buy on the rock."

"My cell is in my bag."

John held his satellite cell phone up for her to see.

"Besides, unless you have a satellite cell, yours won't work anyway. If you need to make a call you can use mine."

John didn't give her a chance to concoct a new excuse to get in the tram.

"Come on, my car is right over there. If we hurry, I can get you back in time to buy you dinner."

Sarah paused for a moment.

"Fine, let's go."

Dinner might be the best place to explain her commitment to Dan.

John chatted about her book, looking forward to the time

he'd have alone with her on the rock. Sarah stepped into the small boat with John holding her hand for support as the boat bobbed beside the dock.

The trip didn't take as long since the water wasn't so choppy. Still, Sarah had a queasy unsettling feeling in the pit of her stomach. She hoped she wasn't getting seasick since she hadn't taken an anti-motion sickness pill.

Frankly, she wished she hadn't agreed to come out here with him. Maybe she could rush him by telling him she was starving. When they docked at the rock, Sarah watched as he secured the boat with a chain and padlock.

"Why all the security," Sarah motioned to the lock?

John was amused considering all the security she had around her house.

"Sometimes kids think it's funny to set the boat adrift. I've had to replace the boat once because the last one burst apart on the rocks when kids untied it. The surf crashing on Tilly is wild; I've had boulders smash through the tower windows before."

John smiled and took her by the elbow walking her to the door as he pocketed the key. The sound of the pounding surf was bearable inside the building, and they no longer had to shout at one another to be heard.

"Excuse me Sarah, I'll get the photos, make yourself at home."

Sarah couldn't begin to imagine this place as home. The upset in her stomach continued to make her uneasy but she didn't dare say anything to John, because she needed the excuse of dinner to get off this rock as soon as possible.

The inside of Tilly was all stone walls which stayed slightly damp and somewhat creepy. How did he do it, stay here day in and day out, and why would he want to?

John placed the keys and cell on the desk in his private room and quickly pulled two bottled waters out of the mini fridge. It didn't take long to spike one with a syringe filled with the sedative used to quiet the predators that Duplicity brought to him.

She was in the tower room when he found her, and she didn't look good.

"Sarah, what's wrong? You look sick."

"I think I'm seasick. No, I was feeling funny before we got on the boat."

Sarah amended what she said because she really needed to get out of here. She needed to get back to shore even if she was seasick. She was fine with vomiting all the way back to shore.

"Please, John, can we go now? I need to get home."

"Of course we can. Here, I brought you some water, drink it and then we'll go."

John's voice was calming, and it had a lilt to it that she hadn't heard before. He was trying to reassure her as one would with a sick child. John cracked the cap on a water bottle and handed it to her. Sarah drank it, nearly all of it, it tasted so good. He helped her down the stairs of the tower and sat her in a deep chair.

"I'll get the keys to the boat Sarah; everything will be fine."

Sarah watched through a haze as John left her to get the keys.

John watched her sleep. He had moved her to his bed when she was completely under. He could do anything he wanted, and all he wanted was to watch her sleep. He would never take advantage of her the way his worthless mother had done to him.

Lying in his bed like that made him wonder what it would be like to make love to her whenever he wanted to. Two days, the storm would last nearly two days, which would give him a chance to get to know her. After two days, she would know he was better for her than the PI was.

Dan had tried to call Sarah numerous times on her cell and the landline, she never picked up, so he called Melinda.

"Yes, she called around 1:30 Dan. Is everything alright?"

"I don't know Melinda. She should have her cell on her, but who knows, the battery could be dead."

"Do you want me to go over there; I don't mind and now I'm worried too?"

"Yes I do, and Melinda, call me back as soon as you can."

Melinda drove to Sarah's house in ten minutes. From the gate she pressed the call button numerous times, no one answered. Through the trees and shrubs, she could see the bumper of Sarah's car, so she had to be home, or she took the tram down to the beach. Melinda punched in Dan's cell number; he answered on the first ring.

"Dan her car is in the drive, but she doesn't answer the call from the gate."

"What about the tram?"

"Hang on, I'm climbing the hill it will take a minute or two. If the tram is up how do I get in to check on her?"

"If the tram is up call, Billy, he'll know what to do."

"Dan, I can't see the tram, it's not up. Hang on I want to look over the cliff. Dan the tram is down on the beach."

Relief filled him, he was so relieved but what about her cell and why had she been gone for hours?

"Melinda, do you mind checking around to see if she turns up and please call me either way."

"Absolutely, I'm sure she's having dinner somewhere in town. Don't worry, you know I'll track her down."

Melinda tried to act unconcerned, but she had a nagging feeling that something was wrong here. When she got off the phone with Dan, she called Josh and got him on the phone, calling the businesses around town. Someone would have seen her in town.

Next, she called Billy, but Dan had already called him. Sugar Mama's Bakery reported seeing Sarah around 2:15 or so. From there, Mrs. Grissom, a local beachcomber saw Sarah walking toward Tillamook Head along the beach.

There were still a lot of tourists on the beach, but Mrs. Grissom saw Sarah heading toward the tram. Then she was gone, and everyone was thinking about the two college kids and the fact that they had simply disappeared as well.

Dan caught a tail wind and flew home in record time. Billy picked him up at the airport and filled him in on the nothing that they had on Sarah's whereabouts.

"What the hell is going on here Billy? First those rapists go missing and now Sarah!"

Billy let Dan rant for a minute, he had a right to.

"Dan, I need your calm. Sarah needs your calm. We're going to find her."

Billy put his hand on his friends' shoulder. He'd never seen Dan this upset, not even during his divorce.

"Billy, I've got my entire agency coming in tomorrow. I'd appreciate it if your guys shared any information they may have, and we'll do the same."

"You got it, buddy. It's going to be okay."

Billy had gotten the security company to send a technician to Sarah's house long before Dan flew in. Now, her house was a command station full of police by the time Billy arrived with Dan. It made Dan sick to see that many police in her house and knowing it was because something terrible may have happened to her.

Zane briefed Dan within minutes of him entering the house.

"Sarah's purse, her phone, and car keys are all here. It looks as though she changed clothes after her meeting with the

Historical Society and there is no sign of a struggle. The security system was fully operational and in good working order. The house was locked up and there was no sign of any intruder or guest for that matter. She was seen at the bakery, and she was seen walking back toward her tram. The tram was on the beach and after we dusted for prints inside the tram, we had security override the system and we had it brought back up. The last call made from her phone was to Melinda and Josh's shop. The last dozen or so in-coming calls were from you and Melinda." Zane took a breath.

"My men have already been canvassing businesses and beach front properties looking for anyone who may have seen her. Your friends and hers have been out looking as well. If she's in this town we will find her," Billy added.

"What if she's not, Billy? What if someone took her out of town? What then?" Billy looked from Dan to Zane, and back to Dan, he had no answer.

Dan walked to the deck overlooking the sea and hit a number on his cell.

"Hunter, Sarah needs your help and so do I."

***

Sarah woke groggy. And she had one hell of a headache. Where was she; she tried to remember. This wasn't her bed, and not her house. Sarah tried to get up, but her head was spinning, and she fell back against the pillow."

"Sarah you're awake, are you okay? I've been so worried about you."

That's not Dan's voice, whose voice… "Where—where am I?"

"Sarah it's me, it's John. You're here with me. We're at the lighthouse. Don't you remember?"

John knew she would be disoriented it was to be expected. The drug did that to its victim, but it was short lived. She would come around shortly now.

"Do you need anything?" concern in his voice.

"Why—why am I here, I don't understand?"

Bits and pieces were beginning to come back to her. *She was sick and then John was—he was—what, she couldn't remember.*

"You were sick, do you remember?" he gently asked.

"Yes, I was sick, and we were going back."

"We were going back but you fainted, and I tried to use the satellite cell, but it wouldn't work. It must have been the storm coming in, I had no signal. I was afraid to chance taking you out in the boat because a heavy fog rolled in, so we stayed here."

"I need to leave. I need to go home now."

Sarah tried to get up again but fell back on the bed. *What's wrong with me, why am I so weak she worried?*

"I would take you home Sarah, honestly I would but there's a storm today a terrible storm and we'd never make it. I'm so sorry. Can I get you anything?"

"I need to call Dan, can I call?"

"I'm sorry, we have no signal, it's the storm."

Sarah could hear the storm outside now; she had thought the noise was in her head that it was part of her sickness. *Dan must be out of his mind worrying about me she thought, I never should have come here.*

"Coffee, may I have some coffee? Maybe that will help to clear my head."

"Of course, Sarah, I have some made. Luckily, I have a generator, so we have electricity."

John went to the counter in his small quarters and poured a cup.

"Do you take milk or sugar?" he asked.

"Milk please."

Sarah could sit up now, and she put the pillow behind her back. She felt achy like when she had the flu.

"Thank you John."

Sarah took the cup and sipped the hot liquid.

"It's good, I needed this."

She sipped the coffee quietly for a few minutes. John was quiet too, but he watched her, and it bothered her.

"Are you hungry, I'd be happy to make you something?"

Sarah's stomach lurched; the thought of food made her feel nauseous again.

"May I use the bathroom? I'm feeling a little sick."

"Right through there, do you need help?" John wanted her to need him.

"No, I can do it, thank you though." She was a little

wobbly, but she was able to make it under her own power.

John was glad she seemed to be coming out of the fog of the drug. He was afraid he might have given her too much but, in his defense, it never really mattered if the others had gotten too much of the sedative.

The water was cold, ice-cold coming out of the faucet and it helped to clear her head as she splashed it on her face and neck. She hated that she didn't have her purse with her. Sarah felt better, the nausea had passed, and she did remember most of yesterday.

So, what happened last night that made it impossible for them to return to shore, and how long was this storm going to last? Sarah rinsed her mouth out with the cold water and opened the door. John was waiting patiently just as she had left him.

"Better now? You certainly look like you feel better."

"Yes, thank you John."

He liked the way she said his name; too bad it wasn't his real name though. He would have liked that better.

"How long will the storm last?" she asked.

John contemplated how long it would take for the drug to be out of her system.

"A day or two I guess."

The drug was like alcohol, a day or two and it wouldn't show up on a test. John smiled, he had a day or two to show her what he had to offer her.

***

The storm raged along the coast keeping most people indoors

Justifiable: Oregon

but not Dan and not Hunter. Their teams were out in it as well.
They were knocking on doors and asking questions. Melinda
phoned anyone and everyone in between the cell signal being lost
and regained. Dan had not slept, and he had not eaten. His bubba
keg of coffee kept him moving. Fritz and Gina tried to get him to
eat or lie down, but he wouldn't, so they left him alone.

How can a person simply vanish with no witnesses and no
evidence left behind? The only lead in recent vanishings had been
the little drug pusher, Pete. He had seen some guy walking the
same direction as the two rapists that's it; that's nothing to go on!

It had been twenty hours since Sarah had gone missing.
Twenty hours translates into a thousand man-hours of searching
because there was at least fifty people looking for her.

The storm continued throughout the day. Not always
raining but raging winds swept limbs and debris across roads and
property, pulling shingles and siding from the buildings. Those out
in the storm either struggled to push against the wind or were
driven forward, often running to stay a foot.

Terrible Tilly was built to withstand these storms but the
isolation the rock brought to those inside was mind numbing to
Sarah.

John had forced her to eat by harassing her until she did.
The steak and baked potato were quite good, and they ate while
John spoke of wines he had tried and places he had visited. Sarah
feigned interest just to pass the time. She asked the appropriate
questions, laughed at his jokes and watched the clock all the while

the storm slammed the rock.

Sarah thought back to the party she had given, which seemed like a lifetime ago. She remembered James and Joe Bartlett, and the night Joe drowned here near the rock. What a horrible way to go, being beaten against rock like John's boat that busted apart. Or worse, having the ocean pull you under, refusing to release you. Sarah remembered the flicker of light she had seen that night, and she instinctively knew not to ask John about it.

"What about you Sarah, have you traveled?"

"I haven't traveled a great deal. The few places I did travel to were with my late husband. We did love wine country in Napa Valley and Martha's Vineyard of course."

John was pensive as he watched her talk about her travels with her late husband.

"Have you ever been married John?"

John said nothing for a long moment, and Sarah worried she may have overstepped her bounds.

"No, no ex-wives and no children left behind."

What a funny way of putting it, Sarah thought though she would never voice it. There were many things she wouldn't feel comfortable voicing to John.

Afternoon flowed into evening and Sarah grew tired of the questions that never seemed to end. John seemed eager to find out everything he could about her, from birth to present and frankly, it was exhausting. Sarah felt it best to humor John as she would with a five-year-old with a penchant for talking, although she could turn the tables on him. Most people liked talking about themselves.

"Were you born in Seaside John?"

Sarah watched as John thought before he spoke. *Why would he have to think about that question,* she wondered?

"No, I wasn't."

Sarah waited for him to tell her where he had been born. He didn't.

"Do you have family here?"

"My family is all gone, my parents both died when I was very young, and I had no siblings."

John fed her the canned monologue knowing she would assume the subject was upsetting to him and stop asking questions about his childhood.

Sarah pretended to accept John's little attempt to squelch her questions about his life. So, she moved on to trivial conversation about his travels. He seemed quite happy to regale her with what he thought were amusing anecdotes he had experienced regarding language and cultural differences.

"Excuse me Sarah."

John left the room and was gone for a long time, which was odd. Sarah grew restless and wandered back up to the tower. The table under the window was where she had stood the day she and Dan had come to photograph the lighthouse. Sarah climbed on the table again and stood on her toes, she wanted to see how bad the storm still was.

Sarah hadn't heard John come up behind her as he violently jerked her from the table, one hand twisted in her shirt the other breaking her fall.

***

Hunter had Dan holed up in the room where he had sparred with Sarah. The same room, Sarah, had kicked both their butts in.

"You know as well as I do, the cartel kidnap, it's their specialty second to murder," Hunter stated.

Dan felt sick to his stomach as he thought of what Doc and his wife's final moments must have been like for them to endure. He raked his hands through his hair erasing the thought from his mind. Sarah needed his full attention.

"So, you think the cartel took her on the beach?"

Dan swallowed hard as he looked Hunter in the eye.

"No, I don't. We've checked our sources, everything available to us which are considerable and there is nothing to support that theory. I don't think they killed her either because her body would have surfaced by now. They would want you to know that they killed her, as a warning to back off."

"Who then, and why would someone kidnap her? If it was for her money they would have contacted someone probably me by now, wouldn't they? What about, Ben, he knows her finances as well as she does, wouldn't she have had her kidnappers contact Ben by now?" Dan knew he was ranting, rambling on about every conceivable possibility.

"Ben has not been contacted but he's calling in some favors right now. He's got the FBI running a check on any known predators in the area." Hunter let that sink in for a second.

"Predators?"

"Serial rapists or serial murderers. Those college kids may not have run. If they had there would have been a trail, they weren't rocket scientists," Hunter said.

Dan thought about what Hunter had just said.

"Bull shit… Sarah kicked your ass and mine. She would have stomped some guy into the ground right there on the beach if he'd tried to force her to leave with him!"

Dan was angry, not with Hunter, just angry.

"She would have fought; you know she would have fought back!"

"Maybe she couldn't fight back; it would take only a few seconds to stick her with a syringe filled with a sedative. Even the right hold when caught off guard can incapacitate long enough to maneuver someone off the beach."

"I got it, ok, I got it."

Dan knew Hunter was right, even the wariest of people can be caught off guard.

"Where do we go from here?" Dan asked.

"We continue to search and when we get the profiles from the FBI, we track the sons-of-bitches down and get information any way we can."

"How can we track them down if the FBI hasn't been able

to?"

"We don't play by the same rules as law enforcement brother, you better understand that."

Dan thought about that for a minute and he knew there were things Sarah wouldn't condone, things she wouldn't want him or Hunter to do on her behalf.

"I don't care about your methods just hunt the bastards down. I'll do whatever it takes to get her back."

***

John had Sarah on the floor before she knew what hit her. He was very strong, and she was still weak from the sedative he had spiked her water with.

"ARE YOU CRAZY? WHAT'S WRONG WITH YOU?" Sarah shouted!

She was more angry than scared. Weak or not, she was pissed off right now.

John immediately released her and moved back with his arms outstretched as a sign of surrender. He watched her as one would a wounded animal waiting for it to strike back.

"Sarah calm down," his voice had that lilt again. "I'm sorry I scared you, but you scared me too. Do you remember I told you that storms can ram boulders through the glass in this tower? I've seen it! You could have been killed!"

Sarah sat up and glared at John, incredulous that he should expect her to thank him for yanking her off the table and slamming her to the floor. Slowly she got to her feet, never taking her eyes off him. She heard Greg's voice in her head, telling her to be ready.

"Are you ok Sarah?"

She'd had enough of his mock sincerity.

"John, why didn't you just tell me to get down from the table?"

"I'm sorry, I overreacted. I hope you're not angry with me?"

John smiled. Only this time, Sarah did not think him so benign. This time she looked at him and clearly understood her circumstances.

She was in an inaccessible lighthouse off the coast of Oregon with a man who thought he was in complete control and to a degree, he was. He had the only phone and the only way off this rock, that's if the boat wasn't a pile of kindling smashed on the rocks outside. No one knew where she was or who she was with, and she had no idea what he was capable of.

Having summed up her situation she was compelled to keep her skills of survival to herself for the moment. She would make no mistake; she would assume the worst and act accordingly just as Greg had trained her to do. She could play his bullshit game and beat him at it if that's what it took to get out of this miserable place.

"John, I'm not angry. You did scare me but I'm ok now. Just go down the stairs please." Sarah motioned for John to go ahead of her down the stairs.

John didn't move for a moment he seemed to be evaluating her mood. Then he complied, a slight smirk twitched at the corner of his mouth. Sarah really wanted to kick that smirk down his throat. For the time being, she would feign the weakness that was leaving her system fast. Let him think he had the upper hand; this storm couldn't last forever.

"Can I get you water or anything?" John was trying to resume his gracious host role.

"Actually John, I'd like to try using the satellite phone now please."

Sarah waited for him to give her an excuse as to why she couldn't try the phone.

"I'll get it for you. But surely you know, even if it works, it's not safe for any boat in this storm."

Damn him, he was right. She knew Dan would kill himself and anyone else to get to her.

"John your right and I won't risk anyone in this storm, but I also won't leave people I care about to wonder if I'm dead. May I have the phone please?"

Sarah watched John weigh his options, while she weighed hers. Then he shrugged and went to retrieve the phone. Sarah wondered if he'd try to disable it, she knew a thing or two about phones as well. John brought the phone and handed it to Sarah.

"Thank you John."

Sarah punched in the number…nothing. Sarah swore she saw a smile threaten his lips. Sarah looked him in the eye and pulled the phone apart. She took out the battery shook it and then replaced it just as she did with the sim card. John said nothing as she snapped things back in place and made the call again.

"Ben this is Sarah. I'm fine. No, I'm fine. Ben please listen; the phone may go dead any minute. I'm invoking my lawyer/client privilege…

Right now, you have to say nothing, but what I ask you to say to, Dan, understood. Good, I'm ok but I'm stranded at Tillamook Rock Lighthouse and I'm with John. You are not to tell Dan where I'm at. There is a severe storm, and he will die trying to get to me. When the storm is over you can tell him where I am.

Right now, you tell him I'm fine, you tell him I'm trying to get to him and Ben…," Sarah stared straight into John's eyes. "You tell him I love him."

Sarah did not hand the phone back to John, and he did not ask for it. She also didn't tell him that the phone went dead right after she invoked client privilege.

***

Dan and Hunter forced Ben to repeat his short conversation with Sarah a hundred times. She was fine and invoked lawyer/client privilege but privilege for what? Sarah had said nothing that fell under privilege before the phone went dead. Ben had told them he could barely hear her; she didn't sound afraid she sounded angry. He said background noise was loud with lots of static.

"If it's a kidnapping they will call again. My team is in the process of tracking the phone call but that may take a while."

Hunter summed up while Dan tried to analyze Sarah's call to Ben. To, Ben, not to him. It had to mean something. The fact that she was alive gave him strength.

***

Sarah excused herself and took the phone with her to the bathroom. The phone was dead, and she could hear the storm beating against the stone building outside. The phone would stay with her until she got off this stinking pile of rocks. Ben knew she was okay, and he would call Dan or Hunter, at least that much was for sure. John thought she had told Ben where and who she was with so that lie should keep him well behaved.

Sarah was feeling stronger and better in control of the situation now. The storm was all that remained between her and the mainland. John may be a snake, and he apparently liked having the upper hand, but he had no idea who he was dealing with. Greg's hard work at training her to defend herself was her little ace in the hole and if push came to shove with John. He would be leaving this rock on a stretcher.

John was aware of the change in Sarah's demeanor. The fact that she told someone named Ben of her whereabouts and his name—changed things considerably. His plans to woo her over a couple of days while waiting out the storm were compromised. Not to mention the adamant profession of her undying love for the PI put a crimp in things as well. Maybe she wasn't as intelligent and interesting as he had hoped.

When Sarah came back into the room with John he had assumed a polite but aloof attitude that suited Sarah just fine. Both would simply have to endure the others company until the storm let up enough to allow them to boat back to Seaside or at least call for help.

John thought about asking Sarah for his phone back but the glint in her eye gave him pause and he thought better of it. Let her keep her security blanket, the sooner she got out of here the better anyway.

John offered Sarah his bed for the night though he really didn't want to. Sarah was not interested in his bed, him, or his condescending tone.

"Actually John, I'm not tired."

Let her sit up all night, John thought as he took his leave and went to bed.

Morning light brought with it a calmer yet still raining forecast. Sarah opened the door of the lighthouse and stepped out to check on the boat. A light drizzle couldn't keep her trapped in the old stone building another minute.

The boat was pretty banged up. The motor was bent slightly to the left and may have damaged the fiberglass where it attached to the boat. The last thing she needed was to be cast adrift in a small boat with John. One of them would not make it to shore. Sarah said a little prayer and made the call to Dan.

"Morrison!"

The urgency in Dan's voice made her voice break when

she spoke.

"Dan…I…It's me."

"Sarah, thank God! Where are you?"

"I'm at the lighthouse!"

She wasn't taking any chances with the phone this time. Dan would know where she was, and he would come and get her.

"I'm on my way. Stay on the phone with me, please don't hang up."

"I won't. I need to hear your voice too."

Dan could hear the tension in her voice, and he had a million questions to ask her but was unsure of where to begin. *Are you okay? Why are you out there? What's going on? What the hell were you thinking*? These were just a few of the questions he wanted some answers to but for now all he needed to know was, *was she okay.*

"Sarah, are you okay? Are you hurt?"

"No, I'm okay now that you know where I am. I've been trying to reach you, but the phone kept losing the signal and… and it doesn't matter. We can't get to shore because the boat is messed up and we're stranded."

"By we, you mean, John, too?"

"Yes, John, too. Though I think he will be glad to be rid of me too. The sooner the better for both of us."

"What did he do?"

Dan could feel his pent-up emotion threatening to blow and taking it out on John sounded pretty good right about now.

"He didn't do anything and yet I would like to kick him in the head. I just need to get back to you, to home. Dan be careful, but please—hurry!"

"Hunter has been listening in, and he's already made arrangements for a boat. We're on our way; it won't be long now. Sarah... I... everyone has been so worried about you."

"I'm so sorry. I didn't know about the storm coming in or I never would have agreed to come out here."

"Why did you go out there?"

"John said he'd found some old photographs of the lighthouse and of the keepers and I wanted them for my book."

"But your phone and your cameras, you left them all behind. It made no sense to anyone. We thought you were taken... you just disappeared."

"Oh Dan, I'm so sorry. Cells don't work out here; John has a satellite cell and sometimes it doesn't work either. I didn't need any more shots of the lighthouse. I just wanted the old photos John found."

"Honey, why didn't you call or leave a note before you went?"

"I was on the beach when John found me, and I had nothing with me at the time. I thought I could get out to the rock and back in an hour or so. I wasn't prepared. I didn't think about the possibilities. I can't apologize enough to everyone. Poor Hunter, I've wasted everyone's time."

"Sarah, Hunter wants to say something to you."

"Ahh, ohh."

"Sarah, Hunter here. I'd threaten to kick your ass, but now I'm just too glad you're okay. Plus, I'd have to kick Dan's first just to get to yours and, well, I'm still sore from the last match with you."

"Hunter, I'd stand there and let you kick mine if it meant I'd get back home sooner."

"We're on our way. We'll be there in thirty minutes. Here's Dan."

"Hey baby, you said, John found you on the beach?"

"Yea, I was getting some exercise, and I was headed back to the tram when I ran into John. He had asked me out to lunch earlier and I had said no. Then, there he was…"

"There he was. He asked you out, you said no…and then, there he was!"

"I thought about that, Dan, but he said he was getting some exercise, and it seemed plausible at the time. Plus, I really wanted the photos."

"Do you have the photos?"

"No, we never actually got around to getting them yet. I got sick."

"This keeps getting worse Sarah. You're sick?"

"No, I was sick. I got seasick coming out here and then we were going to come back, but I fainted and John decided we needed to stay put but then the storm hit and…"

"Please don't tell me anymore until I can actually see you.

I don't know if I should thank John for taking care of you or smash his face in for taking you out there in the first place. I'm leaning heavily toward smashing his face in though."

"Dan, please don't do that. Can't we just get back home?"

"Fine, Hunter can do it after we leave."

Dan changed the subject to please Sarah and kept her on the phone for the entire length of time it took for the boat to reach the lighthouse.

John had stood in the doorway watching her while she kept watch toward the coastline. *Weak, she was weak*, John thought with disgust. Staying on the rock had proved more than she could bear.

Plus, she was so easily manipulated. The promise of a few photos brought her straight into his hands and under his will. He could have done anything to her while sedated. He chose what happened and what didn't. Sarah would never know how lucky she was that he wasn't like those he interrogated.

John felt superior to her just as he felt superior to those he interrogated. He had no patience for women who through their own negligence find themselves victim to the men who abuse them.

Young women and children, he held to a different standard. They were not equipped to evaluate or analyze situations or motives of adults that are intent on harming them. Just as John had no voice or choice as a child and was subjected to the will of vile adults that used and abused him with the consent of his own mother.

Somewhere deep inside, John, he knew he was highly critical of women. Women who were near the same age his mother had been when she had hurt him so badly. He knew it and he couldn't change it even if he had wanted to.

John watched as the boat closed in on the mooring station that still held his small boat secure. He wondered what she had told her PI.

Hunter steered the boat close to the rock while Dan leaped to the rock and quickly secured the rope to the pilings. Sarah closed the distance between them and Dan gathered her to him, burying his face in her hair. Neither one said a word they just both were so grateful to be together.

Hunter's eyes traveled up the walkway to the door of the lighthouse to the man in the doorway. He watched as the man watched Sarah and Dan and then focused his attention on Hunter. The man raised his hand in a friendly acknowledgement that didn't feel all that friendly.

Hunter was out of the boat and stood next to Sarah, and once again, Sarah had the overpowering urge to hug him. He tolerated it a little better this time.

"Let's get your things and get out of here, what do you say?" Hunter asked.

Sarah couldn't say much of anything as she wiped the tears off her cheek with the back of her hand and bobbed her head a couple of times. Together the three headed to the entry door and to John.

John quickly made a mental checklist of all his prepared answers and of his private quarters he had sanitized while Sarah had spent the last thirty minutes or so outside.

"Dan, welcome, we're sure glad to see you aren't we Sarah?"

John smiled as he opened the door wide inviting them in.

"John." Dan acknowledged John without offering to shake his hand and John didn't extend his either.

Sarah was the one to quickly introduce Hunter to John. Hunter leaned into the space between him and John, with his arm extended. John stepped forward and shook Hunter's hand. It all seemed normal yet nothing about John rang true, Sarah noticed. Even simple gestures appeared ill at ease when done by John.

"John," Hunter acknowledged.

Hunter had a way of commanding a room that wasn't really threatening yet effectively influenced good behavior. Sarah thought it was a good thing at this moment. Dan seemed intent on remaining polite yet distant with John while John pretended not to notice.

"The boat has some damage John. You may need to come with us. I wouldn't want you to be trapped out here without a boat."

Sarah's matter-of-fact tone put John in the position of having to answer directly to her.

"I see, maybe your right."

"John, before we go, I'd like those photos I came here for."

"Of course, I'll get them for you."

John didn't particularly care for Sarah's slight tone, but what choice did he have now? Funny how polite she had been when she first woke during the storm, when she'd needed him and the shelter he'd provided.

"Do you have everything else Sarah?" John inquired as he turned to get the photos.

"I didn't bring anything John. By the way, here's your phone." Sarah held the cell out and John smiled as he took it from her.

"Thank you, I'm just glad it finally worked."

The exchange between Sarah and John instantly triggered a question, Dan had been meaning to ask Sarah.

"Sarah that reminds me, why did you invoke lawyer/client privilege when you called Ben yesterday?"

John stopped and turned, wanting to hear what Sarah would say to Dan.

"John reminded me that the storm was dangerous to any boat on the water. I knew you would come anyway so I called Ben instead. I invoked privilege to keep Ben from telling you where I was until the storm was over," she said.

Sarah reached for Dan's hand, hoping that would be the end of his questions until they were away from John. It wasn't.

"We couldn't figure out why you would invoke privilege,

and neither could…"

"We need to go, brother, before the storm kicks back up."

Hunter had put his hand on Dan's shoulder and Dan instantly knew, to change the subject.

"Hunter's right, we need to go. John if you'll get the photos we'll be on our way."

John nodded and turned to his private quarters. John knew something was up but short of demanding an explanation, he had no other option but to go along.

There were six photos in all. Two were virtually the same shot of the lighthouse and the other four were of various keepers in the early 1900's. Now that Sarah had them in her possession, it made her sick to think that she had caused everyone so much trouble over six such inconsequential photographs.

The boat ride back to the shore was tense with the waves at least seven-foot-high causing the boat to rise and slap back down on the surface of the water over and over as they made their way.

Sarah stayed close to Dan as Hunter manned the boat, while John sat patiently in the rear playing with the cell phone. It didn't occur to Sarah that John might be checking the number of minutes the phone maintained a connection during her short conversation with Ben last night.

John knew that the phone had connected but for how long. The odd behavior over the PI's question had him curious and he had nothing better to do.

Eight seconds, the conversation lasted for eight seconds. The cells' memory clearly showed him that Sarah lost contact shortly after making her call. Eight seconds was probably just enough time for her to have invoked privilege and nothing else. All that, *"'I'm stranded at Tillamook Rock lighthouse with John'"* was a con and it had worked.

Well, well, Sarah wasn't quite the weak little victim he had thought her to be after all. John cut his eyes over to, Sarah, and she was staring back. Yes, there was more to, Sarah Knight, than met the eye. John smiled and nodded to her.

Sarah hated John's little smiles. One day she may have to wipe one right off his face for him. The best part was she knew he had absolutely no idea that she could.

The short drive to town was quiet and over before they knew it.

"Thank you John, for all your hospitality."

Sarah said the right words for everyone's benefit though her eyes bore coldly into John's, as he got out of the car.

"You're welcome Sarah. I'm sorry it was under such unpleasant circumstances. Thanks for the ride."

With that, John was at last away from her.

Dan and Hunter wanted to grill her about their time together on the rock, but both felt it better to give her a break. Besides, if John did anything wrong, they knew where to find him. Sarah leaned into Dan and nearly fell asleep after her sleepless night keeping watch on John's damn bedroom door.

Billy and Zane had clued everyone in on, Sarah's whereabouts long ago and the search and worry had ended shortly after her call to, Dan, earlier today. Both, Dan's agents and Hunter's men had packed up and left as soon as the boat had docked in Seaside. Hunter was all that was left of the search party.

"Hunter, please stay the night at least. We'll take you out for dinner or order in, whatever you want."

Sarah was feeling embarrassed by all the worry and intense searching done on her behalf.

"Sarah, listen to me. This wasn't your fault. I'm going back to Portland, and you should get some sleep by the looks of you. Did you sleep at all?" Hunter seemed genuinely concerned.

"Not for a while, I couldn't. I now know why the keepers went mad out there. I don't know how John can stay out there. Maybe, John, is mad. He certainly is strange, isn't he?"

"Oh yeah, he's strange alright," Hunter confirmed the obvious.

Sarah let Dan pull her out of the car and wrap his arm around her waist as they said their goodbyes to Hunter, before he drove off.

"Let's get you in the house before you fall down, Sarah."

While she showered and brushed her teeth, Dan ordered in and waited for the delivery of the food. Sarah walked out onto her deck overlooking the sea. Purposefully she looked toward the lighthouse, yep; the attraction was gone for good. No more snooping with the telescope, the lighthouse was the last place she had any desire to check out.

The scent of delicious food drew her to the kitchen where she found Dan, plating freshly caught and prepared seafood and crisp salads. Chardonnay was already poured into stemware, and she took several slow sips while Dan worked over the table.

"Scallops, they're my favorite," she mused.

The gesture made her want to tear up, but she fought it and pretended to look for something in the cabinet while she got it under control.

Dan was behind her his hands on her shoulders, his thumbs kneading her stiff muscles. A deep sigh escaped her as she melted into him, she had no idea she had been this tense, and his touch was so comforting after two days of John.

"Let's eat while the food is still hot and then I'll give you a serious massage before bed."

"A massage?"

"Only a massage tonight, you'll be asleep anyway before I'm through working out those kinks in your back. You need to sleep, and I'll be right here when you wake up."

Dan never asked her any questions about the lighthouse or John. He'd let her tell him what she chose to tell. He told her of all the people that stepped up in the search to find her.

He reassured her that it wasn't her fault, and he did not tell her that John would most certainly have known of the impending storm. Anyone living in a lighthouse offshore would be aware of those types of eminent weather patterns developing. Granted,

Sarah got sick, but that didn't relieve John of responsibility here.

The deep muscle, back, and neck massage along with a couple of glasses of chardonnay put Sarah under for nearly twelve hours of deep sleep. Sleep she needed in her bed and under the safety of Dan's watch.

The phones had been turned off except for Dan's cell, and he kept it on vibrate so she wouldn't hear it ring and ring and ring. People all over town wanted to call and express relief that she had been found and was alright.

Dan was very tired of explaining her disappearance and found himself saying her work on the book had trapped her at the lighthouse during the storm. Everyone knew she was dedicated to the book and accepted the facts without hesitation.

Plus, Dan knew public speculation regarding her and John would upset Sarah, greatly. One minute with the two of them together more than confirmed her disdain for him.

Eventually, Sarah would tell him everything that happened on the rock. He knew John had not attempted to get physical with her. He knew this because John wasn't hurt. He was more the salesman type. Dan figured he had tried to sell Sarah on what he considered to be his outstanding qualities, but Sarah wasn't buying any of them.

CHAPTER 35

COMMITMENTS

By noon, Sarah was in the shower and she felt good. Thursday, she couldn't believe it was Thursday and she hadn't completed the two separate book layouts for the committee to approve their final choice.

Today was going to be spent inside pouring over the layouts and her final text. Either choice they made had Dan's photo of the bridge and their photo of the lush waterfall scene. So, she would be satisfied regardless of their choice.

The storm had passed but left many with minor and not so minor damage to repair on their homes and businesses. Dan left Sarah mid-afternoon, to check on his beach house.

She was sprawled out on the living room floor with text and photos spread around her. Sarah made last minute changes of minor details that she would fret about until the books were handed in tomorrow afternoon. The changes kept her occupied and gave her pleasure as well. Sarah had not liked feeling as if she was controlled and she had felt controlled by John, and the storm.

Dan was lucky; the beach house had lost a few shingles and a small tree from a neighboring yard had fallen across his driveway. The neighbor was an elderly man yet was trying his best to use a small chainsaw to cut the tree up.

"Mr. Monroe please let me cut that up for you."

"I can do it, Dan. Your dad and I used to cut Christmas trees together every year for both houses."

"I remember, Mr. Monroe. They are some of my best memories too. Do you remember the time we went into the mountains looking for the perfect tree and dad told me to be careful not to fall into a hole?"

"Yes son I do. There was snow in the mountains, and it covered everything. Your dad knew the snow would hide fallen logs and crevices and such."

"Dad had barely gotten the warning out of his mouth when suddenly he all but disappeared into a hole. Just his head was sticking out."

The men were laughing and enjoying a shared memory, so much so that, Mr. Monroe, relinquished the saw to, Dan, and allowed him to cut it up. When it was done, Dan helped him to stack the small logs alongside his neighbor's house. The man needed to feel useful and who was Dan to stop him.

Before leaving, Dan inspected both houses and made a list of things to get at the hardware store.

"I'll be back to help you. We're both lucky, the damage was minimal."

Sarah's house also sustained minor damage, but she wasn't about to let, Dan, make the repairs. She knew he would put her house before his and that was unacceptable to her. The handyman the Realtor had recommended was busy, but he said he would make time for her repairs and that would give, Dan, the time needed for Mr. Monroe and his own house.

Friday afternoon came and her presentation was anti-climactic to say the least. The committee wanted her to leave both layouts for their consideration, and their decision would be made in a couple of weeks.

Oh well, she thought, it was out of her hands now. Sarah felt good about her work and a little disappointed that it was over.

Now what was she supposed to do with herself? She couldn't go back to doing nothing, having a goal with deadlines and achievements had kept her motivated and excited. Sarah was not the type of woman that could sit around or shop and do lunch. Something would have to be done.

The coast was overrun with small art galleries, boutiques, and eateries, none of those types of businesses held any interest for her. The Signal would give her a byline, but what would she write about week in and week out. This would take serious consideration and some input from Dan would be helpful as well.

Dan was back at Sarah's by 7:00 pm and she had prepared a simple dinner for them.

"Melinda called while you were gone. She wanted to know if dinner tomorrow night was still on or if we needed to cancel."

"What did you tell her?" he asked.

"I told her we were still on. If you would rather cancel, I

can call her back."

"No, we'll go as long as you're up to it."

"Dan, I'm fine. Nothing happened except John is weird, and I was trapped by the storm. My biggest concern was for you and the worry I put you through. I want to go because I need some advice from all of you."

"What kind of advice?"

"Now that the book is all but complete, I find myself out of a job with nothing to do and I have to do something worthwhile. I need some input because I've been wracking my brain and haven't come up with a single viable idea."

Dan thought about what she had said and knew she was right, she would need to have an outlet, something motivating

.   "You're right, everyone needs stimulating work to do. Some people have hobbies but that isn't you. You're far too complicated and sensitive to not have your goals and ambitions realized. What moves you, Sarah? What gets your blood boiling?"

Sarah hadn't thought of it in those terms and when, Dan phrased it that way it got her to thinking about the last days before Greg died.

The neo-natal unit was two floors down from ICU at the hospital in Boston. One day, Sarah was lost in thought and worry and mistakenly got off the elevator at the neo-natal unit. She couldn't take her eyes off the newborn babies in their clear bassinets behind the bank of glass windows. Children had not yet been part of her and Greg's lives, one day they planned to have a child, but the accident took that dream along with Greg.

Sarah found herself going to that bank of windows each day and a pediatric nurse spoke to her of the miracles a good neo-natal unit could perform. The right equipment and the right staff could drastically reduce infant mortality rates.

That nurse taught her that life's work can bring about miracles in people's lives. There had been no miracles for Greg at that hospital but for so many others, life was given when hope was nearly lost.

"I know that look. What are you thinking about?"

Dan knew he had sparked an idea, and he wanted to know what it was.

"How good is the neo-natal unit here?"

That question came so far out of left field that Dan had no answer for her.

"What do you mean?"

Sarah became completely animated as she explained her experience in Boston and the nurse that had dedicated her life to saving newborn infants. Dan listened and saw the excitement well up in her as she talked about making a difference in people's lives, in children's lives.

"I have so many resources Dan. I'm not just talking about the money. I'm talking about the contacts and the ability to bring people to the table that can make things happen. Ben alone is invaluable in so many ways."

"Tell me about it, between Ben and Hunter, no one and

nothing stands a chance against those two."

"See what I'm saying? The right mix of people and planning can change anything."

They talked into the night, bouncing ideas off one another until Sarah had the beginning of a solid plan to work on.

Cocktails with Josh and Melinda turned out to be a replay of Sarah's experience on the rock with John. Both Dan and Sarah downplayed the creepy caretaker's role and blamed the whole ordeal on the storm and the book layout.

Dinner was enjoyed at Lil Bayou, a very relaxed atmosphere and laid-back eatery with New Orleans flair. The restaurant seemed odd on the Northwest coast. Regardless, the French Quarter pastries and coffee with chicory was ridiculously good and Sarah knew a hundred laps in the pool wouldn't make it right. Still, she ate her share and damned the consequences.

The conversation turned to the idea Sarah had on improving the neo-natal unit in Seaside's hospital. Improvements would make it unnecessary for infants to be air-lifted to Portland or some other pediatric hospital. In addition, parents wouldn't be forced to incur additional bills for lodging and food away from home as they would if their baby was hospitalized in another city or state.

Melinda was almost as animated about the project as Sarah was and the two presented a powerful alliance. Dan enjoyed seeing Sarah come alive with anticipation and resigned himself to the fact that life was going to get hectic real soon.

The following week kept Dan in his office in Portland and Sarah, in conference calls with top fundraiser specialists that Ben had introduced her to. Melinda and Sarah had planned to meet with the hospital administrator along with the neo-natal physicians and ob-gyn s on staff. Several fundraiser ideas had been tossed around, and several seemed quite ambitious but profitable.

One idea seemed intense and would take a year or more to pull off. All businesses would be invited to become involved in the building of a dream house.

Local designers and architects as well as landscapers would come together to design and build the house. Tickets to win the house in a drawing would be sold for one hundred dollars per ticket over the course of a year and the profits would go to the hospital. People from all over the country would want a coastal vacation home especially if it helped children.

Somewhere in the back of Dan's mind he wondered if Sarah's interest in an improved neo-natal unit had to do with Greg, and the lost vision of having a child with him. Somewhere in the back of Dan's mind, he wondered if Sarah had ever envisioned having a child with him.

CHAPTER 36

MARCUS' PRISON

Jackman sat in his stateroom and looked at the wedding photo he always carried with him. Emily was every man's dream. She had been his and no other woman since had ever been given a fair opportunity with Marcus. Emily was always with him; she was the fire he pursued predators with, and she was always just out of reach as he pursued her through the mist of his dreams.

Duplicity was his hope and his prison. The yacht provided him the perfect backdrop for hunting the traffickers maybe even the very animals that had taken Emily, and in a way his life from him.

Marcus knew the small flicker of hope he had left in finding Emily alive was all but extinguished. He also knew he was bound by the vessel and the opportunity it provided him to find the ones who destroyed their lives together. That hope and opportunity was all that kept Marcus alive and motivated in tracking the elite predators.

The yacht had been prepared and was ready for his new guests to board. Marcus needed the moments he took for himself alone in his stateroom; to gather the strength he needed to become the charming host to the scum that would be boarding Duplicity.

John had rented a small outboard while his boat was being repaired. The weekend had been spent in preparing, Tilly, for the new subjects that would soon be coming under his interrogation.

Jackman had seemed more distant than usual though he doubted the overseer of Duplicity knew of his most recent guest. Even if Jackman were aware, it was he who had agreed that the journalist must have access to the rock.

Once again, all the tools of the trade were on display, and his mirrors were again placed for maximum visual affect. Frankly, John was looking forward to resuming his interrogations. The disappointment he had with Sarah had left him feeling agitated. The control that John needed in order to feel centered came with each successful interrogation. Successful interrogations came when information was gleaned from a subject that offered up another predator to the team.

John knew what Jackman was waiting for. It's what Jackman had been waiting on for many years now. While John didn't fully understand the devastation Jackman felt over having lost his wife after all this time, he did understand the rage of having something taken from you by force. That rage alone kept John on task when he interrogated the bastards on Jackman's behalf.

By the time the subjects were before John, and his staged set, so to speak, they were ready to spill anything they knew.

Including any knowledge they may have of Jackman's Emily. John hoped one day he would have the information Jackman was waiting for. Not because he cared about Jackman's obsession but because Jackman would owe him and he never knew when he might need to call in a favor.

CHAPTER 37

INTENSE

Melinda had come by Sarah's house for a planning session and before they knew it several hours had passed. Melinda stretched and yawned as she rose from her chair.

"Sorry Sarah, but I've got to get the kids off the bus. If they're home alone for ten minutes the house won't be left standing."

"Please, I've met your kids, they're great but I understand. We've covered a lot of details, and I like the outline we've put together. If you come up with any changes or new ideas jot them down and I'll do the same."

"When is Dan coming back to the coast?"

"Probably this weekend, why?"

"Josh wanted to play a round of golf with him if he's up for it. What about you, do you play?"

"Melinda, you're brilliant!"

"What? I mean of course I'm brilliant, but what am I brilliant about this time?"

"We could sponsor a golf tournament. A tournament

would bring in funds for the hospital and the people coming in for the tournament would be great for the area businesses as well. Plus, we could get plenty of free press to promote our *Dream House* give away."

"I know the owner of the golf course, he's great. I'll bet he'll have some insight into staging a successful tournament. Do you want me to talk to him?" Melinda offered as she gathered her notes and stuffed them into the leather binder she'd brought.

"Absolutely, oh and I'll have Dan call Josh about golfing this weekend."

"okay, I've got to go but I'll call you tomorrow. See you soon."

"Bye."

Sarah pushed the buttons opening the front gate for Melinda to drive through. She watched until her car got out on the road before she closed the gate again.

Sarah's call went straight to Dan's voice mail.

"Hey Dan, it's me, I just wanted to talk for a minute. Josh needs a golf partner this weekend and I need a partner too but not for golf. Call when you get a minute, bye."

***

Dan's meeting with Wayne at the ME's office had been less than fruitful. Wayne had been emphatic that there was no evidence to support anything but a murder/suicide at the hand of Dr. Bennett, and if the police had any evidence to the contrary, they weren't disclosing it to anyone.

The police had no intention of sharing information with Dan, unless he had something of interest for them first and as of right now, he didn't.

Ed at the Falcon's had made it clear when he'd said, "I want this over!"

Dan had pushed as far as he could with the Bennett case, without digging up new evidence to support what he knew to be a double murder. The cartel had proved to be a threat to anyone including Sarah. Given the lethal stance they took with Doc and his wife; Dan would choose very carefully his next steps.

Hunter may be the key here Dan thought as he evaluated his options. Hunter had proved invaluable as an ally when Sarah went missing. He had no illusions; Hunter would be equally adept as an opponent.

Sarah would be caught in the middle, she would side with Dan in the end, but at what cost to their relationship? Dan didn't want any of this conflict, but could he live with the knowledge that he'd walked away from a double murder. Worst of all, could he ever allow Americans to be murdered by low-life drug-running cartel members, especially on American soil. Even when Americans were involved as he knew Doc had been.

Dan checked his messages when he left the ME's office and called Sarah back.

"Hey, what did you have in mind besides golf?"

"I have some ideas, but I'm open to suggestions."

"Let me think about it, I don't want to shortchange myself

here."

"Dan, there's nothing shortchanged about you."

"I'm glad you noticed."

Their usual banter lifted his spirits, and he was looking forward to the weekend with Sarah.

"Tell Josh, I'll play 18 holes on Saturday unless you prefer Sunday instead."

"No, Saturday is good. Melinda and I can work on the fundraiser if she's available."

"Why can't we all golf? I know you golf and I've seen Melinda on the course before."

"She did ask me if I golfed, but we never got around to talking about it because we got caught up in fund-raising ideas."

"Personally, I would like to spend the day with you but if you need to work, I'll understand."

"Get serious, I need to be with you too. Which brings us back to partnering up, doesn't it Dan."

"Yes it does," he said.

"I still have a key to your apartment."

"How soon can you get here?"

That afternoon, Dan let himself into his apartment and found, Sarah, wrapped in a towel her hair wet from the shower. Neither said a word as she watched him take his clothes off and walk to her. He didn't smile. He didn't have to and the look in his eyes was dark and intense, the sexy kind of dangerous that Sarah had always loved about him. The dangerous side of, Dan, was what women were willing to do for and to him.

With one hand, he reached out and took the towel from her body. Sarah took a step toward Dan, but without a word he put his palm against her stomach, stopping her. He could feel her tremble beneath his hand as he circled behind her lifting a single strand of her wet fragrant hair, breathing in the scent of it, of her.

Dan slowly slid his other hand down the front of her thigh and gently moved it back up cupping her while she leaned back against him, waiting. He moved his mouth up her neck to her ear and whispered.

"Sarah."

"Yes," she breathed.

"I don't want to make love to you."

"I don't want you to." She whispered under her breath, his touch.

Hours later, before she left for the coast, Dan had his hands braced against the sides of the shower, Sarah pressed between his arms, the warm water washing over their skin.

"I can't get enough of you," he breathed against her mouth, kissing her, tasting her, telling her all the things he hadn't said earlier.

***

Tuesday meetings were held all day for Sarah and Melinda.

"I called you last night; did you get my message?" Melinda asked as she reapplied her lipstick in the visor mirror of Sarah's car.

"Actually, I got in so late I just went to bed and this morning I had forgotten about it until now. I'm sorry."

"Don't be silly. I thought Dan was in Portland?"

"He is. I went to Portland yesterday after you left."

"Wow, I remember when Josh and I couldn't be apart for longer than a day. Damn, I miss those days."

Sarah smiled, remembering how he had looked at her, how he had wanted her and the feel of Dan's…everything.

"Hey, I offered to babysit anytime. You can bring the kids over to my house so you and Josh can go wild in your own home."

"You do know your house isn't kid proof, don't you?"

"I can put the cleaners up and my gun is in a locked safe."

"I mean your house isn't safe from them."

"Oh!" Sarah laughed. "Anyway, I'm serious, you and Josh need a romantic evening."

"Josh's idea of a romantic evening is me rubbing his feet while he watches the Dallas Cowboys on TV."

"Not if the only thing you're wearing is his football jersey and those kitten heels you have."

"Oh please, I'd have to wear chaps and spurs."

They both cracked up.

"Umm Melinda, I've been meaning to ask you something."

"okay, shoot."

"Can you see my swimming pool on the upper deck from your house?"

"I'm pretty sure that's a no, why?"

"Just wondering," Sarah was so relieved.

CHAPTER 38

THE BROTHEL

Duplicity dropped anchor in a quiet cove south of Terrible Tilly. The evening served two South American businessmen. Men who had been relieved of vast amounts of money in expectation of a shipment of young beautiful girls. Girls they believed were bought for their Brazilian brothels.

The girls they expected in the morning were to have come from places like Venice Beach and Malibu. Tall, tan, thin, and blond was the order. Six in all, and the men greatly anticipated initiating the girls into the life themselves aboard the ship on the voyage back.

Marcus had regaled them with make-believe exploits of the capture of the Gold Coast beauties. The South Americans could barely contain their enthusiasm as they looked forward to morning light, when the girls would be brought on board for their pleasure.

Marcus shared a final story with the men, of a young bride snatch from her groom as they honeymooned in the Caribbean. The photograph he passed to the men of the young woman failed to spark recognition in either of the men and as they remarked on her beauty new drinks were offered and accepted and soon both were deeply asleep, dreaming their twisted dreams aboard Duplicity.

Late that night, John, met the outboard as usual and the Brazilians were rolled into, Tilly, under darkness and the fog that had crept in.

One was strapped to a gurney and left in an adjacent room to wait his turn though he didn't know it, while in his drug induced sleep. The other was strapped to a gurney in full view of the autopsy room and tools of the trade.

Morning would find John in his assumed position. Standing perfectly still and solemnly quiet as the first to be interrogated woke to find he was trapped and terrorized into giving up anything John asked of him. The furnace was ignited and would be more than ready to receive the two soulless bastards.

CHAPTER 39

BOGIE

Saturday's golf game was fun and everyone near evenly matched. In fact, they were scratch golfers and boasting accompanied drinks on the nineteenth hole.

"I want a recount Melinda; how many drinks has Josh had because he's impaired if he thinks he's won?"

Dan cocked his brow at Josh and Josh raised his glass to Dan, with a wide grin plastered across his face.

"Count the cards yourself. I got an eagle on the third hole while you got a bogie."

"Yeah, yeah, yeah, you're Tiger Woods."

"I'm hungry, is the Partee room open yet?" Melinda looked at her watch.

"Me too, I want a steak." Josh smiled at his wife. "This has been a great day. First, you in my jersey and now I beat Dan in golf."

Melinda turned three shades of red before she cut her eyes at Sarah while Sarah tried to contain the laughter threatening to spill out.

"Come on everyone, let's go eat."

Sarah led the way up the stairs to the dining room. The dining room was not yet filled, and they snagged a table overlooking the green with a straight shot down the fairway. The service was quick, because they already knew what they wanted for dinner.

The guys ordered steaks while Sarah ordered the seared tuna. Melinda was intent on having fresh salmon and asparagus spears with lemon wedges. The room quickly filled with people enjoying themselves and the four of them lingered over coffee for several hours before calling it a night.

Sunday morning was lazy and laid back just as it should be. A late breakfast in the kitchen and a trip to the beach in the tram helped to clear their heads after the drinks from the night before. Thank goodness neither had a hangover though they wondered if Josh had fared so well. Sarah wondered if the chaps and spurs had made another appearance.

The beach was chilly and a bit windy, but the walk did them both some good. Dan found a perfect starfish that he added to the collection of a little girl who gushed over it as he held it in his hand for her to see, her mom standing guard a foot or two away. The water was murky gray and quite choppy without a ship or sail in sight.

Clam diggers were looking for the tell-tale dimples in the sand showing them the hiding places of the razor clams beneath. Even experienced clam diggers with their canvas bags draped over their necks and narrow clam shovels often missed as the quick clam made its escape.

Sarah remembered her parents bringing home fresh dug clams for her to pry open and wash. She washed and rinsed them forever, only to find that fine particles of sand remained here and there. Her parents didn't fuss too much as they chewed the grit along with the fried clams.

Even though they'd had breakfast an hour before they couldn't resist Sugar Mamma's coffee and caramel apple twists to enjoy on the slow walk back to the tram.

"I have a love/hate relationship with Sundays," Sarah mused as they started the tram up.

"Why is that?" Dan had his arms wrapped around Sarah's waist from behind as her head lay back against his chest, his chin resting on top of her head.

"We both go our separate ways during the week even though we have our impromptu get together every now and again, which is really great. I guess it's just when you leave, I feel a little lonely."

Dan kissed the top of her head.

"I love you too, baby."

Dan decided to wait until early Monday morning to head to the Portland office because he didn't want her alone. Sarah didn't feel guilty when he told her of his change in plans, she enjoyed their lazy evening together.

Monday morning came all too soon for both, when Dan

had left. Sarah began her day by going over her notes before her 9:00 am meeting with hospital attorneys. Melinda had called at 7:30 to beg off the meeting since her youngest had kept her and Josh up all night with an earache.

"No problem, I can handle the meeting. It shouldn't run over an hour anyway. Is there anything I can do for you?"

"No, Josh is going to the shop and I'll take Kyle to the pediatrician. Call me later and tell me how the meeting went."

"You've got it, bye." Sarah said.

***

Serious satellite was playing Fox news for Dan on his early morning drive to the agency. A ranch ninety miles over the Mexican border from California was swarming with Mexican police.

More than seventy men and women were found shot to death and piled up in rotting carcasses. This was not the work of a demented serial killer. This was the work of a Mexican drug cartel. More bodies were expected to be found, and the police were overwhelmed by the stench and the sheer horrific scene around them.

One lone guy had made his escape before anyone knew. Had he not, nearly eighty more bodies would have been ready for cremation.

The Mexican people were so eager to leave their own country they willingly took risky chances. They took chances with transporters, those who take money from poor Mexicans in exchange for a way across the border into the US. Only there are many transporters that take their money and transport them to their own people, Cartel members, to be used as the catalyst needed to enhance the new performance drug creeping into pro-sports.

Eighty bodies seized, damn, that was a hit on their product, and the cartel would have to make the loss up and soon.

The Mexican officials and the American border cities as well had no idea that this ranch was only one of many peppered along the border. This was a new day in the life of cartel business.

Desperate Mexicans no longer simply worked the labs churning out product or acted as mules for transport for the cartel. Desperate Mexicans were now a key ingredient in the product itself.

The transporters, coyotes as they were called had found a way to be paid twice for their haul. They had no conscience and no remorse; they simply wanted paid for the haul and twice was better than once.

The impoverished Mexicans paid the coyotes more for their exodus from Mexico than the cartel paid to have them rounded up for cremation. Hell, those Mexicans only made it out of Mexico as cartel product.

The cartel would lose the ranch of course, at least for the time being but it was a small price to pay in the long run. The next shipment of human bondage would have to be monitored more effectively. The cartel wasn't used to this aspect of the new inventory, the fact that the key ingredient might escape.

Dan was very interested in anything coming out of Mexico, especially when it had cartel written all over it. What would possibly be the purpose of killing these people, their people? *This cartel was a new breed of animal, he thought and a sick breed at that.*

Cannibal came to mind, a group of ruthless people killing their own with no more thought than killing flies in a barn.

***

The agency was much calmer since the Falcons debacle with Scott Rader. The tension resolved when toxicology came up clean in the deceased twenty-three-year-old athlete.

The threat of the cartel seemed to vanish overnight; especially with the disappearance of the two Mexicans in the black Escalade. No mysterious cars following Dan to or from Seaside. No more break-ins or suspicious characters lurking around corners. Everything seemed back to normal, except the fact that for Scott Rader, Doc, his wife, and a teen tennis star nothing would ever be normal again for their families.

The deaths of the doctor and his wife seemed almost inconsequential in retrospect, to the Falcons anyway and to the rest of the world. Even Scott and Rhianna were old news, nothing but a foot note in the history of world sports.

Dan was grateful no other team member had died and that gave him some pause in whether Doc's supplements had caused Scott's death. No, the death of Rhianna Ryan was too coincidental, and Dan didn't believe in coincidence.

***

Mark Richardson's mother was waiting for Dan when he got to the office. He knew she loved her son even if that son was a worthless rapist. The problem was he had no information on the whereabouts of her son.

"Mrs. Richardson, how have you been?"

Dan knew the question was ridiculous, how would any mother be with a child missing?

Mrs. Richardson said nothing she simply stood to follow Dan into his private office. Dan held the door for her and told Fritz to hold his calls. Fritz nodded to him and felt sorry for both. This meeting was not going to be pleasant for either.

"Mr. Morrison, is there any news about my son?"

"Mrs. Richardson I'm so sorry, no. Nothing has changed since I called you last Thursday."

"How can there be no witnesses, no evidence, no leads, nothing?"

Her question was more a statement of disbelief and Dan had no answer for her.

"Mrs. Richardson please have a seat; can I get you a coffee or water?"

"Coffee would be good. I haven't been sleeping well."

Dan buzzed Fritz.

"Fritz would you bring Mrs. Richardson a coffee please?"

Fritz brought coffee and packets of cream and sugar just in

case. When he had closed the door behind him, Dan handed the coffee to Mrs. Richardson. Dan had been weighing the words he would say to her while coffee was being rounded up.

"Why didn't your husband come with you today?"

"My husband has decided to distance himself from, Mark, since… since the tests."

Dan knew she was talking about the DNA tests, and the fact that her son along with his friend had indeed raped that girl on the beach the night they both went missing.

"Mrs. Richardson, don't you think it's possible that your son and his friend are in hiding considering what the evidence has proved?"

Dan chose his words carefully. He had no desire to call the men what they were in front of, Mark's mother. Yes, she condoned in a way what he had become but she was still his mother and he her child.

"Mr. Morrison, my son wouldn't let me wait and worry about him like this. I know my son and he would have contacted me by now."

She said she knew her son and Dan wondered if that included what he was. What he had been for a long time now, a misogynous, a woman hater. Dan also wondered why this man had come to hate women so much.

This woman sat before him, desperate to find her son, knowing what he had done. She obviously loved her child, Mark had been loved by his mother, so why did he become the monster he was? Dan knew there were no concrete answers to these questions. Sometimes people choose to be monsters regardless of their upbringing. Regardless of the consequences and regardless of the pain and suffering they inflict on those around them.

"I won't pretend to know what you're going through Mrs. Richardson, because I have no child of my own. I can't in good conscience continue to look for your son with no new leads to go on either. In fact, I have had a check prepared for you. A refund, because I'm not getting anywhere with the leads that I do have."

"I don't want a refund; I want my son. No other agency will even try to find Mark for me. You can't quit, please don't quit looking for my son!"

Mrs. Richardson's voice was pleading, and angry, and frightened all at the same time.

Dan hated this part of the job. Dealing with the overwhelming emotions of family members who's loved ones were lost, maybe forever.

In the end, Dan agreed to keep Mark's case open, to look for new leads if Mrs. Richardson took the refund check. Dan told her if he could track a new lead, he would submit a new bill to her but not until he had something new to go on.

CHAPTER 40

JOHN'S CONTROL

John went about cleaning the instruments and the gurneys in his usual manner, meticulously. The two South Americans had been difficult. They let their pride bring them more pain than was necessary. John did not like being forced to prove he would resort to violent measures with uncooperative subjects.

The two had put on a show of bravado almost as if they failed to realize their circumstances. It wasn't until, John, was prepared to amputate their genitals that the men fully appreciated their predicament.

John had no desire to resort to such measures even though these men had used their genitals as weapons against the women they bought.

He was once again in complete control. The rape he'd witnessed on the beach awhile back had triggered a rage in him that was overwhelming, and he didn't want to experience that lack of control again.

Finally, John had been satisfied; the two gave up several of their wealthy associates dabbling in the skin trade. Though he was sorry they knew nothing of Marcus's Emily. He had nothing new to ingratiate himself to Marcus Jackman. Oh well, maybe next time.

The cleanup gave him something to occupy his time while the furnace consumed the Brazilin trash. He looked forward to a trip to Portland with the new shipment of *minerals* he was to send to the Mexican manufacturing company.

The rock seemed kind of lonely since Sarah left. John had never had an actual guest visit before she came along.

It was rather nice, at first. Meeting her for the first time when she came to photograph, Tilly, even though the PI and boatman were there too. Then the day on the beach helping her with the equipment as she took photos of the sandcastles was mesmerizing. Sarah got as caught up in her work as he did in his.

She did disappoint him though. He would have to remember that so he shouldn't put her on too high a pedestal, he thought as he flushed blood from tubing.

CHAPTER 41

ON HOLD

Sarah had called Melinda after the meeting, but Melinda was still sitting in the doctor's waiting room with a sick child. Apparently, it was a busy Monday morning for the pediatrician. Melinda didn't sound too pleased.

"We always have a long wait here, even when we have an appointment. I can understand this morning because we're walk-ins but it's like this no matter what when we come in here."

"Maybe there's just a shortage of pediatricians in Seaside," Sarah offered.

"Maybe but it gets frustrating. I need to remember to bring paperwork or something to occupy my time, so it doesn't feel like such a waste to sit for a couple of hours in a waiting room."

Kyle's name was called shortly thereafter and Melinda quickly got off the phone with Sarah.

Sarah gave Dan a call, but Fritz told her he had all his calls on hold while he was with a client.

"No problem, Fritz, just tell him I called and tell him it

wasn't important. I don't want to pull him away from work. How are you doing?" she asked.

Fritz liked that about Sarah, she wanted to know how he was doing, the music he liked etc. She wasn't self-absorbed like so many of Dan's other friends had been. Where was his Sarah, Fritz wondered?

Of course, Dan called her back. He was never going to be too busy or put her on hold for too long. The thing about Dan was he didn't have to try to be thoughtful he was just being who he was naturally.

The things he loved about Sarah, her sincerity and loyalty, and complete lack of conceit were the very things that described him. Like Sarah, he didn't even realize he was being exceptional.

Dan needed uplifting after his meeting with Mrs. Richardson. Her husband should have come with her...for her. Dan had seen the man's defeat even before the DNA tests had confirmed his son's guilt. No, he couldn't imagine the gut-wrenching pain of bringing someone like Mark Richardson into this world. The guilt a parent would feel would be near unbearable he suspected.

He thought back to the sandcastle contest and to the six teenage boys that had tried to climb Haystack Rock. When Sarah had said, *no child of ours would act that way*. He wondered if Sarah wanted a child, his child and if she did, did he want a child. He didn't know because he liked his life right now just as it was. One thing was certain, he liked his life because Sarah was in it and if she wanted a child, he would make it happen.

Sarah was grateful it wasn't her sitting up all night with a sick child or for hours in a waiting room to see a pediatrician. Sarah thought back to the time she and, Dan, talked about poor behavior like the poor behavior exhibited by those six teenaged boys that acted so badly on the beach during the sandcastle contest.

They had both joked about using contraceptives and abstinence to avoid having children, but she couldn't help wondering if Dan wanted a child of his own. She had thought she wanted a baby someday. When Greg was alive.

Now, she just didn't know…she was happy being with Dan just as they were. She also knew if Dan wanted her to have a child with him she would, for him. She also knew she would love the baby because she loved him more than she ever intended to.

Loving someone to the point of physical pain when apart from them may not be the healthiest kind of love to experience. Though she didn't care, loving him and being loved by him was all that mattered. Having a baby or not having a baby with, Dan, only mattered if it mattered to him.

Sarah would let him bring that subject up if he chose to and until then she wouldn't worry about it. To be perfectly honest she wasn't even sure she wanted to marry again. Marriage was wonderful with Greg, and now a monogamous relationship with Dan was wonderful as well.

Sarah's life seemed just about perfect now and she wasn't

interested in disturbing the balance of things between her and Dan.

Besides, look at Melinda and Josh, they can't even seem to make time for a sex life with three kids in the house. Sarah never wanted to get to the point where Dan took second place to anyone or anything and she had seen it all too often in the lives of her friends and even with Greg, to a small degree.

She knew Greg had loved her. Loved her more than she had a right to expect but frankly, intimacy had become less frequent in the last few months of their marriage. She thought it was because of his work but a small part of her wondered if he had grown complacent in their marriage.

Like the time she had bought a new negligee to wear for him and he hadn't noticed. Greg saw the hurt and immediately complimented her on how beautiful she looked but it wasn't the same as if he had noticed her in it right away. No, Sarah wanted to keep things just the way they were with Dan.

CHAPTER 42

EMILY

Duplicity sailed into port just as planned. Marcus was not going to give up his search, not ever. Before he died, Marcus Jackman would know what happened to, Emily, his Emily. Before he died, Marcus would be able to let her finally rest and then maybe he could rest with her.

The men coming aboard had been friends of the Producer, Roman Caulfield. The three of them were heavily invested in the TV and film industry. Like the rest of the world, they believed acts of terrorism played a role in the disappearance of their colleague in the industry and colleague as well, in their preference for pre-teen children and young women.

The youngest of the three men had expressed an interest in little boys between the ages of five and eight while the other two preferred to share their degrading exploits with young women between the ages of sixteen and twenty.

Catalogues had been sent and orders had been taken. Money, lots of it, had been deposited into the Cayman account.

The three men had planned and executed their per-arranged and phony vacations as per, Marcus Jackman's required conditions.

Duplicity had docked as scheduled to bring aboard the wealthy men. The opulence of the ship and the crew attending to their every need lulled them into a state of relaxed entitlement.

The dining room awaited the men to sit for dinner. White bone china rimmed in silver with the ships image imprinted in the center sat at each place setting. Fine linen napkins were set like sails at crisp attention above the plates. Sterling flatware flanked the sides of the plates and cut crystal stemware topped the picture-perfect stage.

Rich floras lay along the center and the full length of the table mingled with twinkling lit candles. The flickering of the candles danced off the crystal and silver which brought the table to life. Background music played low and soothing marking time until, Marcus, escorted the men in for their final meal.

Chef had been inspired. Baby spring vegetables and organic field greens feathered the salad plates. Fresh delicate pansies and nasturtiums in reds and golds rimmed the silver edging. Flaky yeast rolls and creamery butter molded in the shape of tiny ships sat daintily on the bread plates at each place setting. Wines were chilling in silver ice buckets; Cabernet was at the ready at room temperature and a decanter of fine cognac from western France waited patiently for dessert to be served.

Marcus led the way followed by Dwight Carradine, a producer in his early forties with a slight paunch and acne scarring left over from his teenage days. With him was his party pal, Matt Houston, fifty plus and a real piece of work of self-promoting, bragging, and inflated ego. Bringing up the rear was the thirty-five-year-old director and small male child pedophile, Richard Lee.

Marcus stood behind his chair as host at the head of the table. Smiling, he spread his arms out in a welcome and asked the men to find their place at the table by choosing the photograph at each place setting that displayed the image of their purchase. The men enjoyed this little parlor game and made a few lusty comments as they took their seats around the table.

Marcus sat and raised his glass to each of the men. "Salute, gentlemen."

"Salute."

"Salute."

"Salute."

Each drank from the cut crystal goblets and the evening began.

Servers quietly brought course after course and took china and flatware as they were used. The main course was a rare beef wellington, topped with caramelized onion, fresh spinach, and heady blue cheese wrapped in buttery puff pastry. Intricate birds in flight also of cut pastry and baked to a golden brown topped the wellingtons. Delicately wrapped bundles of freshly steamed vegetables sprinkled with cut chives gave color and inspiration to the elegant meal.

The scraping of cutlery and the tinkling of stemware were the only sounds heard above the music for a few moments as the men enjoyed the rich foods prepared by chef. The grand finale came in a three-tiered chocolate glazed torte topped with hand sculpted swans of white chocolate filled with fresh tart raspberries.

Cognac, fat cigars, and conversation took them into the wee hours of the night. Marcus would hold off the sedatives until he had an opportunity to share his story of the ill-fated bride and groom honeymooning in the Caribbean.

Until then he was subjected to crass remembrances of seedy exploits to the detriment of children and young women around the world.

The most difficult part of Marcus's job was being forced to smile and put up a pretense of enjoyment as they bragged of their conquests, as if those sold to them had a choice in what happened to them.

Sometimes Marcus envisioned ramming his steak knife through the jugular of one of these animals. His need to find the truth of Emily's disappearance is all that kept him from a rampage aboard Duplicity. That and the fact that Duplicity's owner would bury him at sea if he lost his perspective.

The crew all had their motives that kept them sailing into the lives and deaths of the monsters that sailed with them. Some motives were known among each other while others were not known to anyone but the man or woman aching for a lost loved one.

The crew knew of Marcus's, Emily. They had heard the story of his loss many times and didn't mind because once Marcus knew of Emily's final moments he could begin to heal…they hoped anyway.

Finally, Marcus summoned up the endurance needed to play his role as he produced the photograph of Emily.

"Gentlemen, I have a story for you," he began.

Marcus had the men fascinated by the fabricated story of his involvement in the abduction and sale of the beautiful bride taken in port on a sandy beach of an island resort in the Caribbean.

They were enthralled by the tales of her beauty and the fight she put up as she was dragged from the beach. When the moment was right, Marcus produced a copy of the cherished photograph of his wife. He hated this part, the part where these pigs looked at his wife and touched her image. He would stomach it because hope was all he had left of her anyway.

He watched very carefully as the photograph was passed from man to man. His rehearsed tale continued as he watched the men and then—he saw it.

The flicker of recognition crossed Houston's face as he glanced at his buddy Carradine. Carradine passed a look back to Houston, and Marcus knew, finally, finally he knew.

These two bastards had seen Emily, and they would tell him all they knew before they made the final leg of their journey to Tilly and the caretaker.

Marcus excused himself and went to his stateroom, he had to think. He had to be careful. He couldn't make a mistake, not now. When sedated, the men would be out for hours and he couldn't bare the wait any longer, now that he had answers within his grasp.

There was no way he could have questioned the men when he saw the recognition on their faces. He didn't trust himself not to lose it and choke them to death before the truth was told. No, this would be done the right way…for Emily.

He would require help and Captain Snell would need to prepare, as would the crew members that usually handled situations such as this. Marcus picked up the ship's phone in his stateroom and punched in the number to Captain Snell's quarters.

"Snell, Marcus here. Our guests, Houston and Carradine, need to be secured but not sedated. Go ahead and sedate, Lee, because I don't need him. Snell, they recognized the photograph of my wife."

"Marcus, I don't know what to say. It's been a long time coming; are you ok?"

"No—I don't know—I'll know when I can question them."

"Of course, I'll get on this right away. Where do you want them, Marcus?"

"Put them in the infirmary and, Snell, let's be careful."

"You've got it, I'll call when their secured."

Marcus sat on the edge of his bed and took several deep

breaths. The photo of his wife, Marcus pulled from his breast pocket and stared into her eyes for a long time. The happiness she had felt on their honeymoon shone through her smiling eyes.

He couldn't even imagine what her eyes must have expressed when they took her from him. He couldn't let himself even think of how she must have felt waiting for him to come for her, to save her from all those men. He wondered how long it took for her to give up on him, on hope, on living. The sharp ring of the stateroom phone jarred him out of his moment of self-loathing.

"Yes."

"They're secured, Marcus."

Captain Snell felt worried and slightly sickened by what the next few hours might bring to light. Snell wasn't concerned for the two men tied down in sick bay he was worried for, Marcus. Worried, the two may not have the information, Marcus desperately craved. He worried the information they had would push Marcus over the edge. There was nothing he could do but see this through.

By the time Marcus had gotten to the infirmary the two men had run through the usual furious and indignant monologue all predators used at first. By the time Marcus had gotten to them they were somewhat subdued. Marcus wondered what Snell and his men had said to them, though it didn't matter.

Marcus walked in and looked at each of the men strapped down and then turned to Snell.

"Do I need to know anything?" he asked Snell.

"You need to know I'm going to sue your ass and own this ship before this is over," Houston spewed to everyone in general!

Marcus slowly turned to Houston, a cold humorless smile on his lips.

"Let's get started, shall we?"

Marcus started with Houston, and he was very calm, very controlled. Captain Snell was taken aback by the control Marcus exhibited in his questioning. Houston refused to answer his questions at first, playing the role of a rich pampered elite man failing to grasp his predicament.

Carradine remained silent though he watched wide-eyed and numb with fear because he fully understood the situation they were in.

"Tell me where she was taken from."

Marcus knew the answer to this. He knew a great many things, things that had no impact on finding Emily. He needed to be sure that these men knew a history of her kidnapping on that tropical beach.

Houston remained silent while glaring hard into Marcus' eyes, his arrogance resonated through that stare.

Marcus stared back for a moment before accepting the fact that he didn't have the time it would take to verbally convince Houston to talk to him truthfully.

Without a word he turned and opened a middle drawer of a cabinet within arm's reach. When Marcus pulled out a rather large pair of shears he finally had Houston's attention.

Houston wailed obscenities at Marcus as Marcus began cutting away Houston's clothes. It wasn't until Houston's silk, Lord of the Manor shorts, from Harrods of London, had been cut away that he began to whimper. Then the lion gave way to the coward he had always been, hiding behind his money and fame.

"Tell me where she was taken from."

The shears hovered just above the shriveled and trembling penis of a seriously shaken Houston.

"The beach, she was taken from the beach!"

"What beach?"

Marcus' hand was steady though his long wait and near hopelessness was nearly over. The excitement he should have felt was overshadowed by the fact that no matter what these two told him it would not bring her back to him.

"San Tropez, a beach on San Tropez."

Emily had left their bungalow built on stilts over the water in the bay to get them drinks, from an open bar on the beach. That night had been dark and balmy; moonlight flickered over the water from behind scattered clouds. Emily had bought the drinks and was close, so close to the bungalow when they took her.

The colorful drink glasses laid in the sand. Skewered fruit close by. The rum-soaked white sand showed the exact spot of Emily's abduction from the beach in San Tropez.

"Who took her?"

"I don't know their names, I swear."

Houston whimpered and tears flowed freely down his

pampered and exfoliated face.

"I...I can tell you something about the kidnapping."

Marcus turned to the timid and worried voice to his right. Carradine was anxious to help in any way available to him. Marcus said nothing he simply took a step toward the exam table that Carradine found himself strapped to.

"The bartender was paid to spike the drinks of women he thought would be good candidates for—for purchase."

"The bartender took her is that what you're saying?"

"No, the bartender spikes the drinks and calls the guys that take the women."

"That doesn't make sense, Mr. Carradine, Emily was so close to the bungalow and so was the bar. Emily would have made it back before anyone could have been called and certainly before they could have arrived."

"The bartender had already tagged her from the first time he had seen her. They had planned to take her when she was alone. She was alone on the beach."

"The bartender had already tagged her?" Marcus' questioned.

"He took photos of her and forwarded them to his boss. His job was to know where she stayed, who she was with, and when she would be alone. The men that took her were at the bar that evening. They waited and they watched, then they followed her and took her before she could get back to the bungalow.

"She would have fought, she would have screamed.

Someone would have heard her or seen what was happening to her."

"She was drugged. The bartender made sure she drank before she left the bar and the drug is fast acting."

"How did the bartender make sure she drank before leaving the bar?"

"He offers the drinks for free if the women will only try the new drink he has designed. He tells them he needs their opinion, that he wants to promote his own personal signature drink and the women are all too willing to help him. They're usually flattered or simply want to be kind to the Jamaican bartender. So, they try it, they drink in front of him."

"What if she had refused to try his new drink what would he have done then?"

"It wouldn't have mattered. Both the drinks she took with her were drugged as well. They would have waited until she and her husband were out. And they would have taken her anyway."

"I don't understand, why take her on the beach? Why not wait until both were out to take her?"

"I don't know, Mr. Jackman, maybe they thought her husband would be a problem. Maybe they were in a hurry. Most likely the drug kicked-in and she went down on the beach before she could reach the bungalow, so they took her there."

"How do you know all this? How do you know about the bartender and the drugs?"

Marcus was absurdly calm considering what they were

talking about… Emily. He was talking about Emily, just as he did when he regaled the traffickers with made-up stories and exploits at dinner. Marcus felt disgusted with himself, why wasn't he screaming and swinging at them as he'd always thought he would?

"I know this because I saw her, Mr. Jackman. I saw her in the Cayman's."

What Carradine wasn't saying was he had paid for a night with her in the Cayman's. Carradine was smart enough and scared enough that he wasn't going to admit to having paid for sex with this, Emily person, these guys were so intent on finding.

He wasn't going to tell them how she had begged him not to rape her and of how she had told him of having been drugged and taken from her husband in San Tropez. He wasn't going to tell them how he had finally threatened to call the bouncer if she didn't shut up and cooperate because he didn't care. He wasn't going to give them a reason to cut anything off, not even his clothes.

"You saw her in the Cayman's? Where exactly and when exactly did you see her?"

Marcus momentarily forgot his question hadn't been answered because, Emily had been seen, seen by this man.

Carradine cut his eyes to Houston and Houston stared back revealing neither consent nor a look of warning. So, Carradine continued…cautiously.

"We were in the Cayman's three or four years ago and we

saw her."

Marcus wasn't going to play anymore games with these two sons-of-bitches. He stepped closer to Carradine, with the shears hovering precariously over his groin area. The look of complete resolve regarding the action he would take steeled his face and cold hard eyes.

"When?"

Marcus quietly commanded Carradine and that quiet command frightened Carradine almost as much as the shears did, mere inches from his crotch.

"We…We were on a shoot, filming in the Cayman's. It…It was June, three years ago.

Two years and five months after Emily was taken, she was seen in the Cayman's. Two years and five months after she was taken, Emily was still alive and waiting… waiting for him to save her.

That knowledge tore at his soul and damned near drove him from the room. Damned near except that Emily could still be alive and he would not stop until he knew. He would find her if she was alive and he would do everything he could to give her back some semblance of her life.

Marcus knew she wouldn't want him anymore and he knew why. He should have been with her. He should have found and killed those that took her. He should have found her before anyone could have hurt her. Before any man had the chance to use her as if she were no more than a receptacle for the waste that those men were.

Emily would no longer want him, but he wanted her. He wanted whatever was left of the woman he had loved so very much. He knew she would not be the same, would never be the same, but still he wanted her.

"Where?"

The question was barely audible, but Carradine heard him ask and understood the gravity his answer would bare.

"She was working at a gentleman's club in a casino near the docks."

Marcus' hand tightened around the shears. Captain Snell saw Marcus' jaw tighten. And his grip on the shears drained the blood from his knuckles. Snell feared, Marcus would snap and plunge the shears into the man's body. Then just as suddenly, Marcus got it under control and began to speak.

"Emily was not working, Mr. Carradine. Emily was owned by the casino just as the gaming tables were owned. Just as the slot machines were owned by the casino and used by men just like the two of you, Mr. Carradine. But we won't speak of that just yet. We will talk about the casino and the gentlemen's club, and you will tell me every detail, every face, and every name you encountered, won't you, Mr. Carradine?"

"Yes." Carradine whispered and he knew the odds of him making it off the ship alive were next to zero.

CHAPTER 43

MANIPULATAED

John knew his approach with Sarah had been a mistake. Luring her to the lighthouse was an unfortunate manipulation and Sarah didn't take manipulation well. A straightforward approach was far better suited to her nature. John could see that now and he intended to rectify that error in judgment as soon as possible.

Morrison was in Portland, he had checked. John called to set up a phony appointment with Morrison, for Friday afternoon and planned to speak with Sarah mid-week.

The problem was Duplicity. Jackman had three new subjects, subjects that John's previous interrogations had delivered. Well, he had delivered their names anyway. Names he had gotten from the producer, Roman Caulfield.

Jackman was to send them to John mid-week unless he called with a change of plans. What kind of change of plans, John couldn't imagine, as there had never been a change of plans? Unless... Of course—unless the change had anything to do with his missing wife.

Damn…Jackman was interrogating these guys about his wife. John knew he'd always showed the subjects the photo. They must have recognized her face. John would hate to be them right about now.

John had wanted to be the one to find someone, anyone who had known Marcus' wife. He had wanted, Jackman, to owe him big. Oh well, if Jackman did have a lead to the woman maybe it would give him the time he needed to approach Sarah again.

This time he would think things through more clearly. He would be rational and less intimidating. The storm coupled with the isolation of the lighthouse had backfired on him. Instead of relying on him she had panicked and felt trapped. She couldn't fully appreciate him under those circumstances.

John would find the right opportunity to meet with Sarah again, and when they met, Sarah would have a new appreciation for him and what he had to offer her.

Sarah had teleconferenced all week with Ben and the fund-raising specialists he had introduced her to. The project was just beginning yet had the feel of full swing and the momentum was picking up fast.

Dan was just as busy in Portland not only with current clients but also new ones coming in with new work. Though they were busy they stayed in contact and Sarah was sorry she couldn't make another trip to be with him because she sure wanted to.

Mid-afternoon came and went while Sarah worked on the various options of fund-raising. Her stomach began to growl before she remembered she hadn't eaten all day. The refrigerator had old tuna salad and dried out Chinese food and not much else to offer her.

After a quick glance in the cupboard, she grabbed her car keys and headed for the door. She was in the mood for Norma's clam chowder.

The line at Norma's was relative short and she didn't mind the wait anyway. Sarah ordered a container to go and crusty French bread even though, Norma's was famous for its cornbread. In addition, she ordered a small slice of chocolate cake because she felt sorry for herself without Dan.

The drive home took less than ten minutes, and it was still light out. She would eat and take a long bath before curling up with a good book. With any luck she would be asleep before 9:00.

Sarah pushed the remote control to her gate as she turned into the driveway. She had to hesitate for a few seconds before she could clear the end of the gate and drive through. Sarah had a habit of looking in the rear-view mirror as she pushed the remote to close the gate behind her. When she looked in the mirror, she saw him.

John's car was inches from her bumper, and the gate was closing behind him. Irritation rather than concern enveloped her. Who did he think he was, following her onto her property without an invitation? Once again, he was trying to control a situation with her.

Not this time, she thought. Sarah pushed the remote again, opening the gate so she could order him off her property and out of her life. When she stepped out of the car it was with purpose though John was oblivious to her assertive attitude.

"John!"

His name didn't sound so appealing to him this time when she said it but that didn't dissuade him from his mission with her.

"Sarah, how have you been? I've been worried about you."

Please, Sarah thought. "Why on earth would you be worried about me?"

"Well, you were sick, and I did take care of you if you remember."

His voice had that lilt again and she was beginning to wonder if he had a duel personality.

"I remember you yanking me off a table onto a stone floor too."

"You can't still be angry about that can you? I had to do it for your own safety, surely you know that."

This wasn't going as well as he had hoped but she was going to listen to what he had to say before he left and then maybe she wouldn't want him to leave.

"All right, John, it's obvious to me that I'm going to have to be blunt with you. Please hear me when I say that I am with Dan. We are in a serious relationship and that will not change."

"How serious can it be when he's away all week and sometimes on the weekend as well?"

"How would you know anything about his work schedule

John, unless you were stalking us?"

"That's very dramatic Sarah, but you forget this is a small town and everyone knows everything that goes on around here."

"That may very well be, but our life is not your concern, and you need to leave right now."

"I don't like rude behavior Sarah, especially when I've made an effort to speak with you."

Sarah might have been shocked by John's gall, but now she was too angry to be anything but insistent that he leave.

"I said leave and I mean now!"

John continued to stand there looking at her. He made no attempt to move, which infuriated her further.

"Sarah, if your little tantrum is over, I have a few things to say to you."

The next instant found, John, sprawled out alongside his car face down, after Sarah had stepped into him flipping John smoothly and effortlessly to the ground. Sarah was crouched low waiting for John to pull himself up. When he stood, John turned and the cold hard glare made Sarah prepare for a fight.

"That was a mistake, Sarah. Now I'll have to teach you some manners."

Sarah said nothing as she readied herself just as John sprung at her. Sarah dove away from his car and side-swept his legs knocking him to the ground again before jumping up into a fighting stance.

"You stupid bitch!" John snarled just as, Sarah, performed

a round house kick to the side of his head followed by an axe kick on the top of his head with the heel of her Nike knocking him flat on his stomach again.

"I've wanted to do that since you messed with me at the lighthouse, John, but it would have been rude of me considering all that care you were giving me."

Sarah stood tall and breathed deeply through her mouth and nose while John gathered himself to stand. When he did, she leaned forward to strike again, waiting for John to make a move.

"You're going to pay for this, Sarah, you know that don't you?" John's voice was brittle and threatening.

"I don't like threats, John, so listen and listen well. The moment you leave, and you are leaving one way or the other, I am calling the police, my lawyer, and Hunter. You remember Hunter don't you? The tall muscular special ops guy that came to the rock to get me with Dan?"

Sarah saw an *ahhh ohhh* moment cross John's face.

"Yea, I thought you would remember him. They will be watching you and if you even think of pulling something like this again, they will make this look like a stroll on the beach. Now get the hell off my property and out of my life."

John slowly got to his feet and before he got to his car, he'd wished he hadn't left his stun gun in his room at the lighthouse. Once she told people of his little visit, the operation on Terrible Tilly would be compromised. He needed to smooth this over right now before she called anyone.

"Sarah, listen, I've made a mistake here and I'm sorry. I'm not going to bother you again I promise."

"That's great John, but you'd better remember this, I'm making those calls and as long as I'm left alone and Dan's left alone, you will be left alone."

"You didn't threaten to tell Morrison what happened here, that doesn't sound like you're very serious about him?"

Sarah stared John in the eye, and with a smirk on her face she said.

"Dan would swim to that rock and cut your heart out if he knew how you treated me today and I wouldn't want him in trouble, oh and one more thing John."

Sarah used the heel of her hand, taming her thrust, she drove John's nose to the breaking point without the danger of death. Blood spewed out of his nose as he screamed, clasping his hands to the sides of his nose as if holding it in place.

"I'm just teaching you some manners John. Don't you ever call me a stupid bitch again unless you are prepared for another ass-kicking; now get off my property before I really get angry."

Sarah made those calls the second John was gone, and her alarms were set. She would not take chances again where John was concerned.

Billy had said she should press charges. But Sarah told him she felt sure John had gotten her message loud and clear. Ben being the fatherly type as well as a lawyer had wanted to beat him up, throw him in jail, and sue him all at the same time. As for

Hunter, well let's just say, Hunter was damned proud of Sarah, even though he planned to have a word or two with John himself.

CHAPTER 44

HUNTER'S TEAM

Hunter also told Sarah he would be away for a while, he and the men that had done so much for her and Dan when the cartel was a threat and when she was trapped at the lighthouse with John.

"How long will you be gone?" she asked.

Sarah felt a strange feeling of sadness at the thought of Hunter not being nearby. Not that she thought he should be at her beck and call though he pretty much had been since, Ben had sent him to help her. Sarah noticed her odd need to hold those she cared about close since Greg's death.

"I don't know Sarah, but you'll be okay if today is any indication of your ability to defend yourself."

"I'm not worried about myself. I'm worried about you and the guys."

"You had better not tell them that or you'll find yourself in another butt kicking match, this time with them. They think pretty highly of their skills and so do I."

Sarah laughed at the thought of her kicking any of their

butts, she would be toast and she knew it.

"I don't suppose there's any use in asking where you're going."

"Not likely little sister, need to know and all that."

"I didn't think so it's just been very nice knowing you're a phone call away. I've gotten use to you Hunter."

Sarah's voice was cheerful through the phone because she didn't want Hunter to know she was brushing away tears at the thought of anything bad happening to him. Almost like he was a small piece of Greg's life that had been returned to her and that she wasn't ready to lose again.

"I'll call from time to time just to make sure you haven't gotten yourself lost again."

Hunter had gotten used to Sarah too; used to caring about her, a feeling he had thought was long dead in his soul.

"Hunter," Sarah's voice almost broke.

"What?"

"Please come back to us."

"No worries little sister. I'll always be around. You take care of yourself. I've got to go now."

"Bye."

Sarah didn't know what was wrong with her. She knew what Hunter did, what he and the guys including Greg had done since the Gulf. Why was she so emotional about this mission? Maybe Hunter had felt like family to her because of Greg, and because of Greg, she was afraid of losing someone else. The tears fell freely and the more she tried to stop the harder she cried.

CHAPTER 45

LETTING GO

What Hunter couldn't and wouldn't tell Sarah, was that their mission was extremely dangerous to him and the men. The US government had hired the team to go after the cartels that were involved in the mass killings along the border towns of Mexico.

Mexican Federal officials not only knew of the special ops mission by a US mercenary group, but they also blind sanctioned the operation.

Blind sanctioning an operation and owning it were two separate issues. Much the same way the US hired and sanctioned Hunter's team. Mexico would look the other way if the mission was a success. If otherwise, Mexico would deny any knowledge of the mission and most likely would accuse the US of illegal activity on Mexican soil.

The US government would deny involvement regardless of the outcome of this mission and the team knew this going in. These were the rules of engagement anytime Hunter's team was called in, regardless of where in the world the team was needed.

***

Sarah called Dan, after she got off the phone with Hunter, and after she had pulled it together, but he already knew Hunter's team was leaving.

"How long have you known they were going?"

Sarah wondered if Dan and Hunter were trying to protect her again by keeping her in the dark, but she should have known better.

"Hunter called me this morning with the news. He said he was entrusting me to keep you safe. I took that as a compliment."

"Do you think they'll be okay?"

Sarah felt tears prick her eyes again and she brushed at them with the back of her hand.

"Hunter cares about you too, and yes, I think they'll be fine. They're the best at what they do, who would stand a chance against them?"

Sarah thought about that and she knew Dan was right. Sarah also knew that even the best of the best have been lost, that's how legends are born.

"When are you coming home?"

"I'm on my way, baby. I'm on my way."

Dan didn't need to meet with his appointments for the rest of the week. Fritz could meet with the clients or if his clients so chose, they could reschedule for the following week as far as he was concerned.

Sarah sounded down and he knew there had to be more to

it than Hunter's team leaving for a while. Whatever was bothering her was his priority right now and he was headed to the coast.

In the two hours it took Dan to get back to the coast, Sarah had tried to figure out what was making her so emotional about today. She knew what Hunter and the guys did. What they had always done since the Gulf, what Greg had done until he met her. Their leaving wasn't the issue really though she didn't want them, any of them in harm's way.

The encounter with John should have made her feel empowered it should have given her back the control she had been without while trapped on that damned rock with him for two days. Why didn't it though she wondered, maybe because she had felt the encounter had been orchestrated by John's actions and that was control he had manipulated.

John's attitude and the way he had tried to force her to deal with him today made her feel as if the choice to fight wasn't a choice at all. Once again, John had set the stage for them both.

Sarah wasn't confrontational by nature so having to confront John because of his actions made her feel backed into a corner. Sarah had no choice but to come out swinging. Now that John had no choice but to leave her alone, Sarah could feel in control again and forget John even existed.

Dan was met by Sarah on the front steps of her house when he arrived. The emotional roller-coaster she had been on that day peaked when she touched him. His dark eyes searched her face.

The fact that he had dropped everything to come to her when she needed him made everything that was already sexy about him, heart stopping to her. Sarah never wanted to use his feelings for her to control him or their life but her need for him was overwhelming at times and right now she needed him.

"You're an amazing man, Dan Morrison. In the morning I'm going to tell you that you shouldn't feel compelled to drop everything for me."

Dan cocked his brow at her absurd statement.

"The morning's several hours away so what about right now?"

"Right now, well right now I just hope you're up for what I have in mind."

***

Breakfast was a perfect time for her to share with Dan her feelings and concerns about their relationship. Feelings and concerns she had pushed to the side because she didn't want to risk losing a moment of the happiness she had with him.

Greg's death had brought with it a loss she had never wanted to experience again. It took her ordeal with John, and her sudden attachment to Greg's close friend coupled with Hunter's dangerous mission to bring her feelings to the surface.

Sarah loved Dan but was holding her emotions in check on the end case that something bad might happen. No one wants to experience loss, but loss is a fact of life. Sarah wanted to live all life had to offer and she wanted to live it with Dan.

"I've been struggling with a few things lately."

Dan knew she had been but hoped it wasn't a reflection on their relationship.

"What things, Sarah?"

Dan was intense, his eyes were dark, and concern shone in them as he studied her face. Sarah swallowed hard, not because she didn't want to answer his question but because he literally had no idea how stunning he was when he looked at her that way. She got up from the table and moved away from him.

"Sarah, what is it, what's wrong?"

Dan was up and across the room to her, turning her body to face him.

"Dan please don't."

Her hands were up as if to push him from her.

"I don't understand, just tell me what's wrong."

"What's wrong is I haven't been totally honest with you and I need to be. I need to tell you exactly how I feel, and what I want, and frankly I'm not sure that it won't change things between us."

Dan looked at her worried face and took her by the hand and led her to the living room to the sofa where they had first made love. Sarah thought about that night because she knew what she had to say to him may mean the end of their physical relationship as well as any other they now had.

Sarah gently pulled her hand from his and folded her hands in her lap. Dan watched her do this but said nothing.

"Dan, I've been doing something that I wasn't even aware of until yesterday. Then John showed up and Hunter left and suddenly I was an emotional wreck and…"

The tears began to flow, and Dan was more confused than ever, so he went to gather her to him, but she pushed him away. Frustration nearly got the better of him, and he was about to demand to know why John had shown up but she spoke again.

"I didn't think I wanted more. I thought everything was perfect between us."

"It is perfect, I don't understand."

"It was perfect then something happened and now it's not."

A light bulb went on, and Dan was suddenly aware of what was going on. Instantly he was kneeling in front of her, stroking her hair, telling her everything was fine, that it was all okay. And she had no idea what in the hell he was talking about.

"I love you, Sarah, I can't believe you don't know that."

"I do know it and I love you too but…"

Sarah was about to explain more but Dan went on.

"We aren't the usual age for this sort of thing but so what, who cares what people think. We think it's great and that's all that matters, right?"

Sarah stared at Dan, unable to piece together the conversation they were struggling to have.

"Did you take one of those tests?" he asked.

Dan was still stroking her hair waiting for an answer and

Sarah was horrified as it finally sunk in what he was thinking. *Now what was she supposed to do*, she thought, as she looked into Dan's eyes—eyes that seemed to adore the idea of a baby.

"Dan, oh Dan, I'm so sorry. I didn't mean to make you think that I was pregnant."

Tears rolled down Sarah's face as she watched Dan's expression change from adoration to complete confusion.

"Dan I'm not pregnant and I didn't think I wanted a baby. I didn't think I wanted to ever marry again until everything went crazy yesterday. Then I realized what I was doing, and I don't want to live like that anymore."

"Live like what, Sarah?"

Dan's voice was quiet yet full of emotion because he was no longer sure of anything anymore. He woke up this morning sure of everything in his life and in the space of twenty minutes he thought he had a baby on the way, now he doesn't, and he may not have, Sarah, either.

"Afraid! Afraid of taking a chance again don't you see. I've been holding you at arm's length because I was afraid of losing you. I'm afraid of marriage because something bad might happen. I'm afraid of having a baby because what if I must raise the baby alone? I don't want to be afraid to really live anymore."

"What do you want, Sarah. I need to know what you want from me."

"I want all you have to give, and I want to give all I have to you. Is that okay or do you feel like running?"

Dan cocked his brow at her, a slow smile easing across his breathtakingly beautiful features.

"Sarah, commitment doesn't scare me and I'm not running from anything. I'm in this as far as you want me to go. I know what I want and that hasn't changed. I've been waiting for you to decide how far you want to go."

Sarah slid off the sofa into his lap burying her face in his chest, her arms around his neck.

"Does that include a baby?"

Dan rolled her slowly down to the floor covering her body with his.

"I've been practicing, and I've been told I'm very good at it."

CHAPTER 46

GENOCIDE

Hunter and the others barely broke a sweat in the hundred-degree heat eighty miles on the other side of the Mexican border. The outskirts of Nogales were dusty, dirty and exactly what the team thought it would be. One more hole in a long line of holes the team had put their lives on the line to go into.

Hunter never wanted or needed a hero's welcome when he returned from one of these missions. Which was just as well since he wouldn't get one, ever. No one knew where he went or what he did, not even those who paid him. The only thing those people knew was that the target had been eliminated and the threat neutralized. The world media would have to move on to new threats because the old one simply ceased to exist.

Unfortunately, like Al Qaida, the Mexican drug lords were a dime a dozen and when one was killed ten more stepped up to take his place. The best the team could do was to take out those vicious enough to mass murder their own people as those in power of the cartels were now doing.

The team was a deterrent of sorts; kill enough murdering animals and the new animals coming to take their place would learn to heal… to a degree.

No one, not the US government, not the Mexican government, and certainly not the Mexican's themselves ever expected to heal the drug trade. Not when US citizens were so damned intent on using the very drugs the cartels manufactured and sold.

The team had no illusions, their mission had nothing to do with the drugs coming into the US through Mexico. Their mission was to find out why the cartel was murdering their own people in vast numbers and to eliminate those responsible.

One more thing, the team was to make an example of those responsible for murdering the Mexican men and women. Graphic examples made known to cartel members would send an indelible message to those up-and-coming wannabe's that their aggressive genocide of the Mexican people would not be tolerated.

What Hunter and the other men didn't know but were curious about was why children weren't being murdered along with their parents. They didn't know, though they suspected, that the children of those murdered parents were being sold to human traffickers.

From the cartel's standpoint, there was more money in the sale of those children even though they weren't blond and blue eyed. Their body mass wasn't large enough to bring much to the cartel as food grade minerals for their supplement trade…yet.

When the traffickers and the pedophiles used up what childhood had to offer; what remained as adults would be sold back to the cartel, to be offered up as a final sacrifice. The cartel took their recycling very seriously.

CHAPTER 47

CARRADINE

Dwight Carradine's production company was in a hot seat. The action thriller film was in production and behind schedule. Carradine was out of the country, and he hadn't even checked in let alone answered the constant stream of calls from his assistant and lawyers.

The lawyers were in meetings with investors and Lloyd's of London was threatening to pull the insurance policies covering the film. Carradine's absence was a financial nightmare for the company as well as for the film. The company's money was vested right along with their investors and if the insurance was pulled, the filming would halt and the company would be ruined.

Even Carradine's friends, Houston, and the film's director, Lee, were missing and had not been heard from since the day they left for their four-day golf trip to the Bahamas'. The three had not cleared customs let alone checked into their hotel. The men virtually disappeared once they landed in Paradise.

Lawyers for the company knew this smacked of the same

scenario as the last three VIP's that had vanished once they boarded flights to their various destinations. The two very important differences here were, the three men flew the company jet to the Bahamas'. Dwight was an experienced pilot who often flew himself and others to their destinations. The flight plan had been logged and the plane indeed landed in the Bahamas' where it still sat to this day on the tarmac.

The island had been combed quietly by local police with a hefty incentive paid to expedite the search and the promise of more when the men were found, but without media attention. So far, the locals had turned up nothing, not even a sighting of the men.

The second difference was the lawyers were compelled not to disclose these facts to the authorities, or their investors, let alone Lloyd's of London. Every effort would be made and must be made to find the men without creating media frenzy. Soon it would all be moot if other options were not found.

One option was to bring in another powerhouse to act as the production company. This was something Lloyd's of London would accept, as investors would if it were the right powerhouse. Merging two companies was not unusual even on a temporary and limited basis, it was getting a company to come on board under those conditions without losing the house—that was difficult.

L.A. residents woke Thursday morning to the news that Academy Award winner, Isabella Pasquel, best known for her action thriller movies was dead. Staff had found her body on the bathroom floor of her Malibu Beach home. A half empty bottle of supplements was found near her on the floor. Foul play was not suspected, and an autopsy was pending.

Carradine's film was in the toilet as was the company. Isabella Pasquel, the film's leading lady was dead, and the film was nowhere near complete. Why she died was irrelevant. The fact that the star of the film was dead was all that mattered to the lawyers.

The ME had seen the supplements before, and he knew he would not be able to link them to the death of the actress. Just like he had not been able to link the other like supplements to the tennis star, Rhianna Ryan's death.

***

Carradine was crystal clear on his situation; he was going to die unless he did something to save himself. He had thought he would buy some consideration with his cooperation regarding the woman in the Cayman's, this Emily person. However, it quickly became apparent to him that they had no intention of letting him go.

Lee had not been seen, at least not by him since the dinner on board ship the first night. Houston was an idiot whose arrogance got him put down with a drug they injected into him, right in front of his eyes.

Now he was the only one they seemed interested in. They asked the same questions again and again. Hoping to trip him up as if his story would change or maybe to see if he would or could add anything to what he had already told them.

Funny the things one thinks about when the threat of death is imminent.

Carradine found himself thinking about his project that must be tanking now that he was removed from the picture. He thought about the movies he had wanted to make, including what an amazing thriller film his current circumstances would be, if only he survived this nightmare.

Bargaining his way out of this wasn't going to happen because he had seen firsthand exactly what this ship was about. They wouldn't let him go but maybe he could delay what they had in store for him. A delay could help in some way and he was desperate.

***

Jackman had a decision to make, and it had to be made right now. Did he take Carradine with the ship to the Cayman's or was he to be transported to Terrible Tilly?

Taking Carradine to the Cayman's was a risk to everyone. The longer they kept a predator on board the greater the chances of him being seen, not to mention the threat of an escape was always a possibility. The escape of a predator was the ultimate risk to the team, one they had never come close to experiencing, because they didn't take chances.

This was Jackman's decision to make, and he didn't take lightly this responsibility. Not even with Emily, factored into the equation. The odds of Emily still being at the same casino were infinitesimal but that was irrelevant to Marcus. Emily had been there, and this was the only lead he had ever had since her abduction.

He had thought about flying to the Cayman's the moment Carradine had confirmed seeing her but vetoed a rash move for a more organized and calculated plan of action.

The contacts he had were already putting in place, a plan. A quiet but lethal assault on the casino's gentleman's club. The assault team had Emily's photos and the history of her kidnapping, as well as a description of the trinket she had given him on their wedding day.

Marcus held little hope of, Emily, still being at the casino. Just in case she was, he wanted her to know the team was there to rescue her and that he was coming for her. In the end, Marcus opted to have the team simply keep the casino under surveillance until he was personally there for the mission.

Marcus had been in the business of eradicating traffickers long enough to know they moved the children and women often. Sometimes every few days if the prize was high profile. Like the Danish child, kidnapped from a sidewalk café a few years ago. The world media was so wide, frequent moves were required to stay one step ahead of the authorities.

When the risk grows too strong the traffickers simply eliminate the risk and rid themselves of the evidence. While Emily's kidnapping never got the media attention that the Danish child received or the attention, Natalee Holloway's, case had generated and still generates, the traffickers would have continued to move her regardless.

The muti-billion-dollar industry of sexual slavery was a muti-billion-dollar cash cow because the people running it were cautious and calculating. They leave nothing to chance. Which was why the legal system was so ineffective in shutting them down, which was why the safety of the team was so important.

The team's mission superseded the law when the law failed the people. Now, Marcus would decide how much to risk for the small hope of getting Emily back if she was still alive.

Marcus stood outside the infirmary and debated his options. Surely the producer knew how grave his circumstances were. Given an opportunity, Carradine would say anything to keep himself alive as would anyone in his situation. Still, Marcus had to be sure. Sure he had gleaned every grain of truth out of this man. Steeling his resolve, Marcus entered the infirmary and stared down into the face of Carradine.

"Mr. Carradine let me be frank with you. You are still alive for one reason only. You have the distinction of having seen my wife two and a half years after her abduction. I won't ask you what brought you in contact with, Emily, because I won't compel you to lie to me. I will compel you to think carefully, very carefully before you answer my questions."

"Your wife, she's your wife?"

"Yes, Mr. Carradine, Emily is my wife."

"You said I'm alive because I saw your wife. Does that

mean the others are dead?"

"Really… Mr. Carradine, is that the question you want to ask me?"

"No, I want to know how to stay alive here Mr. Jackman?"

"Very good, Mr. Carradine, a very good question."

Carradine knew, Jackman, would kill him just as soon as he had no more use for him, so he had to make sure, Jackman believed there was a reason for keeping him alive.

"Now you tell me why I am to keep you alive?"

Carradine stared Marcus straight in the eyes and believed every word he was about to say. He had to; his life depended on it.

"I am the one person that can cut through the red tape and find out where they sent, Emily. I am the one person they would trust to…"

"To what, Mr. Carradine?"

"To buy her back."

Marcus turned his back to Carradine and refused to think about Carradine's firsthand knowledge of Emily. He only thought of how he would use him to bring Emily back.

Marcus opened a drawer behind Carradine's head and prepared a sedative, a strong sedative for injection.

"Mr. Jackman, are you going to kill me?"

Marcus stepped into view and held up the syringe as he leaned down eye to eye.

"Hear me well. I have a use for you, and you will deliver because if you don't death will be your choice."

"I will deliver Mr. Jackman, I swear I will."

"This sedative will keep you exactly where I want you until you're of use, do you understand?"

"Yes."

Marcus injected the fluid into Carradine's arm and watched as it began its work.

"I'm not going to survive this am I?"

"I told you the truth Mr. Carradine, this is a sedative."

"I mean after I deliver."

"Ask yourself this, do you deserve to survive this? Did any of your victims deserve what you did to them?"

The black fury of Marcus' pupils bore into Carradine's brain and that memory he took with him as he lost consciousness.

***

John took possession of two subjects instead of the three he had been prepared for. The crew members would only say that Jackman would be handling the situation with the third subject. When John questioned them he was brought up short when they suggested he contact Jackman personally with his questions.

"What happened to your nose?"

The older of the two crewmen asked, John.

"That's none of your business."

John glared at the men through his blackened eyes.

The crewmen smiled at, John, as they pushed off and sped back toward the yacht. The yacht would soon be in open water and headed for Panama.

Marcus pulled the cell out of his pocket and called his contact in the Cayman's.

"Is everything in place?"

"Yes, do you want us to proceed?"

"No, I want to be there."

"Is that wise?"

"I'm bringing someone."

"Who?"

"An insider who knows Emily."

"Damn!"

"I'll give you a heads up when we're close."

"We'll be ready."

Marcus checked Carradine's pulse and estimated another six hours before a new injection would have to be administered to keep him under. Marcus would handle him with Kidd gloves until he got what he needed.

The fact remained this man was a rapist, a trafficker, and a bastard that may have raped Emily. He had probably raped too many women to count in his lifetime and even if he managed to recover Emily; to buy her as he had put it, it wouldn't make anything right. Marcus gave him one more glance before he left the infirmary and called Captain Snell.

"Captain, will you have someone watch our guest please? He's under for six more hours at least. Call me when he wakes and, Captain, he's not to be untied for any reason other than using the head."

***

John didn't need those two crewmen to find out the information that had him curious. John had two subjects to interrogate and by the time he was finished with them they would spill their guts, figuratively of course. John smiled wryly at the little play on words flitting through his thoughts.

Three subjects were to have been added to his retirement fund, now there were only two. John would have to consider his options again though he may have to branch out to other coastal towns.

Missing vagrants was never a priority in any town but too many missing from one area would force law enforcement to investigate. Too many other options existed, so he could avoid that risk.

The control John felt with the interrogations did not erase the anger he had felt after the phone call he had received from the pony-tailed ex-op's friend of Sarah's. The arrogant son of a bitch threatened him. The problem was, John knew he would make good on that threat. For the time being, John would bide his time, keep his distance, and not cross paths with Sarah. Let them think he was history; it served his purpose for now anyway.

CHAPTER 48

THE Cayman's

Duplicity entered the Panama Canal paying a hefty toll for its use. Yachts were favorite targets wherever they sailed, and Panama was no different. The cruise to the Atlantic was smooth and uneventful. Soon they would dock in the Cayman's and every nautical mile they sailed twisted his stomach in knots and raised his hopes of finding Emily.

The Cayman's were beautiful, tropical and full of people from all over the world, intent on having the time of their lives. The Island stood as a destination point meant to provide secrecy for all manner of vice. The Cayman's were a playground for those who wish to wallow in illicit behavior, including human trafficking and most especially the prostitution of young girls and women.

Marcus had stayed in constant contact with his associates. Under his orders they had not entered the gentleman's club or the casino. Marcus knew it wasn't the wisest choice for him to pose as a high roller in the casino, but he had to get in there because Emily may still be there.

The evening Duplicity docked was golden with rays of sun glistening off the top of the sea water, giving energy to the festive atmosphere of the islands.

Marcus met with two of his associates on board before he prepared himself for an evening at the casino. The three had interviewed, Carradine, in the infirmary. The information they asked for was already known to the associates. Carradine was being offered an opportunity to be straight and above board. The answers he gave were consistent with what the men knew to be accurate.

Carradine confirmed the customary procedure one would need to know in order to gain access to the select merchandise the club had to offer. Without the required procedures, Marcus would never sidestep the safeguards that were set in place to protect their skin trade activities.

Carradine had been allowed to use the restroom and to shower each day. Showering and using the bathroom while having a gun trained on you was an appalling experience that he had never anticipated having.

Not once did it ever cross his mind that having men like him pay for sex against their will was not an experience those women had ever anticipated either.

That experience for those women happened every day of their lives with no hope of ever being released. They all knew and saw many women that were killed in front of them; the women that fought back too hard or the women that wouldn't accept their lot even after the beatings.

Carradine didn't think of the women as victims he thought of them as a convenience. He was a busy man, away from home, and had no time to strike up a conversation with a woman that may or may not lead to a date, let alone sex.

Carradine simply had the unfortunate luck to have been with one of these women that still had family looking for them. None of these thoughts would escape his lips though because these guys weren't playing around, his life was on the line and he knew it. He was still breathing and that meant there was a chance he would walk away from this. He just had to convince them that he was no threat to them. They had to know he would never want his little secret to come out, even though Hollywood was extremely forgiving of such things. They had to know he had no interest in turning them in, but if they didn't know these things, he would find another way to survive this nightmare.

Marcus came to see him before leaving the ship.

"Carradine."

Marcus acknowledged him as he lay secured to the exam table.

"I see you're dressed for the part."

Carradine appraised the tux Marcus wore. It was new and expensive with a European cut by a well-known designer.

"Just following your instructions. Before I go, I want to know if there is anything you may have left out. Do you wish to amend anything?"

"No, Mr. Jackman, I've told you everything I know. I want this to be over as quickly as possible and as favorable as possible for all of us."

"I'm sure you do, Mr. Carradine, and for your sake I hope it does end favorably for all of us."

"Does that include me as well?"

Marcus was already on his way out the door when Carradine posed the question. Marcus chose not to answer him. Let him wait and worry he had earned it.

The small outboard ferried Marcus and two of his associates to the island where a limo waited at the dock to take them to the casino. The casino was large, loud, and catered to gamblers from the upper echelon of society.

Posing as high rollers required attitude, a sense of entitlement, and receiving a long line of credit by providing the credentials to back it up; all of which they possessed.

Gambling, drinking, and pretending to ogle the attractive servers were part of the ploy as was the unpleasant task of losing large to the house. Pretending the vast amount was a drop in the bucket of his wealth and of no consequence to him wasn't too difficult either. The money came from a long line of wealth, wealth attached to the scum of pedophiles, rapist, and traffickers.

Marcus knew they were about to exterminate the largest nest of vermin they had ever encountered. Not that it would be showy or even draw worldwide media; something they always avoided. No, this extermination would be quietly done, one on one, over an extended period.

The women, whether Emily was among them or not, would be returned to their families if that is what they chose. On occasion, a woman felt she couldn't face her family, and some had no family to return too. In those cases, the team made sure the woman was given a financial opportunity to begin a life of her choosing wherever she chose to live. The ample stake was courtesy of the animals that had kept her enslaved.

Marcus was anxious to move on to the gentleman's club yet maintained a reserve he never thought possible. He was restrained because he felt in his soul, Emily, would be long gone and because once he knew she wasn't there, his dream and his hope would be gone too.

***

With high security cameras and spy-ware throughout the casino, the men were intent on playing their roles to the hilt. Security was packing and they were not. With the exception of course of the fast-acting sedatives they always carried.

An opportunity may not present to bring any of them down long enough to release the women. In fact, they didn't expect to release anyone tonight. Tonight's mission was a fact-finding mission unless of course they found Emily.

Coming face to face with any of the women held captive would be very difficult to ignore tonight, but they would play their part. The women would have no idea they were meeting the men intent on freeing them.

The men had prepared their pretext, should they be expected to perform sexually with the women. The women would be told the man's preference was to talk and to listen. The women would not be told of their impending rescue, but the women would be encouraged to share the story of their capture, with the men.

Marcus had no worries of the pimps bursting through the bedroom doors because his men would pay for a full night with the women. The men had devices that detected surveillance equipment and the rooms would be swept prior to conversation.

The women would never disclose the fact that they didn't perform because they didn't want to be beaten by their captors. This fact-finding mission would give the men the information they needed to discover, Emily, or at least when she was sent away...or killed.

The next couple of days would be spent, one on one, eliminating the pimps when they were away from the casino. By the time the team was done there wouldn't be enough personnel to run the casino let alone the trade behind the scenes. Then the women would simply disappear in the dead of night aboard the ship.

Once the women were on board and the ship was in open water, Duplicity would offer the women all the luxury and comfort they deserved. Then they would discover all that had been done on their behalf, and their options would be presented to them for their deliberation.

Marcus would not be present to witness that part of the rescue. Because without Emily's rescue, he would be holed up in his stateroom, he knew himself. The others, the men, would share with the women the prepared fabrication of their rescue devised to protect them and the ships' purpose.

Once again under cover of night the women would be released on American soil with money and prepaid cell phones to reunite them with their families that had been left behind when they had been taken.

Marcus liked to think ahead to the moments that made these missions worthwhile. However, they hadn't even got past the craps tables let alone a behind the scenes pass to the women.

Losing large again was a signal to approach casino personnel with their request for top dollar escorts for the night. Marcus used the right words, and the process was rather simple.

Apparently, the pimps were complacent and only concerned with payment for their merchandise. The men were ushered into a room with deep seated leather furnishings and an open bar complete with a beautiful blond girl serving the drinks of their choice.

They placed their drink orders and made the obligatory sexual comments to the girl complete with raunchy jokes and laughter to complete the act. Once the men were seated the show began and woman after woman filed out from behind a closed curtain. Dressed in Victoria Secret fashion the ladies paraded for the men with smiles painted on their faces just like the makeup they wore was painted on them.

What struck Marcus most was the smile that never reached their eyes. Most had a dead vacant look in her eyes, a look that came from hopelessness and giving up.

Selections were to be made by the men. They were to choose one each, two each, or several, to be exchanged throughout the night. The men knew the more women they tried to include the more likely the risk would be for discovery, so they had agreed to stick with one woman each through the night. More women could be brought to safety after the traffickers had been taken care of. The sedatives were available when they needed them.

The time to choose was now and quite frankly it didn't really matter which women were chosen they simply needed to get on with the extraction. Emily of course was not among the women that had been paraded before them just as, Marcus had known she wouldn't be.

Marcus was the last to choose because he still held the tiniest bit of hope but choose, he did. The woman escorted him to a rather plush room that was fresh and luxurious. He didn't know why he was surprised but he was. The trade was so contemptible to him that luxury seemed inappropriate in the same context with sexual slavery.

CHAPTER 49

LORI

Prostitution by choice was still slavery to a degree. Most women didn't choose the trade because it was a lifelong pursuit. They chose the trade because they needed quick money and there was always a customer available.

Marcus scanned the room for electronic devises with the small instrument concealed in his hand. The woman was behind him and waited patiently for him to make his requests known to her. She didn't even notice the devise or what he was doing.

The woman was more concerned with how quiet and inattentive, Marcus, was being. Usually, men had their clothes off and were tearing at hers by now. If she failed to excite him, failed to perform for him, she would suffer. All he had to do was open the door and call for one of the men that kept watch over them, if he did that …

"Please, sir."

Her voice was barely more than a whisper and Marcus turned to face her.

"Yes."

Yes, was all he could manage as he waited for her to say something more?

"If you're not happy with me, I promise I'll do better. Whatever you want, please, sir."

The fear shown on her face made Marcus snap out of his darkness.

"No, no I'm very happy with you. You are doing everything just right, please don't be afraid."

The woman was barely more than a girl. She looked confused but said nothing as she waited.

"Look, I've paid for the entire night because I want to talk and get to know you a little bit first. Is that ok with you?"

She slowly nodded her head and seemed to relax just a bit though she was still visibly confused by Marcus.

"Please, have a seat and tell me your name, let's start with your name."

"They call me, Fire, because of my red hair."

She spoke shyly glancing up at Marcus, through her lashes.

Marcus sat in a chair and motioned for Fire, to sit in the chair opposite him.

"Fire is a nice name, but I'd like to know the name your parents gave you, what is your given name?"

Fire tensed again and Marcus saw an almost imperceptible tremble as she evaluated her answer.

"I, I'm not supposed to talk about that."

"I understand but I promise you they will never know what you tell me."

"Sir, is this—a trick?"

"A trick. You mean am I one of them?"

Fire barely nodded once, her eyes wary and sure of a set-up.

"No honey, I'm not a plant sent to hurt you. I'm a man who cares about you and just so we're clear I will tell you about my life and my family first, okay?"

Again, Fire gave a tiny nod, and Marcus began the rehearsed background scenario he had prepared for himself. Marcus talked about a childhood in Montana and a working-class family that attended church on Sundays. He shared make believe stories about sibling rivalry and funny anecdotes that truly did happen between him and his sisters. It helped to lend credibility to the story. He told her about horses he never owned and dates he never went on and, in the end, Fire smiled now and again as Marcus pulled out all the stops on his considerable charm.

"Lori, my name is Lori."

Lori softly spoke her name, using a reverence one uses in church, and her name sounded foreign to her, and it made her want to cry but she didn't dare.

"Lori is a lovely name thank you for sharing it with me, and in the morning, I will assure those men that, Fire was worth every penny that I paid for her company."

Marcus was rewarded with another tiny smile, and he saw

a hesitant trust in her eyes. So, he continued with his monologue hoping to draw her out a bit to share her story with him.

"I lost my wife nearly six years ago and I find it difficult to spend the time it takes to meet someone new."

The only part of Marcus' story that was true opened the door just a crack.

"I grew up in California, Lori whispered, as if she were sharing state secrets with a counter spy."

"California is a wonderful place to grow up. Were you near the ocean?"

"Yes, Sir, I was going surfing…that day."

"That day?"

"When they…"

Lori looked frightened and she looked toward the bedroom door, waiting for them to bust through to shut her up.

"Lori, no one's coming in and they will not hurt you I promise."

Marcus watched as a single tear slid down her face followed by a stream of tears as she told Marcus of the day she had been taken and the endless nightmare of men and destinations that had followed. The gut-wrenching story was not only Lori's but Emily's, and every other sexual slave that has ever been captured, used, and sold by traffickers.

Marcus, spoke of Emily as if she were a close family friend that had disappeared years ago in a similar fashion. Marcus described Emily to Lori and asked her if she had ever seen her here or anywhere else. Lori had not just as Marcus had feared.

Lori and Marcus talked through the night and sometime in the early morning light, they pulled covers and sheets strewing them about the bed as if it had been thoroughly used in a rambunctious tryst. Marcus smiled across the bed at Lori.

"Do you remember what you're supposed to say if questioned by them?"

"Yes, Sir."

Lori smiled back, she truly smiled back, and that simple true smile gave Marcus a reason to continue to live in fact. Every, Lori, found and freed was Emily, in a small way. Maybe, if he freed enough, Lori's, he could let Emily rest just a bit.

Just to be safe and to make Lori feel safe, Marcus rehearsed their story a few more times with her, he even resorted to calling her, Fire, as if reassuring her of his sincerity.

When it was time to leave the room, Marcus held out his hand to shake hers.

"It's been a joy to meet you, Fire, and last night was truly one of the best night's I've shared with anyone in a very long time."

Marcus leaned in and whispered. "You will always be, Lori, to me," Marcus patted his chest, covering his heart, "in here."

Lori wiped at her eyes with the back of her hand and Marcus watched her turn from, Lori to, Fire, before his eyes and he hated it.

Fire had no idea she would be aboard Duplicity very soon or that Marcus was to be her savior. She only knew that last night had been but a moment to her. A moment that she would carry as the only hope she had experienced since her kidnapping over two years ago on her ninetieth birthday.

When they opened the bedroom door and stepped into the hall a large rough looking man was waiting for them.

"Everything okay?"

He asked Marcus gruffly.

His eyes cutting from, Marcus to, Fire, and back again?

"Buddy, everything is right as rain. Fire here is just what I needed, and you can bet I'll be back real soon."

"That's what we like to hear. Come back soon."

"You can count on it. Bye Fire, I hope you're here the next time I'm here."

"Thank you, Sir, I hope so too," and she meant it.

The other two met Marcus outside the casino and they took a taxi to the dock where the outboard waited for them. The three didn't speak of last night until they were on board Duplicity as per-agreed upon. They would take no chances with prying taxi drivers or anyone else who may be listening.

The conference room was prepped and waiting but Marcus wanted to check on Carradine first.

Captain Snell had been diligent as always in his role as jailer.

"Mr. Carradine, I trust you have been treated well?"

"If you can call being trussed up treated well then yes, I've been treated well."

Carradine was not as submissive as he had been.

"Well at least you haven't had an endless parade of men assaulting you day and night, have you?"

Carradine chose to remain silent as he waited to hear what Jackman had found behind the scenes at the gentleman's club.

"My wife is no longer there, Mr. Carradine, so we have need of you once again. My associates and I have obtained the names and photos of the men who operate the casino and the club. You will look at everything we have and tell us who we are to approach for information about my wife's whereabouts. Is that clear?"

Carradine saw the contempt on Jackman's face and was no longer terrified. He knew as sure as he was tied to the table that this man would kill him just as soon as he was of no further use.

"Yes, Mr. Jackman, it is crystal clear."

Carradine had no illusions. He may die but he sure as hell would die fighting to jump ship any way he could. He had already worked several plans out in his mind. One opportunity was all he needed for a chance to break free.

Marcus left Carradine and met with the others in the conference room to plan their next course of action.

The tiny camera film had already been processed aboard ship while Marcus had met with Carradine. The three had each been able to take dozens of shots inside the casino and club without anyone's knowledge. Even the young women had been oblivious of their photos being taken. Cameras were available in any form and size.

The color photos were spread out across the conference table and the men worked together to identify the photos of those that were in charge. The backs of the photos were labeled according to where in the casino or club the men worked or had been seen. Next, they labeled the photos of the women and cross referenced them with the guards assigned to each woman. Suite numbers were printed on the backs as well; of the women they had each chosen to stay the night with. Marcus looked forward to the moment, Lori would be freed from that place.

The next few hours were spent preparing their plan and when they wrapped it up, Marcus headed back to the infirmary with a folder full of photos for Carradine to view.

Carradine was able to put names to several men in the photographs, valuable information that Marcus didn't have. The women though were a different matter; Carradine swore he knew none of them.

"I told you Mr. Jackman, they move the women around frequently."

"I want to know how you know so much about their operation."

Carradine was prepared for this question, and he answered truthfully and without reservation.

"I come here a lot Mr. Jackman. I gamble, I relax, and I

frequent that casino whenever I'm here. The staff knows me because I'm a regular and over the years I've seen how things work."

"That's good, Mr. Carradine. You will be able to fill us in on critical aspects regarding procedure that the club employs. Now I want to know which of these men will have information about my wife and where she is now."

Carradine pointed out two men. Men, Marcus had already identified as men in charge. Carradine was also compelled to point out another fact or two.

"Mr. Jackman, sometimes the women are sold and if that happens, the men at the club won't know where she was sent. And she could have been sent many different places by now, depending on how long ago she left."

"Why exactly are you offering me information? Given your current circumstances I doubt you want to assist me in any way."

"Given my current circumstances, Mr. Jackman, I have nothing to gain by lying to you."

"What makes you think you have anything to gain by being truthful, Mr. Carradine?"

"In case you hadn't noticed Mr. Jackman, I'm winging it here, moment by moment."

"Indeed."

Marcus left to get some rest before their assault on the traffickers began.

The next morning, Marcus rose and took coffee with his associates as they fine-tuned the plan. Night would bring them back to the casino and after that the team would wait for the shift workers guarding the women to change so they could be followed and dealt with.

The team would then have several hours, before those same men were supposed to report for work, to make their extraction of the women. Several hours before an alarm would be sounded because it would take that long for those in charge to put the pieces together. Each team member would carry enough sedative to put down a small army. The sedative was an inhalant and it would only take a moment or two to incapacitate a large man. With the guards down and no new shift coming to take their place the extraction would stand a better chance of success.

Marcus and his men had spent a full night with the three captive women to earn their trust, so that when they came to free them, those three would help to convince the rest of the women to comply quickly and quietly.

The background work had already been done on the three women, and the team had all the information they could get on their disappearances and on their families. While their families had no idea they had been found, Marcus would tell the women their families had hired his team to track them down and bring them home.

This lie was necessary to make the extraction as safe as possible for everyone. Marcus knew the women dreamed of their families coming to their rescue and banked on those emotions to compel the others to follow suit.

Once Duplicity was in open waters, Marcus would deal with the questions the women had to the best of his ability, not that truth would be a top priority, because the anonymity of Duplicity's mission was top priority.

When the time was right the team left Duplicity and made their way to the casino where they enjoyed a few hours at the tables, this time winning and losing throughout the evening.

Approximately an hour before the shift change, the team quietly left the casino and waited patiently for the guards to head home. Each had their assigned guard to follow and put down. Crew members from the ship were also at the ready to quickly dispose of the bodies in deep water. Under cover of darkness this plan was relatively simple and easily implemented.

Marcus' assigned mark was one of the two men in charge of the operation. He was one of the two men in charge who might know where Emily was sent or to whom she was sold. He would be transported to the ship for interrogation.

The other man in charge would be on premises in the gentleman's club and quite possibly with the women behind the scenes.

Regardless of where the man was, Marcus had to find him. Marcus had to transport him back to the ship as well because there would be no time for an interrogation in the club. The ship needed to sail as quickly as possible.

The guards straggled out of the casino periodically and as they did the team member assigned to each one followed them into the darkness and brought them down one by one, handing them off to the crew members.

Marcus' target was last to leave and like the others paid little or no attention to his surroundings, which made it easy for Marcus to slip behind him and putting him under, in moments.

The two crew members were at the ready and knew this man was to be delivered to the ship where, Captain Snell would supervise his confinement in the infirmary. Marcus had no worries of the two captives working out any plans because these guys would be out for several hours.

Within thirty minutes of Marcus' take down, the three team members were once again in the casino making their request for escorts for the night. Those in charge remembered the men and welcomed them back as they took their money and invited them to make a choice of the women available.

"I would like to know if, Fire, is available."

Marcus rubbed his hands together as if his evening with Fire had been the best he'd ever had and was eager for an encore.

"I'll check for you."

The guard seemed unfazed by the request. When he returned, he told Marcus, Fire would be available shortly.

Marcus wanted to gut the guard right there. Fire was expected to be handed from man to man in the space of a few minutes. He hoped she didn't overreact when she saw him. She was still very young and probably unpredictable.

The other two chose from the women available in the parade and let themselves be escorted to the rooms for the night or so the guards thought. Having been there the night before, helped put the guards at ease and gave the team an opportunity to prepare for the next phase.

Marcus was ushered to a room where he was to wait for Fire to arrive. The room they had stayed in before was apparently occupied and Marcus hoped it wasn't being used by the man with Fire. Marcus checked his watch and five minutes had passed since he was brought to the room. He had checked for spy-ware again and found nothing.

His back was to the door when he heard it open. Marcus turned around and saw, Fire, being brought in by a large man. He had her by the elbow and Marcus wanted to break his jaw for him.

When Fire saw Marcus, her eyes lit up, but she said nothing and quickly looked down hiding her relief from her guard. Marcus thanked the guard and sent him out as quickly as he could and shut the door. When he turned, he held his finger to his lips to silence her questions.

"Fire, I couldn't stay away, come here."

Marcus spoke for the guard's benefit and took her by the hand, and they moved to the chairs across the room.

"Lori, are you ok?"

"I'm ok. I can't believe you came back so soon. Why are you here?"

"Lori, listen to me and stay very quiet, do you understand?"

Lori said nothing but nodded her head, trying to be as still as possible and her compliance almost broke his heart. Her spirit was nearly broken, and compliance was now second nature to her.

"What I'm about to tell you is very wonderful, but you mustn't overreact. You have to stay quiet and calm, can you do that, because everything depends on you staying calm."

Again, she said nothing and barely nodded her head as if to prove she could do as he asked.

"I'm not here by accident, Lori. I'm here to take you home to your mother."

Marcus let that bit of information sink in for a moment. Lori didn't move she didn't speak in fact nothing was registering, and he wondered if she had heard him at all.

"Honey, did you hear what I just said?"

Lori stared into Marcus' eyes and a tiny nod of her head let him know she had heard him.

"Are you okay, we don't have a lot of time, and I have a lot to do to make this happen?"

Marcus took her hands in his and they were ice-cold and she began to shake as if her blood sugar level had dropped, and she was about to pass out.

Marcus jumped up and grabbed the comforter from the bed and wrapped it around her body rubbing her shoulders quickly to build heat.

"Lori, listen to me you have to pull it together right now. Do you hear me?"

Marcus' voice was low but firm and his no nonsense tone snapped her back and she bobbed her head, again in compliance.

"Good. You have a job to do too because my friends and I can't pull this off without your help, do you understand?"

"Yes, I understand, I'm ok I promise."

"Good girl, now listen carefully we don't have much time left."

Marcus fed her the lie of a phantom family sending his team to find and bring the women home. Marcus used the information they had researched after he had questioned her the first night. Lori wanted to believe, she needed to believe her mother as well as other families had never given up hope of finding them. It was so easy to deceive her it made him sick even if it was in her best interest.

Lori was to stay in the room until Marcus came to get her then she was to convince the other girls that her mother had sent the team to take them back to the States, back to their families if that is what they wanted.

"I need you to be strong can you do that for me?"

"Yes, I can do this. I will do this, I promise."

"That's my girl. Everything's going to be okay. Now stay here until I come for you. Don't come out no matter what you hear—understand?"

"Yes."

Marcus looked at his watch and waited for the exact moment he was to leave.

Then he left her wide-eyed and very afraid but determined to do as she was asked.

"Hey buddy."

Marcus motioned for the guard to come to him and he did.

"Is there a problem with the girl?"

"No not at all, it's just that we need some drinks maybe some ice too, can you get that for us?"

"Why didn't you just call room service, Sir?"

Clearly the guard was put out that Marcus wanted him to provide service for him and the girl.

"Oh, I'm sorry I didn't think about it I just thought…."

Marcus watched as his associate slipped behind the guard and covered his mouth and nose with the sedative soaked mask. The guard barely had time to acknowledge what was happening to him before he was out. The two dragged the guard into Marcus' room while a wild-eyed, Lori, stood gaping at the men.

Before they left again, they were joined by the third team member and both other women, right on schedule. The men left to clear the way for their escape to the boat while, Lori was left to explain what was happening here. Within minutes they were bringing in another unconscious guard. Three in all had been manning the hallways and exits and now three guards were laid out in the room.

Once the team had the women on the street, crew members

would be at the ready to get everyone to the dock quickly and unseen. The women showed, Marcus, where they kept the parade of women, the women that weren't currently being forced to service men that is.

Those were the women they would offer freedom to. Marcus hated the fact that every woman couldn't be removed from the club at this moment, but if they had any hope of getting any of them home, this difficult choice had to be made right now.

The room went deadly quiet as they entered with Lori and the other two women.

"Ladies listen to us right now, please, we don't have much time. We need you to be quiet and do not overreact. We are an extraction team sent to take you to the United States and back to your families."

Two seconds of silence followed by an eruption of hysteria ensued and the team hissed for the women to quiet down. Lori stepped forward and slapped the hell out of the closest loud woman; the others immediately fell silent.

"I'm sorry," Lori whispered looking up into Marcus' surprised face.

"It's okay honey, you did good, you did really well. Ladies listen up if you want to get the hell out of here! Be quiet and do everything we say, do you understand?"

Quiet yeses could be heard among the women as they waited for Marcus' instructions.

"Before we leave, I need to know exactly where this man

is right now. Does anyone know where this man is?"

Marcus held up the color photo of the second man in charge of operations and after a moment of hesitation one tall, dark-haired girl of about eighteen raised her hand.

"I know where he is," she said quietly looking down as she spoke. "He's with the girl they call, Scarlett, but that's not her real name."

"Where is Scarlett?"

"She's in her room, its number 546."

Marcus turned to the other men and told them to get the women out.

"Marcus, that's not a good idea, we had a plan let's stick to it."

"You know I can't do that. Go now! Get them on the ship, I'll be right behind you."

The men hesitated for a moment and then turned to the women.

"Ladies, we're leaving now and there are men outside that are waiting to help us, so do exactly as they say, and we will be on our ship in no time at all."

Lori turned to Marcus and took his hand. Marcus looked down at her and squeezed her hand before he let it go. "You go with them Lori, do what they say, and I'll be on the ship very soon."

"Please come now, I don't want to go without you."

"Lori you promised to be strong and I'm going to hold you

to it. Now go with the others, right now."

"okay," she whispered.

She threw her arms around his waist, and he could feel her tremble as he gently pulled her arms from around him.

"Take her now."

Marcus said to his friends as he turned to find room 546.

The women were eased out a side door, and the crew members loaded the women into a waiting van and took them to the dock. Inside of thirty minutes the women were on board and the crew was waiting on, Marcus.

Captain Snell was now in command and would give the order to set sail whether Marcus was on board or not. The ship and crew would not be held by a foreign government, on charges that would imprison them for decades, that's if they survived the assault.

The owner of Duplicity would not step forward to claim responsibility, let alone the ship. The ships ownership was registered to a dummy corporation with little hope of anyone unraveling the identity of the owner.

This safeguard was established to protect the work that Marcus' team provided, just as many other teams provided similar work around the globe. The goal was to take down traffickers, wherever they operated.

Marcus would be on his own very soon which is why two men, his friends, had reentered the club using the same side door they had used to free the women. The crew members took the women the rest of the way and got them safely on-board ship.

Marcus was outside room 546 when his friends joined him. Marcus was angry but not surprised and the look of irritation on his faced summed it up for the other two guys. One gave, Marcus, a wry smile while the other grinned and shrugged, then they turned their attention to the door. All the while not a word was said.

Marcus had taken a master key card from one of the guards, after they took him down earlier. Now the team took their positions as they prepared to enter the room. Since Marcus had the sedative ready, the other two would tackle him and hold him while Marcus knocked him out. The girl had better not start screaming or she would be drugged as well and dragging two people to the ship would be unwise because time was critical.

One last nod to each other and Marcus slid the key in and out quickly throwing the door open and his friends were on top of both the club manager and the girl in the bed. The man had no time to act before the soaked mask had him out. The girl struggled while hands covered her mouth.

"Shut up, do you hear me?"

Marcus' whisper was harsh and more menacing than he had intended to sound but it got her attention. The men hauled the guy off the girl while, Marcus, grabbed her clothes from the floor.

"Put these on fast," he ordered, and she complied quickly.

When she was ready the men grabbed the man and dragged him from the room while, Marcus, in a less threatening tone quickly began his explanation, as he too moved her physically from the room.

The outboard was waiting for them at the dock and within moments they were speeding to the ship. The girl had said nothing since Marcus had silenced her in the room. She didn't believe she was being rescued. She believed this was just another move to a new group of owners, and soon, she would be forced to service these three and more.

The crew was ready to quickly pull the five aboard so the captain could leave port as soon as possible. The trafficker was taken to the infirmary and tied like the other two; while the girl was led to the main salon where the other women waited.

Lori looked around for, Marcus, but he wasn't there, only the other two men were there, and she didn't know what to think. Lori could feel herself begin to shut down again, she had to, it was the only way to survive, so she simply slid to the floor and curled into a ball.

Marcus had entered the room just as she went down and instantly, he was by her side and gathering her up into his arms.

"Lori what is it, what's wrong?"

Marcus was brushing her hair out of her face, checking her pulse, and ordering water, now!

Lori looked up into his face and began to cry.

"You were gone. I thought it was a dream. I didn't think you were real."

"Honey, I'm as real as you are and we're both ok."

Marcus sat with her rubbing her cold hands, reassuring her.

"Lori listen, I need to talk to everyone, so they know what to expect, ok."

Lori nodded never taking her eyes off Marcus, as if seeing him made her rescue real somehow.

Marcus stood and asked everyone to be quiet and to sit down. They did. Marcus moved to the bar in front of the main salon and when he turned to face everyone. Lori was right there beside him, looking at him. This was going to be difficult, Marcus realized. Maybe it was some sort of Stockholm syndrome. For the next hour or so, as Marcus spoke to the women and answered their questions; when he moved, she moved.

Captain Snell and the men noticed this new little twist and they understood. The psychological damage these young women endured would be with them throughout their lives. Marcus represented this girl's freedom, and she was hanging on for dear life.

By the time Marcus had explained everything, and questions had been asked and answered he felt exhausted and needed a break from everyone. He looked down into Lori's face and knew that wasn't going to happen any time soon.

He smiled, she smiled, if he frowned, her eyes widened with worry. What the hell was he supposed to do? A tiny dose of sedative did cross his mind though. When he looked into her eyes, he caved because in her eyes, he saw his own pain and sorrow, as was the sorrow mirrored in the eyes of Lori.

The next few days would be spent in interrogation with the three in sickbay. Marcus would have to find a way to keep Lori occupied so that he could continue with his work. Her need to be near him was exhausting and he felt compelled to be there for her, it was fast becoming a vicious cycle and emotionally draining for both.

The usual procedure for the team was to speak with each young woman and record all background information they could garner from each. Sometimes a woman would be able to shed light on the operation of the traffickers as well as give a history of her previous owners and destinations. The team was always very careful not to add trauma to their already fragile state of mind.

This was a very important part of processing that the team relied on for future raids on trafficking operations. Recording the interviews with the women insured no pertinent information was ever lost in translation or viewpoint. This was a valuable job that Lori could perform for Marcus, yet a job she couldn't botch even in a fragile state of mind. Plus, Lori was more apt to gather information that the women may feel uncomfortable sharing with the men. Marcus took Lori aside and told her he needed her help with the other women.

"I don't want to push you, Lori, but I have many things I have to do and if you're up to it, I could use your help."

"I want to help you."

Marcus was rewarded with a small shy smile and the ever-increasing look of adoration that he wasn't at all sure he deserved.

He had in fact lied to her about almost everything since he had met her.

"That's my girl. We have a room, an interview room set up with video equipment. I need you to interview each woman separately, because we need to find out everything we can about their capture and the places they've been so we can help other women escape as well. Can you do that for me?"

"I don't know what to ask them."

Lori was afraid she would disappoint Marcus, and she would hate to do that.

"Not to worry, we have a written list of questions to ask during the interview. See, we need help too in order to be thorough.

Lori smiled and nodded her head.

"I'd like to help you; you've done everything for me...Marcus."

She spoke his name shyly almost reverently like she was seeking consent to address him by his given name.

Marcus smiled at her and patted her shoulder giving his approval.

"Come on, I'll show you where to set up and I'll give you the list of questions to go over before you get started, ok?"

Lori stood and followed behind Marcus, grateful for an opportunity to help him. An hour later, Lori was set up in the interview room and had read over the list of questions numerous times.

She was determined to do an exceptional job for Marcus. This was, after all, the first non-sexual job she'd had in two years. This was the first job in two years that had been requested of her rather than forced on her and it felt great.

It felt great to have someone think she could handle an important job, a job that would help other women. It felt especially great that it was Marcus, who believed in her.

Lori wasn't stupid, she knew she was fixated on Marcus. She knew she was trailing after him like a love-struck child and she did love Marcus. She loved that he put his life on the line for her and the other women. She loved that he cared about how she felt, and what she wanted, and the fact that he had never looked down on her, as if she were a whore.

Marcus was the only man she had ever known in her entire life that had treated her with respect, and the only man that had ever protected her.

That included her own father, a man that had walked out on her and her mother when she was a baby. The boyfriends her mother had gone through had either ignored her or hit on her, so she had spent her time avoiding them at all cost.

Lori took her job very seriously and spent an inordinate amount of time with each woman, and as they shared their experiences with her, she began to focus less on herself. There was something healing about sharing traumatic experiences.

For Lori, videotaping the women, hearing their painful stories and offering her compassion, put her in the role of caregiver, and she felt powerful and in control. Something she had not felt in a very long time was control and power.

***

Marcus was prepared for the worst. He felt he would hear that his Emily was gone, dead, that she had been dead for quite some time. Still, he had to know, he had to find out, and these two men would tell him everything.

The men were separated and one man at a time was interrogated by Marcus. Marcus started the process by holding up the photo of Emily. He was tired and had no patience for game playing.

"This is my wife, where is she?"

The club's day manager looked from Marcus to the picture and then away, refusing to acknowledge either. Marcus reached into the middle drawer again and brought out the shears.

"You have exactly five seconds to tell me where she is."

Marcus had enough cat and mouse games to last a lifetime. This pig was about to find out how serious Marcus was. Five seconds were up.

Marcus Jackman rammed the shears through the fabric of the manager's shirt and began cutting the material without regard to the gouging of his skin. The manager screamed in terror, but it wasn't until Jackman shoved the blades of the shears down the front of his pants that he screamed repeatedly.

"I'll tell you, I'll tell you. Stop, I'll tell you!"

It took massive restraint to stop but, Jackman pulled it

together, though he still held the shears in place.

"Where is she?"

"She was sold; she was sold!"

"When?"

"A year ago."

"Where was she sent?"

"I don't know, I swear. Once they're sold, we don't know where they're taken."

"Who bought her?"

"Two men from Brazil, they bought her and others."

"Their names you son of a bitch, give me their names?"

Jackman gouged the shears into flesh causing the manager to scream out a Brazilian name. The recorder captured the entire interrogation and in Jackman's state of mind he would need the recording to remember what had been said…by both.

The second interrogation found Jackman slightly more in control of his emotions. The night manager of the club had seen the shredded clothing of the day manager and had seen the smudges of blood that had seeped from the gouges in his skin, and he wanted none of that, so he was quite compliant when it was his turn to talk.

Marcus held the photo of his wife up so the second manager could get a good look at her.

"Where is my wife?"

"Brazil, I think, we sold her last year."

The guy was straight forward, fearful, but straight forward.

Why was she sold?"

"Why?"

The guy repeated the question as if confused by it. Jackman was less than patient and stepped closer to the guy, shears in hand.

"Because she was trouble! We sold her because she caused trouble!"

"Explain?"

"She kept telling everyone she was kidnapped no matter what we did, she wouldn't stop. So, we sold her because she was too much trouble."

"Names, I want names and contact information."

"There's no contact information bro! Those dudes from Brazil were customers. They offered to buy, we sold, that's it, end of story."

"That's it, end of story, is that what you think? Let me tell you the end of the story for you." Jackman told him that he would be shown mercy by injecting him with a strong sedative prior to being thrown overboard in open water hundreds of miles from shore.

He was tired, Marcus was so tired. Emily had been sold to men from Brazil, maybe even the Brazilians that had been aboard Duplicity, though the name he'd heard tonight was not one that had sailed with them to Terrible Tilly.

A lead, at least he had a lead to go on and tomorrow he would find out more about the Brazilian bastards that had bought

Emily. Tomorrow the team would plan the next leg of their mission—to Brazil. Where Emily was last known to be and where Emily was, more women would also be.

First though, Lori, and the others would have to be taken to Miami, to safety where they could reunite with their families; after Duplicity had set sail of course.

Marcus wanted to check in on Lori before calling it a night. The three men were secured for the evening; the guards would make sure of that. Marcus would take no chances with these three animals, animals that had known his Emily.

Carradine watched Jackman walk out the door of the infirmary and down the corridor. He'd also heard Jackman tell the casino manager what was going to happen to him once they were in open water. And Carradine knew, Jackman meant what he had threatened.

***

"How's the interviews going?"

Lori turned to smile at Marcus, and she showed teeth this time.

"It's going good… slow but good. How are you doing?"

Marcus couldn't remember the last time someone asked him how he was doing. Well, anyone besides Captain Snell that is.

"It's ok, take your time. Get all the information you can, it will be very helpful. And I'm doing good, thanks for asking."

"I was going to take a break and go out on deck before the next interview. Do you want to walk with me?" she asked.

"Sure, for a minute or two then I have to get some sleep. Shouldn't you be sleeping too?"

"I'm too excited to sleep besides I'm not tired. Some of the women can't sleep yet so, I thought I'd use the time to videotape some interviews."

"You're doing great Lori, I'm proud of you."

Lori stopped walking with Marcus and looked up at him. No one had been proud of her for a very long time, not even herself. Marcus looked down at Lori, moonlight cast a soft glow on her red curls. He was about to excuse himself to go to his cabin, when the sound of men shouting and running caught their attention.

"Stop him! Look out, he has a gun!"

Marcus saw Carradine running toward them just as, Carradine saw Marcus and Lori. Marcus was about to lunge forward to grab Carradine. Only Carradine raised his right arm with gun in hand, pointing it at them.

In the instant it took for Marcus to grasp the situation, he threw himself into, Lori, knocking her to the deck just as he saw the flash from the pistol. The force of the bullet spun Marcus backward into the railing of the ship.

Marcus heard Lori scream his name as he slid to the deck unable to stop the scene before him. Marcus tried to shout as he saw Carradine raise the gun again, just as a second shot rang out, this one fired by Captain Snell. Carradine was hit in the back, the force of the impact flipping his body over the railing and into the sea below.

Marcus' breath was coming in short, ragged gasps, and his sight was fading into pinpoint vision and the last face he saw was that of, Lori, hovering over him.

Lori wouldn't leave his bedside, not when the ship docked in Miami nor when given an opportunity to contact her mother. Marcus had saved her. He saved her from the endless line of men in the Cayman's, and he had saved her from the man with the gun. Most of all, he had saved her from giving up. No, she would not leave, Marcus, not when he needed her as much as she still needed him.

In the six days that had passed since the shooting, Marcus had drifted in and out of consciousness. The doctor had administered pain killers and antibiotics on a regular basis.

The doctor had given up on trying to convince Lori to return to her family let alone leave the ship. Now they were back at sea, and it was too late for any of that anyway.

Captain Snell had thrown his hands up in frustration and allowed Lori to remain by Marcus' side. Lori left to shower, but she slept in the chair beside his bed and she rarely ate.

The bullet had entered and exited Marcus' chest and back narrowly missing the aorta and spine. Marcus was extremely lucky though he wouldn't know it, from the wracking pain in his chest. The doctor was mostly concerned that infection would set up in the wound.

Carradine had waited for Jackman to be out of ear shot

before asking his guard to let him use the head. It took a split second and adrenaline pumping hard through his veins to give him massive strength to overpower his guard and take the pistol from his belt.

Carradine had no plan, other than to jump ship alive. His desperate attempt to escape led him straight into the path of Jackman. And Jackman was going to kill him, just as he planned to kill the two casino managers.

Shooting Jackman was not planned. It was to his mind, kill or be killed, and it gave Carradine a second of hope just before a bullet tore through his own body sending him straight to hell.

Captain Snell had many contacts around the world. Some of the contacts owed the team. Some were parents or relatives of women or children that had been found and returned by the team. One such relative was a surgeon and he came aboard Duplicity to perform surgery on Marcus in Miami.

The team couldn't do the work they did without those quietly giving aid in the background. Just as those in the background, wouldn't find their loved ones without Duplicity and the team that sailed her around the world, searching always searching for the lost and the taken.

Marcus woke to find Lori peering intently into his eyes, her hand holding his own.

"Marcus," Lori whispered looking worried and exhausted.

"Are you alright, honey," he asked as she bent over his bed?

"Marcus," Lori cried and laughed at the same time, "only you would worry about me after being shot. You're alive so yes, I'm great."

"How long has it been?"

"Six days, Marcus, it's been six days. I've been so worried, you had all of us worried but you're going to be fine. I need to get Captain Snell now."

Lori waited on Marcus hand and foot for the next couple of weeks and Marcus had to admit he needed the help.

When he learned of how she refused to leave the ship, and that she had stayed with him around the clock, he was grateful but disheartened that she chose to stay with him over reuniting with her mother.

"Lori is it fair to let your family go on waiting and wondering what happened to you?"

"Of course it's not fair, Marcus, but my mother is the only family I have and I'm just not ready yet. There's a lot of hurt and resentment that I haven't worked out yet. I need a little time and besides I feel closer to you than I do to her."

"Don't you think that may be because of the circumstances that brought us together and not because of me so much?"

"Marcus, why do you do that?"

"Why do I do what?"

"Why do you discount how wonderful you are?"

"I think you may be biased just a bit," he said.

"I am biased but that doesn't make it untrue. I'm also

selfish. I'm not ready to let you go yet. I need you, Marcus, and every day I'm with you I get stronger and I need to feel strong again. So please, just let me stay a little longer."

"Lori you do know I'm looking for my wife, don't you?"

"Yes, and I hope you find her. I wish I could find her for you. I owe you so much."

"You don't owe me anything, honey, and I kind of like having you around too. Maybe we can help each other to stay strong. So, let's just see how things go for a while."

Lori put her arm through his, as they took that walk on deck that they started nearly three weeks ago.

Justifiable: Oregon

THE END

TILLY

EPILOGUE:

SEPTEMBER 1, 1957

FINAL ENTRY

Farewell, Tillamook Rock Light Station. An era has ended. With this final entry, and not without sentiment, I return thee to the elements. You, one of the most notorious and yet fascinating of the sea-swept sentinels in the world; long the friend of the tempest-tossed mariner. Through howling gale, thick fog and driving rain your beacon has been a star of hope and your foghorn a voice of encouragement. May the elements of nature be kind to you. For 77 years you have beamed your light across desolate acres of ocean. Keepers have come and gone; men lived and died; but you were faithful to the end. May your sunset years be good years. Your purpose is now only a symbol, but the lives you have saved and the service you have rendered are worthy of the highest respect. A protector of life and property to all, may old-timers, newcomers and travelers along the way pause from thee shore in memory of your humanitarian role.

Keeper: Oswald Allik
September1, 1957

COMING SOON!

GHOST SAVIORS

A Novel

By: Pamela Crist-Wright

AN EXCERPT FROM GHOST SAVIORS

Allistor prayed his daughter was dead—rather than imagine the abuses she suffered at the hands of sadistic traffickers—and the endless succession of Godless pedophiles and johns.

Allistor tried hard not to think about the abuses his baby girl had endured at the will of her captors. He didn't know if praying she'd died long ago to end her suffering was natural for a father. He only knew he would never stop searching for her—nor the savages that stole her.

There are those who say everything happens for a reason. A tragic event for some spurs their wrath. The wrath for some makes the difference between them becoming a victim or a warrior.

Allistor became a warrior the day his child was taken and sold into slavery by traffickers. His wealth became his sword—and he wielded it to accrue lethal and heroic teams to combat traffickers around the world.

Little did he know an equally lethal and rogue military unit was about to match forces with his teams in Mexico. Nor that his surrogate daughter, McKinley Martinez, would soon be caught in the crossfire of a vicious cartel and the *Ghost Saviors* bent on taking them down.

FROM THE AUTHOR

Justifiable: Oregon

Dear Readers,

      GHOST SAVIORS bring beloved characters like Jake Hunter, Dan Morrison, Sarah Knight, Marcus Jackman, and Lori back to the fight for the freedom of all people.

      While introducing the amazing wounded warriors, made whole with superior technology that catapults them to superhero status as they join forces with the lethal forces of, Marcus Jackman and Jake Hunter.

      You will love these characters and this new installment of THE JUSTIFIABLE SERIES as much as I loved writing it.

      I've laughed and I've cried through the writing of GHOST SAVIORS, and I know you will love the story, as the characters come to life on the pages.

      The non-stop action, colorful characters, and romance of these loved heroes will draw you in and take you on a roller-coaster ride you will not soon forget.

      Know that I am deep into the next installment of the series titled MONSTER.

Warmest Wishes,

Pamela Crist-Wright